THE PILLARS

BUILDING THE CIRCLE - BOOK 5

MAGGIE M LILY

Cover design by Melony Paradise of Paradise Cover Design

Standard Print ISBN: 978-1-7353887-8-6

2020 takes no prisoners. This one's for all of us survivors, hanging on and making the best of it.

Chin up, otherwise the tiara slips.

I hope you enjoy this mental break from reality.

PROLOGUE

TEN YEARS AGO

For a reminder of the characters and relationships in this series, please refer to the back matter.

"Boys!" Darla Trellis yelled down the basement stairs. "Get up! If you miss the bus, you're walking to school."

"Ma, I'll drive us!" Noah yelled back, pulling the pillow over his head.

"No, you won't! Get up. The last time you drove, you got pulled over," Darla hollered down, throwing the switch to turn all the basement lights on at once.

"GAH!" Luke yelled. "Holy fuck! My head, I'm going to puke. Turn the lights off, Mom! I'm up!"

"Did you just swear at me?" Darla roared.

Luke fell out of his bed, dry heaving with a bloody nose. "Mom, I'm sick. Please turn out the lights!"

The overhead lights flicked off before the sound of Darla's angry stomps down the basement stairs reached the boys.

"What do you mean you're sick? Get up!" Darla demanded. "What happened?"

"I dunno," Luke groaned. "My head. Too bright."

Darla rolled her eyes. "Were you drinking? I thought you were too smart for that crap."

"No, Mom. Not drinking," Luke muttered, holding one hand over his eyes.

"Boys! Why did you let him drink?" Darla yelled. "Noah, this is your fault. I know it!"

"Ma, we haven't been drinking," Noah objected, pillow still over his head.

"Then get up! You and Matthew are going to be late. Luke, stay home."

Noah sighed. "Okay. We've been drinking. We split a bottle of bourbon last night."

"Then you all get up," Darla replied, tone sweet. "Matthew, get up!"

"Uh, I'm awake, Mom. Been awake for a while. Sorry," Matthew muttered, staring off into space.

"Then what are you doing? You're going to be late."

"Um. Thinking, I guess. Sorry. I'm up. Luke, you okay?" Matthew asked.

"Something's wrong with my eyes," Luke replied. "I don't know."

"Get ready for school," Darla said, frowning at Matthew. The two younger boys didn't cause problems. This was unusual.

"Yeah, school." Matthew nodded, distracted, as he headed for the upstairs bathroom. Noah had snuck into the basement bathroom while Matthew was talking with their mother.

Convinced she'd find a half-full bottle of liquor, Darla began picking up dirty clothes and other crap that had gathered on the floor of the basement.

Putting the teenage boys in the basement together kept the crap contained. But the basement had acquired a definite odor after hosting eight boys. It smelled of sweat socks and old food.

The boys didn't seem to notice or care.

It took her a few minutes to make her way over to Matthew's

corner and then another minute in the darkness to realize that there was dried blood on the pillowcase.

"NOAH MICHAEL TRELLIS, YOU'RE GROUNDED!"

"What? I didn't—" Noah charged out of the bathroom, pants around his ankles.

"What did you do to your brothers? They both have bloody noses! If this is another stupid ten-dollar bet like trying to snort Jell-O, we're going to have words!"

"Ma, I didn't—"

"Last time, you tried to get them to chug a gallon of milk! The living room still smells sour!"

"Ma, I got a date tonight!"

"Then you shouldn't have done whatever it is you did to your brothers!"

"She's super cute. Can I be grounded tomorrow? Double grounding?"

"DON'T YOU TRY TO NEGOTIATE WITH ME!"

"I DIDN'T EVEN DO ANYTHING!"

"What the fuck did you and Luke do last night?" Noah asked as they walked toward the bus stop.

"Nothing," Matthew muttered, rubbing his forehead. "I fell asleep early. Maybe a little after nine. Not sure what's with Luke."

"You were both out when I got downstairs around eleven. Why does Mom always blame me?"

Matthew shrugged. "Because you usually do something."

"Okay, yeah, but this time, I'm innocent. I have a date with Nicole tonight. I can't be grounded."

Matthew rolled his eyes.

"Don't roll your eyes. She's super cute. I'm going to take her to prom. She's great. This might be it for me—high school sweethearts and all that," Noah suggested, ever the optimist.

"She wears a dog collar, Noah."

"So. Fucking. Hot!"

"You're a strange dude," Matthew muttered, shaking his head.

"Yeah, yeah. Not your type; prim and proper for you. I get it, but you don't know what you're missing. Stacey was boring, man. And she cheated on you with that football player. She's a boring cheater. Move on. New girlfriend time!"

"Meh."

"What's your problem? You're all distracted this morning."

"I dunno. Sorry. I guess I don't feel right, either. My ears keep crackling," Matthew admitted as they got on the bus and grabbed seats across the aisle from each other.

Resting his head back on the seat, Matthew closed his eyes to focus on his hearing. The crackling sounded almost like it had words in it.

"*Let go,*" a high-pitched whisper suddenly said through the crackling. Matthew flinched back from the sound, losing his concentration and focus.

At the same time, the front right tire on the school bus blew out, causing the bus to drive into the semi-truck next to them.

Matthew's face slammed into the seat in front of him, slashing his face open and breaking his nose. Of the eighteen kids on the bus, Matthew's injuries were the worst.

"I know. I know my face was bleeding a little bit. It's fine. I don't think I'm even bleeding anymore. Please. Would you please check my ears?" Matthew repeated to the emergency room doctor for the third time.

"Son, your ears look fine. There's no fluid or anything in them, no scratches or visible damage. Why are you worried about your ears?"

"Because I keep hearing a crackling noise!" Matthew objected. "Something is wrong with my ears."

"Matthew," the nurse said, coming into the triage area, "your mom is here. She's signing the consent for treatment forms and said to tell you she'll be right here."

"Tell her I'm fine. She's going to be pissed. Tell her I'm fine, okay?" Matthew requested, sounding slightly panicked.

"We told her. She's calm. Mostly." The nurse gave a sickly smile.

Yeah, right, Matthew thought. *What fool decided she needed to fill out forms?*

"Here, I'm going to pull the compress off your face and start cleaning the wound so we can stitch…" The doctor's voice trailed off as he looked at the wound and then looked at the compress.

"Well, I think you were right, Matthew." The doctor smiled. "Your face is only bleeding a little bit. It certainly seemed like a much bigger cut when we put the compress on. I can tell from the type of compress they used. I don't think we're even going to stitch this—"

"Where is he?" Darla roared, stomping through the emergency room like an enraged T-Rex. "I signed all the damn forms! Where's my kid?"

"Mrs. Trellis. So nice to see you again," the doctor hedged, looking uncomfortable. "I haven't seen you since Beth broke Noah's arm."

"You," Darla growled.

"He's fine. Just a little cut and a banged-up nose," the doctor offered, biting back a smile.

The exploits of the Trellis children were the stuff of emergency room legend.

"Matthew?" Darla asked, still glaring at the doctor.

"Fine, Mom. I'm fine. How are you?" Matthew asked innocently, provoking a snort of choked laughter from the doctor.

Sorry, man. Seemed like the thing to do, Matthew winced, internally sighing.

Darla turned her scowl on her child.

"Okay. Dumb question. Sorry. Hey, my ears keep crackling," Matthew continued.

"There's nothing wrong with his ears," the doctor responded

immediately. "I've checked. Could be drainage through the sinuses from his nose."

"You're fine?" Darla asked Matthew.

"Uh-huh. Don't even need stitches."

"What are you doing, then? Get up! Let's go home," Darla complained.

"I just want to slap a couple of butterflies on that cut. No stitches, but we'll make sure it stays closed. Just a minute, and we'll have you out of here," the doctor offered.

"Fine." Darla's glare was less icy.

"I'll be right back. Just sit back and relax, Matthew. Just a minute." The doctor was up and moving.

Laying back on the cot, Matthew closed his eyes and focused on the crackling in his ears again.

So weird, he thought.

"*—with me,*" the tiny whisper said through the crackle again.

"Did you hear that?" Matthew asked his mom.

"Hear what?" Darla asked, eyes scanning the bay.

"It was like a little whisper. You didn't hear it?"

Darla shook her head. "You got bopped pretty good, Matthew. Relax. If your hearing is still wonky tomorrow, we'll get it checked."

"All right."

The whisper was still there, indistinct in the crackling noise. He focused on it again. "*Pl-Play.*"

Fuck this, Matthew thought, forcefully pushing the crackling noise out of his mind to stare at the ceiling overhead.

The visitor chair broke to pieces under Darla as she sat gingerly down next to Matthew to wait on the doctor.

"Are you kidding me with this?" she yelled at no one in particular.

"I don't know. It's weird. Everything is hazy. Everyone has a colored haze around them," Luke explained the following Monday as they walked into the main school building. "How are your ears?"

"Still crackling." Matthew sighed. "This sucks. Everyone is staring at us."

"They're not staring at us. They're staring at you—the bus crash victim." Luke laughed. "People have been gossiping all weekend about how you were maimed by fate on Friday. And here you are, perfectly fine."

Matthew groaned in disgust. "It was a little cut. It's already healed. People are too fucking dramatic."

"Woo, you're grumpy today." Luke grinned. "Dropping f-bombs before lunch is so unlike you."

Matthew glared at his younger brother. "Fuck you."

Luke shook with laughter that died abruptly as Matthew's ex-girlfriend ran over to them.

"Ohmygosh, Matthew! I heard what happened," Stacey simpered, squeezing Matthew's hand. "But you look fine."

"I am fine," Matthew replied, tone flat.

"It must have been so scary! My poor honey bunny!"

Luke snorted. Matthew hated being called by nicknames, especially lovey-dovey nicknames.

Stacey sneered at Luke. "Run along, little brother. You're not wanted here."

Luke grinned. "Stacey, he dumped your ass after you skanked it up with Hunter. He's not your *honey bunny* anymore."

Stacey scowled at Lucas and then turned a sunny smile on Matthew. "It was all a big—"

"Luke is not wrong," Matthew interrupted, shaking off her hand. "I'm not interested in whatever you're doing, Stacey."

"Matty," she whined. "Listen—"

Matthew's anger spiked as his ears popped. The words came out of his mouth, deep and slow, without conscious thought. "The popularity you're pandering for is bullshit. No one will remember who the junior year homecoming queen was years from now. You'll fade into insignificance and have to deal with your own mediocrity."

Stacey's eyes went wide with shock. Her face crumpled into tears before she bent at the waist, falling to her knees, wailing in agony.

"HOLY SHIT, MATTHEW!" Luke yelled, dropping to the ground and grabbing for the hands that Stacey was raking down her face. "What the fuck?"

"I-I don't know! Oh my God! Stacey, I'm so sorry! I didn't mean it! I don't know where that came from!" Matthew yelled, trying to hold her steady to stop her from thrashing against Luke's grip.

"Stacey, calm down!" Luke yelled as her keening sobs quieted to whimpers of pain.

"Someone get the nurse!" Matthew yelled to the crowd of onlookers.

LAST JULY

Kareem answered his girlfriend's call the same way he always did. "Hi! I love you."

"Did you read them?" Sarah asked, excited. "He posted another one! You have to read them so we can discuss it!"

Kareem sighed. "Honey, I try not to read the group threads."

"Oh, come on! There's great gossip going on about these supposed all-powerful Trellis people. How could you not read it? It's like a soap opera."

"Well, they're disgustingly rich. Of course, they're powerful—"

"Not like that!" Sarah objected. "Like us! Plus, you're moving to Chicago. You need to know the juicy details on the most powerful circle going."

"I really don't," Kareem said, rolling his eyes, glad she couldn't see it.

"Are you rolling your eyes?"

"No, of course not." He rolled his eyes again.

"Go read it!"

"Greggory of Harbor is a fool," Kareem said, tone flat. "I'm not getting sucked into this."

Sarah laughed at that. "I've met him. Twice. He's no fool. Plus, the other corners of the Harbor circle are in on it, too. It'd have to be one hell of a con. Please read it. Please? Maybe we can find a way to get invited to one of the circles. Like maybe if you called around…"

"How was your day otherwise?" Kareem asked, changing the subject.

"No! Go read the posts. I'll call you back in ten minutes." She hung up without another word.

"Love you, too, Kareem. I can't wait until you move here so we can have a real relationship," Kareem muttered to himself as if speaking in his girlfriend's voice.

With another sigh, he opened the messaging platform used by most empowered people around the world to share information. Scrolling, he opened the first message in the thread he'd been avoiding for the last month.

POSTED BY: HarborGregg
DATE: July 16
SUBJECT: The Mistress & Walker have risen!

This evening, Harbor held a special circle welcoming home the Mistress and Walker of legend.

As most of you know, I've long chased the stories of these beings. There has been no substantial, verifiable account of them in over three hundred years. They have risen again, empowered anew to enact change in this world and improve the balance of energy among all living things.

I write this post knowing most of you won't believe me. But I invite you to explore and experience it for yourself. When next your circle closes, feel the change in the energy as it cycles. Pay attention to the sheer volume of energy you encounter throughout your day.

This is real. This is an opportunity for growth and advancement the world has not seen in three centuries. A new day has dawned for those of us empowered with the energy to affect change. This is a cause for celebration and reflection.

Befitting their positions and abilities, the Mistress and Walker now hold the center of the Harbor Circle. I will stand with them as scribe and guide. Neither being has been a part of a traditional circle before tonight.

Nora and Benjamin, the previous cornerstones of Harbor, have also surrendered their places but remain within the circle. Jared, my third corner, has opted not to continue with us of his own accord.

A collection of pillars—beings of such strong, focused energy, they're able to decisively control life and nature around them—now stand in the prominent positions of Harbor. Lords of Fear, Anger, Joy, Lust, Peace, Loyalty, and Chaos have surfaced, along with Ladies of Light, Wind, Love, and Hope.

We live in extraordinary times, friends! I will share more details as Harbor's energy evens out and as the Mistress and Walker deem appropriate. For now, please pay attention to the energy around you. *Feel* the difference in the world.

Our energy, long thought to have been in decline, has resurfaced within this pair and their pillars!

"I'm not reading this shit," Kareem muttered to himself. "What a load of crap. Greggory has lost his grip on reality."

Dialing Sarah's number, he closed his browser window.

"Did you read them already?" Sarah answered.

"No, I read the first one. It was—"

Kareem's words were cut off by squeals of laughter from Sarah's end of the conversation.

"Sarah! Are you all right?" he yelled into the cell phone, instantly concerned.

"I'll call you right back!" she yelled back.

Before she disconnected, he heard muffled words that sounded like, "Don't be like that. I'll talk to him after he's here. His energy is incredibly—"

Kareem frowned at the phone, a sense of foreboding settling in his stomach.

"Fuck my life," Kareem mumbled. "She's going to make me read that stupid message thread. She wants me to request to join Harbor. I just know it."

Kareem bumped his head on the table in front of him.

His energy was focused and intense; he'd be welcome in any circle on the planet. But he preferred to build his own circle. He needed to be picky about who he shared energy with. Sharing power with the wrong people had gotten him into serious trouble throughout his life.

"If Greggory of Harbor is off his rocker, I'm not running to join that circle," Kareem said, staring at his mobile phone. He practiced saying the words out loud, knowing he'd be repeating them to his girlfriend before long.

SEPTEMBER

1

LAST WEEKEND

"Oh! Good, you're home. I worried you wouldn't be home," Miranda squeaked as Lawrence walked in the front door of their house.

"What do you mean by that?" he asked, eyes going to slits. "Where did you expect me to be?"

Miranda blinked. "I just meant that I'm glad you're home. We have Matilda's engagement party tonight. I worried you wouldn't be home in time."

"Oh, that. I'm not going."

"What? Why? You said you would go."

"Benjamin is not going; he doesn't like that family," Lawrence replied with a shrug.

"My grandfather doesn't like that family because they're richer and more powerful than him. He's not going because he treats Matilda poorly. That doesn't mean you shouldn't go to the party!"

"Well, Miranda, I'm angling to inherit from your grandfather, not your sister. I'll make the old man happy. We're not going."

Miranda's expression blanked. Her voice took on a tone of uncharacteristic firmness. "I am going."

"No, you're not. I said no."

"I was invited. I accepted. My sister expects me to be there, and my parents are going."

Lawrence glared at his wife, noticing the set of her shoulders. "Fine. Sit there alone all night. Whatever. I'm not going."

Miranda contemplated the best, non-confrontational path forward as he began walking away from her.

"I'm surprised you're going to skip an opportunity to network with wealthy potential investors." She held her breath.

Lawrence was hungry for investors to grow the business. But she wasn't sure how that shook out against his desire to make her grandfather happy.

"The Trellis family isn't going to invest with me. You know that as well as I do," he called back to her as he made his way down the hallway toward the kitchen.

She exhaled. "But there will be five hundred people at this party—all the friends of the Trellis family that got rich with Sam. You're going to miss out on spending time with them."

Lawrence turned around to face her. "Five hundred people?"

"When I talked to Matty last, she was complaining about the number of people that accepted. It's all wealthy people that she doesn't know," Miranda further baited her trap.

Lawrence chewed his lip, considering the options before him. "Your father is going? Not just your mother?"

"Charles and Megan are both going," Miranda confirmed.

"Fine, but we're leaving if that family starts calling me 'Larry.'"

She nodded, not believing for a second the Trellis family would call him by his preferred name. "The car will be here to collect us at ten minutes to seven."

"WHAT ARE YOU DOING?" Lawrence asked his wife two hours later. He stood in the master bathroom doorway, looking affronted.

"I'm putting on makeup." Miranda frowned at him.

"Why are you doing that here?"

"The lighting is better here. It's easier to do at the vanity," she replied, trying to be reasonable. "I have to lean awkwardly to get proper lighting in the other bathroom."

"Miranda, we've agreed that this is my bathroom."

"Do you need to get in here? I can come back and finish when you're done."

"No. That's not the point. This is *my* bathroom."

"Lawrence, you weren't in here. You don't use the vanity. I just want to do my makeup here. It's evening makeup for a black-tie event. I want to look nice. Don't you want me to look nice?"

"This is my space, Miranda. You can't use this room," he declared.

"I understand that you prefer me to use the other bathroom when you're sleeping. And I don't mind using the smaller shower so my toiletries aren't in your way. I don't spray hairspray in here because it gets everywhere. But why can't I do makeup in here, where it's easier?"

"Because. This is my bathroom."

"I'm at the vanity that you don't use."

"That's not the point. This is my bathroom!" Larry yelled, all but stamping his foot.

"Can we make the smaller bathroom that doesn't have the vanity 'your bathroom?' The vanity makes doing this much more comfortable."

"GET OUT!"

"You're weird about this bathroom thing, just so you know."

"MIRANDA!"

"I'm going."

MIRANDA SAT IN THE BALLROOM, watching Matilda walk into the engagement party on Jake's arm.

So perfect together. So right, she cheered internally.

"She's positively glowing with happiness," Megan murmured, looking in the same direction with a smile.

"Don't ruin it," Miranda chided her mother.

Megan winced. "I swear I wasn't trying to hurt her, Miranda. I want my girls to be happy."

Miranda gave a tiny snort. "You'd be batting five hundred on that, Mom, if you just stayed out of her way."

"Noted." Megan nodded. "I have no intention of saying anything about her relationships again."

"Woo, how do I get on that list of cast-offs? Can you write me off in a similar manner?" Miranda grinned.

"Hush," Megan said, showing a sad smile. "I know I'm a terrible mother. Leave…"

Megan's words trailed off as she watched the remainder of the Trellis family enter the ballroom.

"I should have told you," Miranda admitted, watching Matthew. "I didn't want to talk about him."

Megan's eyebrows climbed up to her hairline.

"Trellis, Mom. Matthew Trellis. He's Jake's brother. I didn't put it together, either, until I was standing in the middle of Darla's living room."

Megan stared at her younger daughter, unblinking.

"I'm fine," Miranda said.

Megan didn't move.

"Just friends," Miranda continued. "Please stop staring at me."

"Miranda," Megan breathed.

"I know."

Megan's eyes lit with fire. "Divorce him. Get out of there. Matthew would help you. He has the means to help you get out of that."

Miranda shook her head. "Sam offered me the means to get out a month ago. Jake and Matty have offered repeatedly. I wouldn't take Matthew's help. I don't need to add 'knight in shining armor' to his list of fine qualities. Stop now, Darla's coming over with Hank."

"Oh, God," Megan muttered, voice tight with anxiety. "This woman is going to hate me. Judge me and hate me."

"Absolutely," Miranda agreed, standing to greet Hank and Darla.

"Darla, you look absolutely stunning." Miranda grinned. "I'm so glad Ellie talked you into the wedding dress!"

"Sweetheart, you look gorgeous as always," Darla said, reaching to give her a kiss.

"Hank and Darla, this is my mom, Megan, and my dad, Charles."

"It's nice to meet you," Hank murmured with a polite, impersonal smile. He shook Megan's hand before turning to Charles.

Wow, Hank does "professionally polite" exceptionally well, Miranda admired.

"I'm sorry you've been unable to make it to dinner before now." Darla's tone was frosty as she shook hands, her body posture stiff.

Ha! Darla's shaking hands. I didn't know she did anything but hugs and kisses!

"It's so nice to finally meet you both." Charles's smile was forced.

"It's a shame Matilda's grandfather couldn't make it," Hank said, adopting Darla's chilly tones.

"No, it's not." Megan snorted. "He's a terrible human being. It's such a lovely occasion, let's be glad he decided to stay out of it."

Miranda burst out laughing as her dad stared at her mom with his mouth agape.

"Oh, don't look at me like that, Charles. You say it yourself. Often."

Hank's face was expressionless, but Darla looked like she was trying not to smile.

Mom scored some points with that one, Miranda allowed.

Lawrence wandered over from a conversation with the people at the next table. "Hank! Darla! Good to see you!"

Ugh. It's the asshole voice again.

"Larry," Hank acknowledged with a nod.

Lawrence glowered at his wife, unhappy, as she failed to hide a smile.

21

The group descended into an awkward silence that Miranda was more than willing to let languish.

As MATTHEW WALKED into the ballroom, he could feel Miranda's eyes on him. He didn't need to look around the room to find her. His energy jumped and danced toward her without warning.

Fuck my life, this is so much worse since she joined the circle. Married woman, married woman, married woman. I'm not looking. I'm not looking. She's married. I can't look.

Unable to resist the urge, he glanced in her direction.

Megan sat next to Miranda, staring at Matthew, and then turning to her daughter with hard eyes. Charles was behind Megan, engrossed in a conversation with the people at the next table. He wasn't sneering, so he hadn't spotted Matthew yet.

Why is Megan making that face? She used to like me. Has something changed? Did Randa tell her about my fucked-up energy?

Matthew's casual glance toward the ladies morphed into a stare as he tried to puzzle through it. Eventually, he recognized that Megan didn't look mad. She looked shocked.

Oh, shit. Did Miranda not tell her parents? Ugh. This might be awkward—on many levels.

As Matthew watched Megan and Miranda urgently whisper to each other, Hank and Darla approached. Megan's expression dropped into anxious fear when she saw them coming.

What the fuck! Someone make popcorn! Mom just shook hands with soon-to-be family members. I wonder if there's going to be a fistfight before the night is over.

Matthew's energy jumped with excitement at the thought.

The excitement shifted to something more sinister as Lawrence approached his wife. The energy clawed at the inside of Matthew's mind, raging for an outlet. Matthew ignored it.

Before meeting Larry, Matthew's energy hung out, just below his conscious thoughts, waiting for some form of madness to present itself. The energy only made itself known when someone around him was leaning toward mental illness or catastrophic behavior.

But the energy didn't like Lawrence. Fighting to the forefront of Matthew's awareness when Larry was within range, it slammed against Matthew's control each time Larry touched Miranda.

Married woman, married woman, married woman, he mentally chanted again.

Matthew was no fool. He heard William's tale of loving Emma and trying to deny the connection. He watched Adrian suffer as he attempted to reject Lucy's role in his life.

The energy's reaction to Miranda was a different slice of the same pie. Matthew's heart had belonged to her since the day they met.

Doesn't change the fact that she's married to a shit-bag!

Watching an uncomfortable silence settle over the parental meeting, he made his way over to the group.

"Well, this looks awkward and strange. Seems like a perfect time to say hello." Matthew chuckled, hugging Megan. "Hello, Charles."

Charles stared in shock at Matthew for a few seconds, missing the offered handshake.

Yep, he still hates me. Matthew's lips turned up at the thought.

He glanced at Miranda, eyebrows raised.

She gave an impish smirk with a minute shrug.

"Hi, Randa!" Sam called, walking up with Adaline in tow. "Are these your parents?"

Miranda smiled with a nod. "Hi, Sam. Hi, Addy. This is Charles and Megan."

Sam nodded politely to both as he "hugged" Miranda, pulling her away from Larry.

Every chance he gets, Sam pulls her away from Larry. I need to ask him about that.

After shaking hands with Sam and exchanging polite words with Adaline, Charles seemed to realize Matthew was still standing there.

"Matthew, I haven't seen you in years." Charles nodded in a cold greeting. "I had no idea you knew Jake and Matilda."

Darla smirked, shooting her own glance at Miranda. "Matthew is my second youngest son."

The color drained from Charles's face.

"Ah. Well, small world," Charles murmured, looking between Matthew and Sam, noticing the resemblance.

"Don't worry, Charles. I won't tell them you hate me." Matthew grinned, teasing.

Darla's polite smile dropped.

"Nonsense!" Charles protested. There was nervous sweat forming on his upper lip. "I don't hate you, Matthew. I just felt, and feel, like you're capable of more than teaching."

"Little kids are fun. It's not a life choice I regret. Let's move on. Do you want to try shaking hands again?"

Huh. I wasn't expecting this to be quite so satisfying. Matthew extended his hand again, making it impossible for Charles to reject his greeting.

"That's better," Matthew praised him. "See, it's fine. I won't let Midas smite you. Again."

Sam's smile was mocking. "You're worried I might go a-smiting? I don't usually do that to family."

Charles fidgeted, uncomfortable.

"I could make an exception, though," Sam offered, asking Matthew a question without words.

"Matthew," Megan laughed, "stop it. You're going to make Charles sick. He doesn't understand your humor. It's wonderful to see you! I had no idea you were related to Jake, but now it's impossible to miss the family resemblance."

Matthew hugged her again. "You look great, Megan. I'm glad you joined us tonight. Have you said hello to Matilda yet?"

"Why would Sam smite Matilda's father?" Hank asked, standing in line for drinks at the bar. The wait staff would bring drinks if asked, but Hank wanted a word with Matthew.

"He hates me." Matthew grinned again.

"I don't understand how that's possible. You are too quietly unassuming and kind for anyone to dislike you."

"Charles is an exception to that general truth," Matthew disagreed.

"Why?"

"You're not going to like this conversation. Can we let this go?"

"We could discuss it over dinner tomorrow," Hank offered.

Matthew sighed. "Megan and Charles visited the campus unexpectedly one weekend. When they showed up, Miranda and I were bickering about literature and being ridiculous in her dorm common room, as we often did."

"I can't imagine either of you bickering, let alone bickering at each other!" Hank laughed.

"We did. She is my favorite person to argue with. She's so gentle, it's fun to get her all worked up over stupid shit. We laughed more than argued, I guess. But anyway, she introduced me to her parents as a friend. Charles looked me up and down in my worn jeans and t-shirt, his disapproval obvious. When he asked what I was studying, I told him I was working on a master's degree in ancient Greek mythology. I explained that I ended up leading undergraduate literature classes as the teacher's assistant."

"And?"

"That's it. He suggested it would be hard to find work without a more substantial degree. We got into a discussion about the merits of liberal arts before I told him I already had a teaching degree and intended to work in early childhood education. I was a lost cause at that point. He wasn't happy."

"He doesn't like you because you have a liberal arts master's degree?" Hank asked, trying to understand.

Matthew cleared his throat as the line moved forward. "He felt I would never make enough money to support his daughter in a way he found agreeable and made no secret of his disapproval. Granted, I failed to mention that Sam had already made enough money for all of us. Miranda and I didn't discuss our families. It seemed wrong to mention it in passing to her parents."

All expression fell off Hank's face, a sign of his anger.

"It's fine, Dad. Miranda and I were never a couple. Not like that."

"Matthew."

"Married woman, married woman, married woman," he chanted aloud.

"You had feelings for her?"

Matthew nodded.

"Like William and Adrian."

It wasn't a question, but Matthew nodded again.

"She had feelings for you?"

The head nod was less pronounced.

"And now?"

"Married woman, married woman, married woman."

Hank glared. "This is a mess, Matthew. He's horrible."

"I don't deserve that glare, Dad. I didn't marry him."

Laughing, Hank smacked Matthew upside the head before ordering drinks.

"WHAT ARE YOU DOING, sitting here all by yourself?" Ethan asked with a grin, flopping down next to Miranda at a back table later that night.

Miranda smiled in return without looking at him. "My parents left about thirty minutes ago."

Following her gaze, Ethan watched as Lawrence petted the shoulder of the woman he was chatting with at the bar.

"Man, he sucks so much."

"He really does," she agreed, laughing.

"Is that an 'I'm going to laugh so I don't cry' kind of laugh?"

"Meh. When he's off pawing someone else, he usually leaves me alone. I was distraught when his girlfriend ended things last week."

Ethan blinked. "How long have you been married, Miranda?"

"Almost six months."

"Dance with me?" he asked after a moment. "I don't have anyone to dance with."

"I thought you and Eric were seeing each other? Didn't you double date with Matty and Jake last week?"

Ethan nodded. "It's not going to work. I was too worried he was reading my mind, and he was too worried that Sam would skewer him if he hurt my feelings. Dance with me?"

She smiled, taking his offered hand. "I'm sorry about Eric."

"He's a friend now. Just no sparks, you know?" Ethan said with a shrug.

Miranda nodded.

After a few moments of quiet swaying, Miranda laughed. "Are we dancing or hugging? I expected better moves from a gay man!"

"You want to dance for reals? We can do that. I can keep up with Luke if you can keep up with Talise. Look at them over there, flinging each other around. But I could use a hug. I thought maybe you could, too."

Miranda's smile fell as she held tighter to Ethan. More than a half foot taller than her five foot six inches, Ethan was broad in the shoulders with a tapered waist. She was eye level with his shoulder, making it easy to rest her head against him.

"I was in love once," Ethan murmured.

"What happened?" Miranda wasn't sure she wanted to hear this story, but it felt rude to not ask.

Ethan nodded, acknowledging her hesitation. "He was a terrible person. Everyone knew it. Sam wouldn't even sit in the same room with him. Darla made him unwelcome at Sunday dinner. They all saw him for what he was. I just saw someone that wanted to be with me, who liked me as I was, without a desire to change me. My family likes me just fine. But romantically, I'm a mess. The gay community is amazing. I just haven't found my place in it."

"What happened?" she asked again.

"I had a falling out with the family. Sam, first. Then everyone else."

Miranda's eyes flicked up to meet his, surprise written all over her face.

Ethan chuckled. "We argue sometimes. Not often, but we do. Darla will only tolerate so much upheaval before she puts her foot down. If I'm Joy and you're Earth, Darla is Hearth and Home. She tends to us all, whether we like it or not."

"I thought she might punch my mom earlier," Miranda admitted.

"I won ten bucks on that!" Ethan laughed. "Will was sure she'd lose her shit on your parents. I'll also win ten bucks if William refrains from punching Larry in the head for the remainder of the night. Emma doesn't think he can lock it down that long. She might be right. I wasn't anticipating Larry hitting on another woman in front of you."

She didn't respond.

"Anyway, once I isolated myself from my family, things shifted. He wanted to be together at all times, wanted access to all my stuff, wanted to control what I did and who I saw. I ended it when he told me I had to quit my job and give up my place at work. So much for liking me as I was."

"You argued with your family over him but wouldn't quit your job?" Miranda asked, hurt on Sam's behalf.

"The job and my family are one and the same. I had to go to work every day and look at Sam, my favorite brother and best friend, knowing that we weren't on good terms. It's hard to control someone when they have a constant reminder that other people in the world love them, even when they're making poor choices."

Ethan turned so they were both looking at Matty and Jake.

"You are better at spotting the asshattery of your husband now that your sister is in your life, aren't you?" Ethan asked, already knowing the answer.

After Miranda's nod of understanding, he continued. "Two weeks after it ended, he called and threatened to share damning pictures, proving my gayness, if I didn't give him three million dollars."

Miranda flinched.

"Yeah," Ethan acknowledged. "He's not a shining example of humanity or intelligence. I didn't even know there *were* pictures. I still don't know if that was a bluff.

"My sexual orientation has never been a secret. I told him to do what he felt was necessary and hung up. Truth be told, if he had called and said that he needed money, I probably would have handed it over. It's not like I don't have enough to share. But he didn't. So I hung up on him."

Ethan paused, taking a deep breath. Miranda hugged him harder, giving up the pretense of dancing. She could feel the tension radiating off him.

"When I walked into my apartment the next day, he was waiting for me with a baseball bat. I spent the night in intensive care. He was arrested and charged with assault, eventually accepting a plea deal in which he served ten days, did extensive community service, and went for counseling. He didn't have so much as a parking ticket in the past. Something in him just snapped with me. Looking back on it now, I wonder if it was the energy. Like, my energy did something to his mind."

"I'm sorry, Ethan. You deserve better," Miranda whispered, voice full of sympathy.

"Ah, now we're to the point. Now I have you where I want you, my pretty!" Ethan grinned, giving a mock-cackle.

She smiled up at him, unable to resist the pull of his amusement.

"You deserve better, too, Miranda. Don't let anyone tell you otherwise."

She nodded, staring at his chest to avoid eye contact. "I know."

"Good. I understand, Randa. I really do. It's hard to walk away from a relationship, knowing you'll be alone. Sam offered you money and resources to get away. Matty and Jake have offered support, too. But I understand the appeal of staying. Your family would be angry if you upset the apple cart. It is horrible to feel like you've failed the people you love the most in the world. But I think you might be failing yourself right now."

Blinking fast to avoid tears, Miranda nodded again. "Before Matty, I didn't have any friends or supportive family. I don't have your family, Ethan. It's easier to make peace with my decisions when my family is not angry with me."

Ethan snorted with quiet laughter. "Actually, you do have my family. And you have me. I won't judge. I won't be upset if you decide to leave him or if you decide to stay with him. Please know I understand, down to the very core of my being.

"We're friends no matter what, okay? You're welcome in my life anytime you want. As a fellow loner, I know you'll understand when I say that being alone gets…lonely. Especially now that all my family is rapidly pairing up, leaving me behind. I'm so happy for them but sad for me."

When Ethan finally fell silent, Miranda rested her head on his chest, listening to his heartbeat through his suit. They swayed in silence, pretending to dance again as she reconsidered her life choices.

2

___

"*N*o way!" Miranda laughed.

"Yes, way," Matilda responded, grinning. "When Luke 'let it slip' that Noah and Talise hooked up, you could have heard a pin drop in that dining room last night! Darla was all, 'She has a gift!' I just about peed my pants from laughing so hard. Jake wanted to make popcorn."

"Popcorn?"

"Didn't I tell you that story? Noah and Sam totally trolled Jake and me when I ran into my ex-boyfriend a couple of months ago. They showed up eating fucking popcorn to watch the drama unfold. Anyway, Noah and Talise! They're a thing. Tonight's circle is going to be awesome."

Miranda considered things for a moment. "I wonder how that's going to go. Luke and Noah are pretty much opposites, personality-wise. I thought she was with Luke. They were dancing and singing at your party."

"Just friends," Matty explained. "It didn't work out between them. Luke thinks of her as a sister, apparently. I'm going to pour my tea into a travel mug. Do you want anything for the road? Jake should be home soon."

"Nope! I'm good. Thanks for letting me ride with you," Miranda said, grateful for the additional time with her sister.

Matty blew her a kiss on the way to the kitchen. "Psh! It gives us time to bullshit without Larry. Thanks for coming over. We don't mind picking you up, but the traffic is easier if we leave from here."

"I don't mind. I have nothing else to do." Miranda sighed.

"Here's an idea," Matty offered, coming back into the room. "Get a job. Volunteer at a worthy organization. What do you do with your days now?"

"Matty, I would love to have a life. Lawrence insists that his wife won't work. And, before that, Charles felt strongly that my time should be spent in 'womanly pursuits.'"

Matilda blinked. "What the fuck are womanly pursuits?"

"I don't know. Husband hunting, child rearing, martini lunches, and weight management?" Miranda offered with a self-mocking smile. "He was appalled when I graduated from school without a husband."

"Has Mom ever worked?" Matilda asked, curious.

"I think for a while when she was with your dad, but otherwise, no. Grandma never did, either. We come from a long line of snobby socialites. But I'm terrible at society stuff. Have you ever tried to have a conversation with another woman in our age group at a fundraiser?"

"Yup. I've attempted it roughly four times," Matilda replied. "They all sneered at me and then made passes at Jake. But that's to be expected with me. I would imagine them welcoming you with open arms!"

Miranda's happy countenance fell.

"I didn't mean it like that!" Matty objected. "You're just so sweet and…eager to please. I'd expect you to fit in wherever you wanted."

"No," Miranda replied, tone subdued. "They'd probably welcome me, but to what end? I don't share their hobbies or interests. I have lunch with a group of women I know from the family brokerage— wives of other traders, for the most part. But that's about it."

A pensive silence fell between them before Miranda spoke again.

"When I was about ten years old, a friend visited me at Grandma and Grandfather's house. It was springtime. Everything had just finished thawing. It wasn't warm enough to plant in the ground yet, so Grandma and I had a small greenhouse going around the side of the house, where it was out of everyone's way. I was trying to impress my friend, showing it off and explaining about cross-pollination. When I suggested my friend plant seeds with me, she declined. Said it would mess up her nails. That was about it for friends and me. She told everyone I played in the dirt and studied science. No one liked me after that."

"You terrible blue-stocking, you. How dare you be interested in a STEM field as a little girl? What is your degree in?"

"Marketing."

"Marketing? What did you plan on marketing?"

"Nothing. Charles insisted my degree be in a business field, and marketing seemed better than accounting or finance."

Matilda scrunched up her face. "Why not tell Charles to fuck off and then choose your own major?"

Miranda exhaled hard. When she finally responded, her voice was strained with shame. "I suspect you won't understand this. But it would have made him unhappy. I'd feel like I was failing him. Like you said, I'm a people-pleaser. I can't stand the thought of him or Mom being angry with me. I'm not strong like you."

"Hello, ladies!" Jake called, coming in the apartment door before Matty could respond. "Are you ready for the high drama that will be tonight's circle? I've been laughing about it all day! Fucking epic!"

I HATE you so much right now, Ethan, Matthew silently bitched, watching his brother hug Miranda. They both broke out in laughter together on the other side of the living room.

The farmhouse that hosted their circles was packed, as always, but Matthew could still find Miranda in any crowd.

"Whatcha doing?" Noah asked.

"Huh?"

"What are you doing right now?" Noah asked again, following Matthew's line of sight.

"Waiting for the circle to start," Matthew replied, sounding innocent.

"No, you're not. You're wishing pain and misery on your brother. I know that look!" Noah laughed. "At least direct it at Jake. He's an asshole. Ethan's too good for your scorn."

"Noah?"

"What?"

"Shut up," Matthew said, voice flat.

"Seriously, I know exactly what you're doing! I was doing it a couple of months ago. It was even directed the same way. Go over there and tell her to dump the shit-bag."

"Noah, you had a run-in with Luke's energy on the car ride out here. You got a firsthand demonstration of what he's capable of. Did you want to go two-for-two?"

"Pfft. You wouldn't."

Matthew looked at his brother, eyebrows raised.

"You wouldn't. Mom would be seriously pissed. Also, there's no telling if Luke would put my mind back together again, given that I stole his girlfriend. You wouldn't chance it."

Matthew rolled his eyes as his ears crackled faintly.

"Fine. Go ahead. I'll take my chance—what the fuck?!" Noah dodged quickly as a chunk of ceiling fell without warning. "That could have killed me!"

"I'm not that lucky," Matthew murmured, walking away.

"WHERE WERE YOU? Why do you have dried mud halfway up your calves?" Lawrence demanded.

Startled, Miranda paused as she entered the front door. "It's Monday night. I was at my circle. There was a mishap with a puddle."

"Stop it with that shit, Miranda," Lawrence yelled. "My wife won't be talking nonsense about circles and psychics. You agreed to never talk about that crap."

"I agreed to never talk about it in public," she corrected. "We're in our home, without company. I can be who I am in our home, Lawrence."

"This is not your house! This is my house! I bought it. I pay for it. It's mine. And I say you will not discuss that nonsense in my house."

Miranda stared, catching the waves of malcontent and frustration coming off him. *Is this his breaking point? I need more time. Get a new girl-friend, Larry.*

"Good night, Lawrence," she whispered, stepping past him toward their bedroom.

"Was he there?"

"Who?" Miranda asked, expecting Lawrence to challenge her about Matthew.

"Who? Who do you think, Miranda? I saw you dancing with him on Saturday! You were all but necking in the middle of the dance floor."

She burst out laughing. "Ethan? You're concerned about Ethan?" *Wrong brother, Larry.*

"He's gay!" She continued laughing at her stupid husband.

"He's not gay! I saw the way he looks at you. Some guys pretend, just to get close to women!"

"Lawrence, that's the dumbest thing you've ever said to me. And that's saying something." The words were out of her mouth before she considered what she was saying.

"How dare you!" he roared. "I keep you comfortable and happy here. Show some damn respect for your betters, Miranda!"

"Show me someone better and I will," she said quietly, forgetting that she didn't want to argue with him.

"You will not see him again! In fact, you will not see Matilda. She's a horrible influence on you, and I don't want her or her boyfriend or his family in our lives."

Miranda's blood went cold. *And that's my breaking point.*

"If you don't want Matty in your life, I understand. I'll see a lawyer in the morning and file papers. I will not give up my sister for this farce of a marriage. Cope with her presence and everything that comes with it or we can just move on."

Fear spiked through Miranda as Lawrence advanced on her with malice.

ETHAN WAS JUST STARTING to drift off to sleep when his cell phone rang. He frowned. His phone automatically switched to Do Not Disturb after ten o'clock. Someone had to call repeatedly for the phone to ring.

His frown deepened after a look at the caller id. "Miranda?"

"Ethan, can you come get me? They won't let me leave on my own, and I don't want to stay here."

He could hear machines beeping in the background.

"Where are you?"

She sighed. "Northwestern Medical. I'm fine, just banged up. It's over. I have to find a lawyer in the morning."

"I'll be right there. Sit tight."

"Thank you," she murmured, the tears obvious in her voice.

"I KNEW he was going to take a swing at me," Miranda continued her story, walking into Ethan's apartment. "I just stood there, frozen. I didn't know what to do. No one's ever hit me before!"

Ethan nodded. "So how did he end up with the broken ribs?"

"Well, after he took a couple swings and broke my face, I was pissed! I shoved him away from me, into our bedroom doorway. The earth energy may have gotten loose, so it was a strong shove. And doorways have all that reinforcement behind them. So I shoved him hard. He fell. Then I called the police. They just assumed he took a bad fall, which wasn't wrong."

"I'm so sorry this happened," Ethan muttered, carefully hugging her. "It's going to be fine. It's better to be done with it now."

"Meh! My face is broken, Ethan! I never thought he'd actually hit me. He's such a coward!"

"Your nose will heal fast, and the bruising, too. Remember how beat up Matty was after banging her face during the seizures? That was so much worse than this. A couple days, you'll be back to normal," he soothed.

"I never thought he'd hit me," Miranda said again. "I should have packed my stuff and left when Sam offered. I wanted to make it a year so I could force him to pay maintenance and claim half the value of the house. That was a bad decision."

Ethan's eyebrows shot up. "You stayed for *money?* Don't ever say that to Sam. He'll lose his damn mind."

"I stayed because I wanted what was mine! Most of our assets were gifts from my family. I knew Sam would help me, but I'm tired of being coddled. I had a plan! I wanted my money from our joint assets so I could get started with what I wanted to do. That's all moot now. There's no equity in the house; we bought it right after we got married. Everything needs to be sold to split evenly." Miranda's voice was resigned and tired. Defeated.

"Do you want to shower now or go to sleep?" Ethan asked.

"Thank you for coming to get me," she slurred. The drugs were starting to weigh heavily on her now that she was safe. "If you don't mind, I'll get cleaned up before sleeping. I know I can't get the stitches wet, so I'll be careful. Then I'll get out of your way in the morning. I'm sorry about the drama."

"I told you that you're welcome here. You're not in my way," Ethan said. "I was actually hoping you'd stay for a while until things got straightened out for you. I have two empty bedrooms. Building security is obscenely good."

"I noticed. Your doorman is armed," she said, eyes blinking slowly.

"Sam went around the bend after I was attacked."

Not unlike what's going to happen when he sees you like this. Good grief, Larry better buckle up, he mentally added. There was no sense in saying it out loud. It would scare her.

"I am Sam's favorite brother. Don't make me unhappy." Ethan gestured down the hallway, grinning. "The good bathroom's back that way."

WHEN THE SHOWER TURNED OFF, he knocked on the master bathroom door. "I found some pajamas for you. Beth had some things here. She used to bop around between brothers until she and Hennessy finally figured things out."

"All the good bits are covered." Miranda tried to smile with her swollen mouth, opening the bathroom door wrapped in a towel.

Holy fuck! Larry punched more than her face, Ethan realized, noticing the bruising around her neck and shoulders.

"I fell backward into the dresser the first time he hit me, so my back is banged up. They took x-rays. Nothing is broken. He pulled me upright by grabbing here." She gestured to the sensitive connective tissue between her neck and shoulder.

"Holy cow," Ethan muttered. "I'm so sorry, sweetheart."

She huffed a cynical snort. "It's like you saw it coming. Are we sure there's not a bit of time walker in you, too? You told me your story on Saturday night. I thought, 'That could *never* happen to me.' Yet here we are, two days later."

"Here. Clothes. I wouldn't want you thinking I'm making a pass at you," Ethan said with an eye-roll.

"How fucking stupid is that?" Miranda couldn't help but laugh.

"Can't fix stupid," Ethan agreed. "Get dressed. Everything will be better in the daylight, after a good night of sleep and a healthy dose of muscle relaxers."

"Thank you for letting me stay," Miranda said, tears in her eyes again. "Thanks for letting me use the big bathroom."

That caught Ethan by surprise. "Huh?"

"I use the guest bathroom at home. Lawrence likes having his own bathroom."

"It's all his now! Once his ribs heal. Have you ever had a broken rib?"

"No."

Ethan smiled. "I have. He's going to be uncomfortable for a while. Couldn't have happened to a bigger asshat!"

Miranda frowned. "I didn't mean to hurt him badly. I just wanted him to stop. He was all but foaming at the mouth. I feel bad that he's going to be in pain for a while."

Ethan snorted. "I don't. And you shouldn't, either."

3

Is that…bacon? And toast? Miranda wondered as she woke up on Tuesday morning. The apartment smelled like a breakfast wonderland.

"Hi," she mumbled, stumbling into the kitchen.

Ethan smiled. "Still a little drugged, huh? You were out like a light once you finally relaxed last night."

"I'm so sorry. I don't remember going to bed. I'm sorry."

Ethan paused, turning to look at her. "What exactly are you sorry for?"

"Um. I'm sorry I didn't put myself to bed, that I needed your help," Miranda eventually responded, looking confused.

"Fortunately, none of that bothered me. You called me for help. I picked you up at the hospital, knowing you'd need help. So there's nothing to apologize for. Agreed?"

Ethan's eyes stayed on her until she nodded.

"How would you like your eggs?" he asked.

"Oh. Um. You don't have to cook for me. I'll be fine with just some coffee if that's okay."

"Nope, that's not okay," he replied simply.

"Huh?"

Ethan smiled again. "I would like it very much if you had breakfast. An actual breakfast. With protein and carbs and fat that your body needs to heal. Not just hot water and caffeine. So a breakfast of coffee isn't acceptable to me. Do you like eggs?"

"I love eggs," Miranda admitted.

"Then why not have eggs and bacon and toast with me?" Ethan asked.

Miranda blinked, thinking for a moment before finally nodding.

"I'm not picky about eggs. I'll eat them however you make them," she acquiesced.

Ethan nodded. "Poached?"

"Poached eggs and toast and bacon. It's like a breakfast fairytale."

Ethan's eyebrows raised. "What do you usually have for breakfast?"

She watched him in silence again, not answering the question. "Miranda?"

"I don't eat much. Lawrence complained if I gained any weight. And when I'm upset or anxious, I get sick easily." She said the words slowly, considering their implication as they came out of her mouth.

Is he going to pity me? Look at me like I'm a pathetic wretch? I can't imagine what he must think of me, Miranda thought.

"Well, let's avoid being anxious, then. You're safe and loved here, just as you are," Ethan said easily, unsurprised by her confession. "Have some fresh-squeezed orange juice. I ran down to the market across the street and got it this morning."

Calm acceptance. I shouldn't have expected anything else. I wonder what life is like to have this kind of support all the time.

"Don't you have to work this morning?" she asked, still thinking.

Ethan scrunched up his face. "I called Hank and told him I was taking a few days off. You're stuck with me. I'll be here to help for a few days at least."

Miranda dropped her gaze, blinking fast.

"Randa?"

I've pulled him away from important things. I'm interrupting his life.

"I'm sorry. You didn't have to do that. I'm fine."

"Seriously?" he asked, laughing.

She looked up, confused.

"You just hobbled your ass down the hallway. I heard you whimper trying to get out of bed."

Miranda's cheeks flushed red. "Sorry."

"For what?" Ethan asked again, his tone clipped.

She sighed, shaking her head. "I don't mean to be a bother."

"You're not! Stop it!"

"I'm sorry!"

"Holy shit, Miranda! You need help. It's fine to need help sometimes. After I was out of the hospital and done recovering with Hank and Darla, at least one brother stayed with me for months until I was comfortable in my space again. One of us lived with Sam for pretty much his entire life until Addy surfaced. This is what family means. This is what true friendship is like!"

I have no idea how to respond to that, but this kindness makes my chest hurt.

They were silent as he finished making breakfast. Sliding a plate of food in front of her, he continued.

"How about this? We'll say thank you for the things we're grateful for. And, we'll say we're sorry when the other person has been hurt in some way. That's how those phrases should be used. I'm sorry you're hurt, Miranda. I wanted better for you. I'm grateful you called me, that you trust me enough to ask for help. Thank you for that. Please don't sully that trust by continually apologizing. It's not necessary."

She sat quietly, eating breakfast and thinking over his words. "Thank you, Ethan. Thank you for helping me, for answering the phone last night, and for breakfast now. I'm glad you'll be here with me for a few days."

Ethan grinned. "See! That wasn't so hard."

She smiled back before her expression turned sad again. "I need to find a lawyer."

"We'll get on that right after breakfast. I'll go pick up your medication once we're dressed."

"Oh. I don't have any clothes," she realized.

"Beth has all kinds of stuff in her room. After we talk to the lawyer, we can call my mom's shopper, Deo, to acquire some clothes for you. Or we can call Hennessy."

"Hennessy?"

"Yup. I'm sure he'd be delighted to go to your place and get all your stuff. I don't think you should go back there, though. If you do decide to go back to the house, do not go alone."

Miranda chewed on her lip. "I'm not ready for everyone to know what happened."

"Meh."

"Meh?"

Ethan rolled his eyes. "Hennessy is Loyalty. He's not going to spill the beans."

"WHAT IS this nonsense about you and Lawrence?" Charles thundered into the phone later that afternoon.

"I'm filing for divorce. Actually, I'm filing as we speak," Miranda said calmly, sitting across from a lawyer in Ethan's living room.

"Fine. Good. You were miserable. No one wants to see you miserable. But that's not what I'm talking about, and you know it!"

Miranda sighed.

"You need to drop those criminal charges right now!" Charles yelled.

Miranda didn't respond.

"He'll lose his security trading license. He'll lose his job at the brokerage. He won't be able to be a financial advisor. Being charged with a felony will end his career. Drop those charges this instant!

"Right now, Miranda!" Charles yelled again.

The silence persisted.

"Miranda?" Charles demanded.

"You didn't even ask how I was doing," she whispered. "You knew he was arrested and charged with beating me. You didn't ask. You're more worried about his securities license than how I'm doing?"

"He said you were fine. The whole thing got blown out of proportion. He's much worse off! Broken ribs! Do you have any idea how much that hurts? No, of course, you don't."

"And you believed him?"

"Fine. How are you, Miranda?" Charles asked, his annoyance and disdain evident, even over the phone.

"My nose is broken. I have eight stitches in my face. I can't move my right shoulder much. The entire length of my back is bruised from hitting the dresser."

"Well, I'm sorry for that. What's wrong with you, arguing over something stupid like that? You should have just let him be!"

"I have to go, Daddy," Miranda choked out, tears dripping down her face.

"Don't hang up. Miranda, you have to drop those charges! It would be dreadful for the family brokerage and for him if you went through with them. You call now and drop them!"

"Do you know what we were arguing about?" she asked, unsure why she didn't hang up.

"He said you called him stupid and then talked about dating a man that was pretending to be gay."

"No, Daddy. He accused me of necking with Ethan Trellis at Matty's party. I said that was stupid. Ethan is gay. He said Ethan was only pretending to be gay to meet women. I said that was the dumbest thing I ever heard. He told me that I couldn't see Matilda anymore. I told him that I'd file for a divorce this morning. Then he attacked me.

"That's the long and the short of it. He broke my face because I refused to stop seeing my sister. Because a gay man gave me a hug. That's it. You're demanding I drop the charges against someone who would do that, Dad. Is that what you want?"

"Yes, Miranda. You need to drop those charges! I'm sorry your feelings got hurt. I'm sorry you didn't get your happily-ever-after with Lawrence. I don't think you even tried. But file for a divorce and start over. Don't destroy the firm and his life because you're pouting about bad life decisions!"

A small piece of Miranda's heart broke at his words. "I have to go, Dad. The lawyer is waiting. Give Mom a kiss from me."

"WHAT AN ABSOLUTE SHIT-BAG," Megan breathed, getting her first glimpse of Miranda's injuries, entering Ethan's apartment on Thursday afternoon.

"Agreed," Ethan said, closing the door behind her. "Hi, Megan."

"Holy cow." Megan winced, ignoring Ethan as she lifted Miranda's shirt to get a look at her back. "This is unbelievable. I would never imagine him being violent."

"Me, neither," Miranda agreed. "I completely froze up at first. I wonder what would have happened if I didn't get a lucky shove in."

"Best not to think about it," Megan admitted. "Ethan, thank you for helping her. But, sweetheart, come home with me. Daddy and I don't want to see you be in anyone's way."

"She's not in my way," Ethan disagreed. "She's going to stay here."

Megan blinked, watching him for a second. "See, and I would swear you're gay."

"I am." Ethan frowned, startled. "What does that have to do with anything?"

"I don't understand why you want her to stay," Megan admitted, looking confused.

Ethan's frown deepened as he looked between the two women. "She's my friend, and I'm glad for the company. I live alone and have plenty of space."

After an awkward silence, he continued. "I don't mean this to come off terribly, Megan. Forgive me; I'm sure it will sound judgmental. But do you have any idea at all how friendship works? Family and friendship? Matty knew friendship but had a limited concept of family. I don't think Miranda knows what either thing is."

Megan rocked back on her heels. "No, Ethan. I don't share your worldview when it comes to family. That was clear on Saturday. 'Family' is something different to you people. I left one daughter and will regret her loneliness for the rest of my life. I won't repeat that mistake."

"I'm going to stay here, Mom. Daddy is unhappy with me. I don't want to deal with that right now. And I don't want to see Lawrence. I know he wants to 'talk' about things. He can talk to my lawyer. I'm staying here."

"Megan, would you like something to drink?" Ethan offered before Megan could respond. "Come in and sit down. I'm sorry we're having deep conversations in the entryway."

Watching Miranda hobble painfully toward the living room, Megan sighed. "Thank you, Ethan. I'm fine. Randa, do you have an ice pack?"

"Heating pad," Miranda said, settling back into the armchair by the wall. "Feels better now that it's been a few days. Sit, Mom. What do you want to order for lunch?"

"Does Matty know you're here?" Megan asked.

"No. I haven't told her yet. I dodged her call this morning. Did you tell her?"

"She doesn't call me. You know that," Megan chided.

"Sorry," Miranda murmured, knowing she had touched a sore spot.

"Why call Ethan instead of Matty or Matthew?" Megan asked, curious. "I never would have expected you to call Ethan."

"We have an understanding," Miranda said with a grin as Ethan handed her another glass of lemonade. "You know I'm going to float away if you keep pushing the fluids on me like this, right?"

"You need them." Ethan smiled. "Anti-inflammatories and muscle relaxers need to be flushed out of your system. Why shouldn't she have called me?"

Megan shook her head. "I just didn't know you were close."

Ethan and Miranda shrugged at the same time.

"Gah! Stop doing that!" Ethan smiled in sympathy at Miranda's wince.

"I forget. But it's getting better."

"Are you going to drop the criminal charges?" Megan asked.

"Nope," Miranda said, unrepentant. "He started swinging. It's on him."

"Charles said that you're being stubborn about this. He said to tell you that you aren't welcome at home until you drop the charges."

"What the hell?" Ethan interjected. "Five minutes ago, you were pressing for her to come home. Now, there's no home for her to return to?"

Miranda sighed, looking at the floor.

"Megan?" Ethan asked. "Can I get an answer to that?"

"I wasn't supposed to want to stay here, Ethan. I was supposed to be eager to go home," Miranda explained. "The one-two punch was ruined when you wanted me here."

Megan sighed. "That's not fair. I want you to come home. Your father wants you to drop the charges. I didn't tell him that I intended to bring you home with me. I thought we'd discuss this like reasonable adults once you were home. There's no way he'd kick you out like this."

"And now?" Miranda asked, still not looking at her mother.

"You're not coming home with me, so I'm trying to make you understand how upset he is about this. Your father loves you more than life itself, and he's upset enough to deny you a welcoming home."

Miranda's head moved in a semblance of a nod, still focused on the floor.

"This is going to hurt the family firm. Hurt all of us, Miranda. Are you sure this is what you want?" Megan pressed. "You want to hurt your family?"

"Goodbye, Megan," Ethan barked.

Megan started, eyes flicking away from her daughter to Ethan's furious gaze.

47

"Get out."

"Ethan, I don't mean to upset anyone, but it's the—"

"Get out, Megan. I will call security."

"Ethan, it's fine," Miranda muttered.

"No, Miranda. It's not. This is not fine. And it's over. Time to go, Megan."

Megan looked around, confused for a minute, before standing to leave. "Feel better, Randa. I wasn't trying to upset anyone. I'm sorry."

"For future reference, *family* doesn't do that. Family doesn't guilt a loved one for standing up for what's right. Family doesn't tell a loved one to take the punch to the face in good humor, for the good of the family business," Ethan scolded as he walked her to the door.

"WE CAN GO," Miranda said, shaking with anxiety.

"Would you please stop it? We don't have to go to Sunday dinner. We all miss it sometimes. I let them know I wasn't coming tonight," Ethan soothed again. "Everything's fine. I was thinking of Thai food for dinner. There's a great place around the corner. What do you think?"

"I'm so sorry, Ethan," she said again, quickly. Nervously.

"Randa, there's nothing to be sorry about. I'm not hurt. Really. Truly. There's no need to be upset. You're not ready to face everyone, so we'll stay home."

"You could go without me," she offered, looking a little sick.

"No, I couldn't."

"You could. I'll be fine."

Ethan chuckled. "I'm confident you'd be fine. However, Darla would have my hide if she thought I left you alone, injured and vulnerable. Absolutely not. Thai food or pizza. Those are my suggestions. What would you prefer?"

Miranda shook her head. "Aren't they upset about you skipping work this week? And now you're not showing up to dinner, too?"

"Sam asked if I met someone. That's about it." Ethan shrugged. "It's fine. Promise. I don't take time off work often, but when I do, it tends to be a few random days at a time. This isn't terribly unusual for me."

"You're really not mad?"

"Well, I'm kind of annoyed you think I'd be mad, but no." He smiled.

"I'm sorry—" she started immediately.

"Miranda! I was teasing. Why are you a bundle of nerves?"

"Because you want to go to Sunday dinner!" she burst out. "I didn't mean that you couldn't go. I meant that I didn't want to go. But we can go."

Ethan blinked, thinking. "Miranda. It's fine to do what you want to do. We can opt to do what you want instead of what I want. People compromise and take turns. Others do that all the time."

"I know," she said, eyes downcast.

"But?"

"I just...I don't know. I just usually do what others want."

"Well, you're in the process of kicking the shit-bag to the curb. Time to think about what you want instead of what he wants."

She made a so-so gesture with her head, still not meeting Ethan's eyes.

"What does that mean?"

Miranda sighed. "I don't know. It's always been like this. Before Lawrence, it was my parents or my grandfather. I'm not supposed to cause waves."

Ethan grinned. "No, waves aren't your thing. Earthquakes. You cause earthquakes, Randa!"

That startled a laugh out of her. "Thai sounds good."

4

---

*T*hirty minutes west of Ethan's apartment, there was a pounding on Hank and Darla Trellis's front door. After a survey of the baffled faces around the table, William got up to answer it.

Expecting trouble, he unholstered the gun at his side before looking through the window next to the double door.

"What the fuck?" he exclaimed, throwing the door open. "What are you doing here?"

"Obviously, I'm interrupting dinner," Micah said. His grin was conspicuous in its absence. "That gun would do you no good against me. The best you could hope for is a bit of a distraction. You people need to learn how to use your energy. Playtime is over."

"Micah!" Sam called, relieved. "Please, we need help. Will you take—"

"Samuel," Micah interrupted. "I need you to find James. I must speak to James and Evelyn. Now. They have failed in one of their primary responsibilities. We are far out of balance."

"I know we're lost, but I don't know why." Sam sighed. "Come in."

"Are you able to reach him?" Micah asked, not moving from the threshold.

"I am. I am not as fast as Addy at finding the binding, but I can do it. Come in," Sam said again.

"No, Walker," Micah refused. "You are too much a man of this age. It is dangerous to invite one like me into the heart of your family circle. I will wait here."

Sam sighed. "Micah, I see you clearly through time, in a way I can find and see few others. You are clearer to me than most of my own family. I can say, with confidence, no matter how lost we are, you are no threat to me or mine. If you forget what I am, what we are, I will take exception to it. But not tonight. I am tired and grieving. Please, come in. We need help. I will find James, and we'll go to him together."

Micah's brow furrowed. "What has happened? You look...different."

Sam nodded, turning from the entryway toward Darla's dining room. "Come on."

Following Sam hesitantly down the hallway, Micah looked around him with interest.

"This is what's known as a family home," William muttered. "There's love and family and strong bindings here. It's what happens when you allow yourself to care about others and them to care about you."

Micah nodded. "Please, don't ever forget that truth, Lord Terror. Those like you are near impossible to contain, short of death, should you lose your moorings."

"That wasn't the point I was trying to make," William responded.

"I know," Micah murmured, a flash of a sad smile crossing his face before he entered the dining room behind Sam.

The family around the table went silent at the sight of him.

"Wow, shit has gone south," Noah muttered.

Micah met his eyes, giving a single nod.

"Micah, this is Talise—" Sam began.

"Lady Water," Micah murmured with deference, staring into Talise's amber eyes, so very like his own.

"Sam and Adaline, you now hold a circle with three of the four elements?" he asked after a moment. "I don't think I've known such a complete circle before."

Sam's eyes narrowed. "Four. Our circle has four corners."

"Yes, of course," Micah said, confused.

"Four elements," Sam clarified.

Micah blinked.

"You know Matilda, Lady Light. You know Lucy, Lady Wind, who is asleep upstairs. This is Talise. Lady Water doesn't sound as awesome as Lady Loch. Just saying."

"That is three, Samuel. Three elements. Elements are not the same as corners. Who stands in the fourth corner?"

"Matilda's younger sister, Miranda, stands as Lady Earth."

Micah's eyes traveled the circumference of the table, pausing briefly at Linda. "You are the child's mother?"

Linda glanced around, uneasy. "My son, Ree, has been in Lucy's care."

"Lady Perseverance?" Micah asked, eyes focused on Linda as she shifted uncomfortably.

"So they tell me."

"So it is," he replied. "Earth does not sit at this table. Joy is also missing. Why is your circle incomplete this evening?"

"Ethan couldn't make dinner," Darla said, looking at Sam, concerned. "Miranda has only joined us for a few meals. She's not normally here."

Micah's brow furrowed in concern. His fear was evident, even to those without extra senses. "We must collect Joy. He is in danger."

Without another word, Samuel and Micah disappeared.

"HOLY FUCK!" Ethan yelled in shock as Samuel and Micah appeared in his living room. "What the fuck, Sam!"

"Where? Where is the danger?" Samuel's eyes were wide with fear and glowing with power as they panned the room, looking for a threat.

All expression dropped from his face when he spotted Miranda, bruised and stitched, in the living room. "Miranda?"

"Hi, Sam," she squeaked as his enraged energy rolled through the room, unchecked.

"Lady Earth," Micah said, bowing his head in greeting. "Ethan, you are not injured?"

"Of course not! What the fuck is happening? Sam? You look like you've been through a war!" Ethan continued to yell.

"Let's go back."

Not waiting for agreement, Sam moved Ethan, Micah, and Miranda with him back to Oak Park in the blink of an eye.

"SO I CALLED Ethan from the hospital. He came to get me and has been helping me for the last few days. I filed divorce papers on Tuesday. It's over," Miranda finished, eyes on the dining room table in front of her—decidedly not looking at her sister.

And not looking at Matthew. In her peripheral vision, she could see him sitting rigid in his chair across from her.

I'm not going to notice Lucas touching his arm. I'm just not going to pay attention. I can't help that, Miranda coached herself.

Matthew's eyes stayed unfocused at half-mast, glassy with rage and chaos that was palpable in the room. No one acknowledged it, so she wouldn't mention it.

He was going to find out eventually, Miranda told herself for the third time. *Still, I wish Ethan told him when I wasn't around.*

She sighed. *I'm such a coward.*

"Why didn't you call me?" Matilda asked, trying to hide her hurt.

I've failed Matty, too. Just when we were getting to be friends. I've failed everyone and made a mess of everything. How do I explain this?

With a small squeeze of Ethan's hand, Miranda thought of her sister's laughter on Monday night as the field where the circle was held turned into a giant puddle. The reminder of past joy helped.

"I didn't want you to see me like this," Miranda admitted, tears leaking down her cheeks as the words fell out of her mouth without thought. "I didn't want anyone to know he hurt me like this. I was so ashamed. I didn't think he'd ever do this, and you all knew he was terrible. I just couldn't call and have you see…to tell you later and have you understand that it happened. Well, that would be one thing. But for you to see…I just couldn't—"

A lightbulb exploded in the overhead fixture. No one reacted. No one glanced at Matthew. Everyone sighed with relief as Luke's energy pulsed through the room.

"I'm sorry," Miranda whispered, back to staring at the table as tears raced down her cheeks.

Before Miranda knew what was happening, Matty had her wrapped in a hug.

"It's over. I'm sorry. I'm so sorry, Miranda. It's over now," Matilda soothed as Miranda wept.

"What happened here?" Ethan asked, eying the unknown, battered woman next to Adaline. He tried to lighten the mood in the room. "Take-out pizza? We had take-out pizza for Sunday dinner, and I missed it?"

Darla glared through her tears as she headed toward the glassy-eyed sisters, joining the hugging and soothing.

A window exploded in the big room.

"Sorry," Matthew slurred. "Trying."

"Sleep?" Hank asked Luke. "Maybe sleep would be best?"

"It's not working," Luke muttered. "He'd normally be out three times over by now. Addy? Maybe?"

She shook her head, gaze traveling between Matthew and Miranda. "Leave him be. You're making it harder for him to control it."

"Sam?" Micah asked with a sigh, unmoved by the family drama.

"I've already told him we need him," Sam said. "He said they'll be here as soon as they can."

"Fine." Micah nodded. "I would also like to know what happened to you tonight."

"I am so tired," Linda muttered, putting her head down on the table.

"Don't sleep there," Adrian said. "Come on, I'll take you up to Lucy and Ree."

"He's really okay?" Linda asked, eyes filling with tears.

"He is fine. Better than he's been in the time that I've known him," Adaline assured her, touching Linda's hand to share peace and safety with her. "Sleep well."

Before Adrian was at the top of the stairs with Linda, there was another knock on the front door.

"It's James and Evelyn," Sam said as he and Adaline stood in unison.

"WHAT DO YOU WANT? We were in the middle of a thing!" James bitched as soon as Sam opened the door. "What the fuck happened to you? You look all...singed!"

Evelyn frowned at Sam then Adaline. "Addy, is that blood on your dress? What has happened?"

"Gah! What are you doing here?" James shouted as Micah came into view.

"Jackass," Micah growled. "You have failed at one of your primary responsibilities! Josiah lives. We are horribly out of balance with three time walkers!"

"That's impossible," James disagreed. "Literally impossible. What's going on? What happened?"

"Would you please come in so we don't have to have this conversation with the front door open?" Sam's fatigue was apparent in his voice. "I don't know what's going on, either, but I also believe we are out of balance."

"Don't invite people into this house, Samuel," Evelyn scolded, stepping into the entryway. "This dwelling holds an incredible amount of latent energy. Do not open it to others so easily."

"And why aren't there wards around this house?" James complained.

"They'd probably know more about these things in general if you, you know, TAUGHT THEM THINGS!" Micah yelled. "But why be responsible for anything? It's only ALL OF LIFE AND TIME that depends on these things."

"No more yelling," Sam muttered. "People are sleeping upstairs. Where are you going, Addy?"

"I will draw wards quickly—"

"No—" Sam started.

"I'll go with her," William said, already following Adaline out of the house.

"Your circle has grown," Evelyn observed, following Sam into the dining room. "Introduce everyone?"

Sam slumped down in his chair, ready to drop into sleep. "You already know almost everyone. That's Talise. This is Miranda. There. Now you know."

"Introduce them," Evelyn insisted. "All of them. Sometimes, taking the names changes things. I am curious about what names are present."

Sam groaned at her. "Later?"

"I'll do it," Jake offered, watching Sam with concern.

"You know William, Fear."

"Lord Terror," Evelyn corrected. "He took the name Terror. Introduce correctly."

Jake rolled his eyes at her. "I don't know everyone's name. Adrian, Rage, is coming down the stairs now from checking on Lucy, who is Wind. She's sleeping—"

"Why is Lady Wind sleeping?" James asked.

"Do you want introductions, or do you want the story?" Jake snapped.

"You're a grouchy Anchor tonight. What's your problem?" James complained before Evelyn could hush him.

"Matilda—"

"Lady Light needs no introduction." James winked.

"Father Time," Samuel, as the Walker, breathed at James. The voice was both pleading and echoing with power. "Please don't make me kill you."

The room was silent while James stared at Sam, assessing.

"I'll be quiet," James said finally.

Jake sighed. "Miranda, Lady Earth, is Matty's sister. Ethan, Lord Jolly, you know. Matthew, Captain Fucking Chaos, you know. I don't know what his actual name is. He didn't say it out loud.

"Luke, Lord Peace or Peacekeeper or whatever. Noah, Lord Lust. Or is it Lord Passion? I don't give a fuck. This is stupid.

"Talise, Lady Water, just took her name on Monday.

"You know Hennessy is Loyalty. That didn't change. You don't know that he almost died tonight. Beth is Hope, and she's a mess. Leave them alone.

"You know my parents, Hank and Darla. You have seen Greggory, Nora, and Ben. And I think you know Addy's family. Blake and Clyde took the girls home, so Ava and Jess, who has all-sight, are here on their own," Jake finished.

"Lord Jolly?" Ethan asked.

"Like that's so much worse than Lord Joy. It's like you were destined to be gay." Jake snorted.

"You could be Lord Gay," Noah offered.

"Stop," Sam's voice cracked through the room.

"Who called you Peacekeeper?" Evelyn asked Luke after an uncomfortable silence.

"Huh?" Luke asked.

"Peacekeeper. Who gave you that name?"

"A friend," Luke said cautiously. "Why?"

"Who? What sort of friend?" Evelyn pressed.

"Why are you asking?"

"The title has significance outside of our circles. I saw the title flare from you when he said it. I know it belongs to you. Where did it come from?"

Luke looked over at Jess. She shrugged.

"All sorts of shit flares around you people. Different names and titles call different bindings and strengths forward. I wouldn't worry about it."

Evelyn continued to stare at Luke.

He shrugged. "I've told you all I'm going to tell you. Stare to your heart's content, Mother Life."

She sighed, unhappy. "You have gathered all four elements and an impressive number of Pillars."

"Perseverance also rests upstairs. She's new to us." Jake grinned, knowing the information made Evelyn uncomfortable.

She met his eyes, expressionless. "If we had not spent so much time building a pair worthy of the names, this circle would be terrifying. As it stands, you are merely frightening."

"Why?" William asked, coming into the room with Adaline.

She shook her head. "It is what it is now. Please, everyone is here. What happened? Why do you think Josiah is alive, Micah? I agree with James. We destroyed his body. There was no life in it. He cannot live now."

"I disagree," Micah said. "He stole all the energy and took fifteen lives in Adaline's clearing two months ago."

5

Talise frowned. "Who's Josiah? Who are you people?"

"Oh. My bad." Jake winced.

"You suck at introductions," Noah commented.

Jake glared at his younger brother. "Do you want to do this?"

"No. I didn't say I was any better at them. I'm just saying you suck at them."

After smacking Noah, Jake explained. "Talise, Miranda, this is Evelyn and James. They were the Walker and Mistress before Sam and Addy took the names. Now, I guess, they're known as Mother Earth and Father Time. They pull away the energy that Sam and Addy push into the world."

Evelyn's smile was condescending. "That's not accurate."

"See? You suck at this," Noah commented, dodging the follow-up head smack.

Evelyn rolled her eyes. "Let's not get sidetracked, boys. Mother Earth is a misnomer. The title belongs to me, but I have no sway over earth energy like you, Miranda. The elements belong to Sam and James. I am more accurately called Mother of Life, but no one says that in practice. We don't take energy from the world. We collect the energy that has expired."

"You're grim reapers?" Jake asked, interested.

"No," Evelyn replied. "James said it well when we were in Texas. If Sam and Adaline are on cooking duty—they create the energy—we're on clean-up patrol. We make sure things stay tidy."

"I don't know what that means." Adrian sighed.

"They collect ghosts, ghouls, and demons and show them the door. They shake out the monsters. They're not grim reapers. They're more like bouncers at a night club. They keep the riff-raff in check," Micah explained.

Evelyn nodded. "Not a bad analogy."

"That's pretty badass!" Noah grinned.

Evelyn rolled her eyes again. "On with it, Micah."

"Wait!" Talise interrupted.

"Josiah was the Walker before James. He was never particularly well-balanced, but he turned a corner eventually and had to be put down. He was hell-bent on world domination," Micah said, guessing her question.

"Thanks. And I'm sorry." Talise gave a sheepish smile. "But who are you?"

Micah's grin exploded briefly. "Apologies, Lady. I am Micah. I was once Lord Hate. I gave up that name long ago and continue on now without my circle. I mean you no harm. I might take a swing at James if I get the chance, though."

"It's completely understandable." Evelyn smiled, patting Micah's hand as she sat down next to him.

"Hey!" James bitched, pulling out the chair on the other side of Evelyn. "I offered good beer in an attempt to make peace. You're the asshole that wouldn't drink it."

"You killed my love. I'll spit in your beer before I drink it," Micah barked.

"I told you! It was an accident," James pouted.

"No, it wasn't! You beheaded him."

"Fine. Not an accident. A misunderstanding," James corrected. "Still, get over it. It's been like three *hundred* years. Talking about carrying a damn torch."

"Enough!" Evelyn yelled. "Just don't look at him, Micah. You can punch him if you get the chance. I'm all for it. It'd be cathartic for me."

With a glance around the table, Micah realized everyone was staring at him. "What?"

"Nothing," Will murmured as everyone looked in another direction.

"Why do you think Josiah is still alive?" Evelyn asked Micah.

Micah shook his head. "Sam first. What happened tonight?"

Sam groaned again, realizing he'd have to tell the story. "A few weeks ago, Jess saw a poisoned binding sapping energy from Ree—"

"Who's Ree?" James asked.

Sam glowered at him. "Lucy's nephew. The one you wouldn't have noticed getting shot. Remember him?"

"Well, now I do," James muttered. "Thanks for making me feel like an asshole, though."

"You make it so easy," Sam murmured back. "We watched for the bad binding again. When it showed up, I took Lucy, Hennessy, and William to the source. Jared was there, all set to do an evil villain monologue. But one of the men who has been stalking Lucy was also there.

"Hennessy shot the stalker six times. The bullets rebounded, so Hennessy is in the back corner, having just recovered from near-fatal gunshot wounds. He would have died if I didn't get him back here quickly."

"You people desperately need to learn to use the energy at your disposal. Hennessy, have you pulled energy to heal from the circle? Do you know how to do that yet?" Micah asked.

"I can't do that. It's not something Loyalty gives me," Hennessy disagreed.

Micah shook his head, glaring at James. "It is not something

Loyalty gives you. It is something the circle gives you. I'm certain Fear would share that power with you. I'll teach you. Later."

Sam nodded. "Thank you. We need to know how to do that."

"James and Evelyn should have taught you."

James shifted uncomfortably without comment.

"Told you," Evelyn muttered.

"There's a ton of pillars for a circle this young. They can lose a few," James whispered to Evelyn.

Sam stared at him again.

"What? It's true!" James objected.

Sam continued to glare.

"Fine. Sorry," James caved. "I don't know how to heal from the circle. How could I teach them?"

Sam continued his story. "Anyway, Lucy and I called lightning and fire, destroying the house—"

"That was you! That was you?" Micah asked. "In Ohio? That was you?"

"I have no idea where we were."

Micah exhaled a sigh of relief. "It was you. It had to be you. That makes sense."

"What happened to Jared? And the guy who stalked Lucy?" Ethan asked.

"Jared ran away when I opened time. The stalker is dead." Sam's voice was flat, emotionless.

Ethan met Sam's eyes, nodding in understanding. They'd discuss it later, in private. "How does Jared fit in?"

"I have no idea," Sam admitted. "I didn't wait for the monologue. Hennessy was down for the count. I was going to toss Jared and the stalker outside of time and deal with them later, but he disappeared. I don't know how he did that."

"Jared? From the restaurant, the one that left?" Micah asked, looking at Nora and Greggory.

Nora nodded. "He was somehow involved with Linda's capture and imprisonment. She spent the last two years in a cage."

Micah's eyebrows shot up. "Perseverance, indeed."

"How do you fit in, Micah?" Evelyn asked. "Not that I'm not delighted to see you."

Micah rolled his eyes. "I will not stand in a circle with him, Evelyn. Sorry."

Evelyn smacked James upside the head. "Why is *everything* so difficult with you?"

"I said I was sorry," James muttered, staring at his hands.

"Micah, why do you think Josiah is alive?" Sam asked, trying to get to the point.

"Over the summer, Adaline's clearing in Texas was harvested by a group of hunters. They went to extreme measures to desecrate the land and left a marker to siphon off any energy that went into repairing things," Micah began.

"How did you become involved in it?" Evelyn asked him, eyes narrowed. "Were you hunting the hunters?"

Micah shook his head. "Adaline asked for my assistance."

Evelyn's brow furrowed. "You were still in the area?"

"No, she built a speech binding to me before they came back to Chicago."

"Break that, right this instant!" Evelyn roared, startling everyone. "What were you thinking?"

"I will not break it," Adaline said simply.

"Adaline, that is extremely dangerous! You don't know what he does!" Evelyn yelled.

"Evie, calm down," James soothed. "She's fine. You can see she's fine."

"He belongs to me, even if he won't admit it yet," Adaline replied. "Sam said he will not die at the hands of a hunter."

Micah sighed. "I've told you repeatedly to break that binding. I will not stand your circle, Adaline. I told you. This is not my place."

"I disagree," Sam said at the same time James muttered, "Wrong."

"William," Darla said, making a show of sniffing.

Will looked at his mother, confused, before taking a deep breath and jumping up. "Ah, shit! Yeah, I'll turn off the natural gas line."

He shot Matthew a dirty look as he headed toward the kitchen.

"Maybe you'd be less grouchy with me if you took your name," James suggested, ignoring the sidebar.

"Tell us about the clearing?" Evelyn asked, trying to gather herself and get back on track. "I will discuss the stupidity of that binding with Adaline later."

"After the children left, I read the marker—"

"What is a marker? What do you mean you 'read' it?" William asked.

Micah nodded. "I will show you. But hush now. I must tell them."

William glowered at him.

"They must know this, Terror," Micah explained, gesturing to James and Evelyn. "They know what I mean. I will explain it to the rest of you later. If the one from the bar, Jared, is involved and the captive woman is now within this home, I am afraid for this circle. Please let me get through the telling."

William nodded in understanding, noticing Micah's speech had lost the cadence of modern times. Micah was worried.

"I read the marker without breaking it then waited. They didn't return. Eventually, I baited and trapped a pair of hunters then unleashed their stolen energy in the clearing."

"You carried stolen energy through Adaline's wards?" James asked, eyebrows raised.

Micah smirked at him. "We share a binding."

Evelyn groaned. "Addy!"

"No," Adaline replied quietly. "He has done me no harm, and I would not have my ward hurt him."

"After the energy was unleashed in the clearing, they resurfaced within a couple of hours—two men in their early twenties. They looked around for the source for close to an hour then gave up. After harvesting the energy, they left through their marker, leaving me a nice trail to follow. It led me to a neighborhood in Ohio. But when I got close to their base of operations, I found a ward I was unwilling to cross."

"I'm still waiting for the part where Josiah jumped out and yelled, 'Boo!'" James said, rolling his eyes. "This smacks of well-organized hunters, not a time walker."

Micah narrowed his eyes at James. "It was such an interesting ward. Those who crossed it, even unwittingly, paid a toll in the form of time. More accurately, they paid for crossing with the minutes, hours, and days of their lives. The ward moved through lifelines and took a small fee at every crossing—just hours or days from each life. But the ward moved through *time*. Affected *time*."

James's eyes narrowed.

"It was not your energy. I know your energy," Micah said with a nod. "And Sam would never draw such a ward. In all of my years, I've only known of one time walker willing to draw something like that. It did not feel like his energy, and you insist he is gone. But I don't know of another that would have the skill. Do you?"

"You're sure it was time? Not life?" Evelyn asked.

"It felt like standing too close to Sam when his eyes glow." Micah shrugged. "If that isn't time, I don't know what is. I am not an expert on either type of energy, Mistress. I will take you to the place if you want to feel it. The ward is gone now; it fell tonight. But the echo was still there when I left."

"Mother," Evelyn correct, lips turned up. "I am Mother now. Mistress no longer."

Micah tried to return the smile. "I know. I will forever think of you as Madrid did, though. You were the joy of her life, Evelyn. Her last thoughts were of how proud she was of you. She wanted you to understand that but was not sure if it ever got through to you. There is more she wanted you to know. Can we discuss it later?"

Evelyn nodded quickly, blinking as tears trickled down her face. "Please. I didn't consider that you might... I didn't consider it."

Micah nodded. "So, the ward was strange. I thought of crossing it. I don't mind the idea of losing some time. But I thought it would likely scare off the hunters if they could feel what I was. So I waited and watched. I was within a thousand feet of the house. I had a good sense of the energy flowing within it.

"Three days after I camped out, I felt someone Walk through space. That was not you, Sam?"

"No," Sam said, shaking his head. "I wasn't there before tonight."

"The guy probably jumped markers," James disagreed. "You're blowing this out of proportion. Evie and I will go find the hunters, but it's not Josiah."

Micah shook his head. "The ward didn't ripple when the hunter crossed it. I only know of one way to move without disturbing a ward."

James chewed on his lip. "You couldn't sense the whole ward. A thousand feet from its center, you wouldn't feel the *whole ward*. It probably reverberated on the opposite side of where you were, Micah."

"I placed markers around it, so I could move quickly when needed. I think they knew I was there. The two men from the clearing came out, looking around a few times. Anyway, I hopped around the markers. There was no movement in the ward. Maybe it is as you say, but I believe someone Walked through space.

"Tonight, I felt it again. The first time would have been Sam's arrival. The second time would have been the other one, Jared, leaving. Sam did it again when he brought Hennessy to safety and again when he returned to Wind. Lightning struck. I felt time open then slam closed, more lightning and fire, then a fifth Walk as Sam and Wind returned with the captive.

"Admittedly, I didn't realize Sam had been there. I thought Jared opened time and called lightning. Still, there was Walking that no one in this room did and the ward that stole time. I believe there is a third Walker, and we are out of balance," Micah finished. "None of the previous Walkers I have known are shining examples of kindness and humanity. Josiah is the only Walker that I've ever known to steal time."

"We'll go look. Show us to the house. Evie and I will investigate. You were right to bring it to us. But there's no way it's Josiah. I destroyed his body myself, Micah. He's gone," James said, trying to sound comforting. "Maybe there is some sort of artifact to account for the ward. Maybe the ripple was small enough that you missed it when the hunter moved to another marker."

"James, I don't—" Micah stopped talking as Matthew slumped over, leaning on Luke, dead asleep.

"Finally," Luke muttered, shoving his favorite brother more solidly into his own chair. "Will?"

"I'll move him later," Will said quietly, returning to the table. "Could have been worse."

"When did the ward fall?" Sam asked, pulling Micah back to the topic at hand.

Micah blinked.

"Did it fall when Jared Walked?" Sam asked.

"When time opened," Micah replied. "The ward fell when time opened. It crashed down without warning."

James's face scrunched up. "What did you do with time open?"

"I sent an asshole to hell," Sam said without inflection.

"No, really? What did you do?" James asked.

Sam sighed.

After a short pause, James grinned. "Really? Do you want to be on cleanup? I'll go back to cooking!"

"Huh?" Sam asked, surprised.

"You snuffed out energy. That's my gig! If you're going to do that, I'll do your gig. Your gig is easier." James laughed.

Sam stared at him, confused.

"That's what Evelyn and I do, Sam. We remove the entities that shouldn't be here. Opening time to do it seems a little...excessive. But you do everything with flair. Whatever. To each his own."

"I cursed someone to hell, and that's your response?" Sam asked, sounding ill.

James snorted. "Hell. Ha! Like we have any sway over that shit.

That's out of our realm, Sam. You took his energy out of circulation. That's it."

James laughed at Sam's shocked expression. "You are incredibly dramatic. I had no idea you'd be this much fun. This is right up there with 'the cold' nonsense. I love it. Evelyn, we did good! I'll buy you a chocolate malt later to celebrate. Extra malty, just the way you like it."

"James," Evelyn chided, recognizing Sam's confusion. "Not helping."

Sam looked around the room at his family. "But the compass moved?"

"Really?" Evelyn perked up. "Let's see. Did the flowers do anything?"

"WHAT COMPASS? What are you talking about?" Micah asked, concerned.

Sam lifted his shirt, exposing the compass marking on his chest.

What the fuck is that? Micah wondered, concerned for Sam.

"Mistress?" Micah murmured.

Adaline turned, unzipping her dress to show the wildflower garden on her back.

"The accordance goes up further than your arm?" Micah asked. "I see some of it wrapping around your side."

"It runs the length of my body on the left side, from shoulder to toes. I wear long dresses or pants now."

Sweet Mistress, what have James and Evelyn done to you? Micah tucked his fear for the young pair aside, pulling forward his rage at James and Evelyn.

"It was a good try, but I still felt that spike of fear," Will muttered. "You're afraid of Adaline!"

Not a bad guess, but incorrect. Micah hid his smile.

"What is this?" he demanded of James and Evelyn. "The damn accordance marks weren't enough? What did you do?"

"We don't know what it is, either," Evelyn said, eyes downcast.

She knows they're in trouble, Micah realized, frowning.

"Eh, you probably hurt your sensitive morals, Sam." James shrugged, ignoring Micah completely. "Get over it. Removing the monsters will be your job eventually. And, yeah, you are the decider of what constitutes a monster. Spoiler alert: I'm probably the first—well, now, I guess, the second—monster you'll drop. But not until I'm truly a monster, okay?"

Ignoring James, Sam addressed Micah. "I don't know what the markings are. We're still us, though." The words were slurred as Sam's fatigue continued to roll through him.

Micah sighed. *He is too tender to stand as Walker, to hold that name.*

"What are we going to do about the third Walker?" Micah asked, trying to get back on track.

James groaned. "There is no third Walker. But I told you. We'll go hunt your hunters down."

"What of the children?" Micah demanded. "You can't leave them like this! They are in danger. Whomever Jared is, he held that woman captive for a reason. He wanted to talk to Sam for a reason."

"Are we 'the children?'" Adrian whispered to Will.

William nodded. "He's like three thousand years old. I'll take it from him. *Father Asshole* pulls that shit out, though, and I'll take umbrage."

"Sounds good," Adrian agreed.

"*The children* are fine," James taunted at William.

"They don't know enough not to invite others into this house," Micah disagreed.

"Their ignorance is charming." James grinned.

Micah and Evelyn glared at him.

"Now? Or are we waiting until after we're done being adults?" Adrian asked.

"You really want to punch him? I can get in on that, I guess." Will shrugged.

"He made fun of Sam."

"True," Will agreed, rising to his feet in time with Adrian.

"What about that 'Do no harm...' thing, *Doctor Adrian?*" James asked, warily watching the brothers approach. "I thought we were just joking around. You guys do that joking around thing..."

Adrian snorted. "You're not my patient. Also, that particular mandate is often irrelevant or misleading. You know nothing about medicine. We don't joke with jackasses."

Will paused. "Well..."

"Fine," Adrian corrected. "We don't joke with unrelated jackasses."

William nodded.

"But I made Sam feel better about sending the guy to hell, and I only made fun of him a little bit," James whined, looking around the room, hoping for intervention.

Sam cleared his throat.

"Boo," William and Micah complained together.

"Let it go," Sam muttered.

Adrian grinned, patted James on the head, and went back to his own chair.

"You weren't going to punch me? You were joking! I knew it!" James sounded outraged.

"You whine worse than a spoiled toddler." Adrian laughed. "Why would you just sit there and wait for us, dumbass?"

James's face fell as he realized his own stupidity.

"You're also fun to mess with. Just so you know," Will taunted.

"Can you see what's coming?" Micah asked James.

"Fuck, I'm terrible at time walking, and you know it," James complained. "Sam, what's coming?"

Sam shook his head before resting it on the table. "We are off course. I agree with Micah. It's better now that Tali is here, but it still feels wrong."

"The circle feels wrong?" Micah asked.

"No, time feels wrong."

James frowned, confused. "Time has no feeling, Sam. That doesn't make sense. Don't sleep yet. What do you mean? Use better words."

"So tired. Why am I so tired?" Sam mumbled.

"You opened time, called fire and lightning, and played taxi for a lot of people," Evelyn replied. "James loses days when he opens time like that. Did you open it twice? Did I hear that correctly? Jared ran away when you opened it the first time. Then you opened it again to get rid of the other guy."

"Mmm," Sam agreed, eyes drifting closed. "Not all the way. I didn't open it all of the way. Most of the way."

"Sam!" James barked. "What do you mean by 'time feels wrong?'"

"Wrong."

"Sit up, Samuel," James demanded. "You are here with most of your circle. Pull the energy you need from them."

"Hmm?" Sam said, unmoving.

"Samuel, look at me." The command in James's voice echoed through the room. Everyone, including Evelyn, stared at him.

Sam shifted to meet James's gaze, head still resting on the table.

"Good," James purred. "Can you feel the energy of your circle around you? Can you feel the organic circle? Feel for your pillars."

Sam's head moved in a slight nod as he slowly blinked.

"Pull energy from it, like inhaling a breath. You use the circle to let go of energy all the time. Do the opposite now. Pull energy to yourself," James said, his voice still heavy with the base sounds of power.

Sam's eyes rolled in his head as he shivered.

"This feels so fucking strange," Jake muttered, "like vertigo."

"Don't like this," Sam groaned. "How do I make it stop?"

"Make what stop?" James asked, power fading from his voice.

"How do I make the energy stop coming to me?"

"Stop pulling it into yourself," James said.

"I'm not pulling it. Please make it stop." Sam groaned again.

"Anchor, re-center the circle," Micah commanded. "He pulled the center from you. Take it back."

"How?" Jake asked. "I don't know what to do. I don't do the organic circle thing on purpose."

"I really am going to fucking punch you," Micah warned James. "Why did you leave them in ignorance like this?"

"Jake, do like Sam did. Pull the energy toward yourself," Ava said, entering the conversation for the first time in hours. "Feel for the circle, and just pull it back."

"I don't know how! I can't feel it. I've never felt it," Jake said, panicking as Sam started to shake.

"Here, Jake," Jess said, extending her hand to him as she walked around the table. "Here, look with me. It'll be easier if you see it. It's all lopsided and strange right now."

"But what do I..." Jake's words trailed off as he looked through Jess's eyes. "Gross. It's wrong. All wrong. There. Better."

Did he just pull me into this circle? I can't be in this fucking circle! Micah thought as he pulled himself out of the energy loop. *For fuck's sake, they're all clueless!*

Sam went still, head resting on the table as he breathed deeply. "Ouch."

"Sorry, Sam!" Jake apologized. "Are you okay? Holy fuck, I don't know what I did wrong."

"What did you do to fix it?" Jess asked. "It happened so fast."

"I have no idea," Jake admitted, "but it's better now. Sam?"

Sam nodded, head still on the table. "Still exhausted mentally and physically. But I have lots of the other energy again."

Micah sighed in frustration as Evelyn's uncontrolled fear rolled through the room.

"You've no right to be afraid of them, Evelyn. You were part of creating this and leaving them in ignorance," Micah scolded.

She nodded in acceptance. "Still terrifying, though."

"Sam, what's wrong with time?" James asked, still focused and severe.

"It feels like it does when I'm lost in it. When I can't find the correct 'now.' Like we're somewhere we shouldn't be," Sam replied, shifting to sit upright.

"Where are we supposed to be?" James asked.

Sam glared at him.

"I have no idea what you're talking about, Sam. But, again, you're much better with time than me. Do you see immediate threats to your circle?"

"No. No threats," Sam admitted. "It just feels wrong. It feels like when I Walk without the indifference and end up in a wrong time."

James's eyebrows shot up in surprise. "You Walk without the indifference on purpose? For more than a second or two?"

Sam nodded. "All the time."

"And yet you seem mentally sound." James's lips tipped upward. "Teach me?"

"Why should he teach you *anything*?" Micah argued. "You've been completely useless to him!"

James sighed. "They're fine, Micah. This circle is fine. They will mature at their own rate. Stop it. They would not be as strong or as tightly bonded as they are if Evie and I intervened earlier. He would not be the savage gentleman necessary to balance life today if he grew up knowing what he was. You quit your job. Stop trying to tell me how to do mine. If their ignorance bothers you so much, stay and teach them."

Micah turned his glare on Evelyn.

"I don't deserve that glare," she objected. "I told you to punch him!"

"Are we about done?" Hank asked tersely. "Matthew's zonked out, Hennessy's not far behind, Beth is barely keeping it together, Addy's covered in dried blood, and Sam's exhausted. Can we wrap this up?"

"Micah, show us the fallen ward. Let's leave them to recover," Evelyn said.

"They are in danger," Micah repeated. "I can feel it. Can't you feel it?"

Evelyn and James shook their heads in time with each other.

"Sam said there's no immediate threat," James offered. "I'd trust that. I agree that whomever Jared is would like a word with them, but he ran tonight. He won't be back for round two before daybreak, and he won't walk through the wards."

"You will stay here tonight? All of you? Behind the wards?" Micah asked, his unhappy, disbelieving gaze circling the table.

"Sam will take us to the lake house. There are better wards there. We have been practicing," Addy offered, stretching to touch Micah's hand and offer comfort.

"I don't know where that is. I won't be able to find you there. But you will all stay behind the wards?"

Sam sighed. "I'll go with you, Evelyn, and James."

"I can take—" Addy started.

"James will bring me back to you," Micah shouted over Adaline, glaring at her. "He will play taxi for me, Sam. Take your flock home. I'll be there soon."

Adaline frowned at Micah's small head shake.

Sam's eyebrows quirked up. "You trust James enough to Walk with him?"

Micah snorted. "I've been trying to get him to end me for three centuries. If he wanted to kill me, he'd have done it by now."

James nodded, shrugging. "That's accurate."

6

---

*M*iranda rolled over in her bed at the lake house. She couldn't stop thinking about the energy and rage rolling off Matthew after she finished recounting her horrible week. She couldn't stop seeing him, slumped over, unconscious, on the table.

My fault. Absolutely my fault. I've made such an awful mess of my life.

At the thought, her energy slammed against Miranda's control again. She'd always maintained a healthy balance with the power. But that evening, it railed against her mind in a wholly new sensation, like it was trying to drive her to do...*something.*

I'd do what it wanted, if I could just figure out what the heck it wanted. She sighed, rolling the other way. She closed her eyes, only to see Matthew's face from earlier in the evening in her mind's eye. His gaze was unfocused when the light bulb had exploded overhead.

The energy slammed through her again.

"I don't know what you want me to do!" she said aloud, keeping her voice quiet. She didn't need to wake everyone in the house by talking to herself.

As the energy shifted, pressure built behind her eyes, causing stabbing pain in her head.

"Oh, no," she muttered, jumping out of bed. Either her nose was going to bleed or she was going to vomit. Maybe both.

Overloaded? I wonder if there's an alarm on the patio door. Maybe I can go outside to ground some of the energy?

Miranda threw on her clothes and headed for the bedroom door.

"Eeek!" she squeaked. When she opened the door, someone fell backward into her room.

"Shh! It's me," Matthew whispered, climbing to his feet. "Sorry."

"What are you doing?"

"Right now? Feeling like an idiot. A minute ago? Sleeping. You okay?"

Miranda shook her head in the darkness. "Sick. I think my energy is overloaded. I was going outside."

"Oh. Goodnight." He walked back into the hallway, starting to pull the door closed behind himself.

"Matthew!" she breathed.

He stopped but didn't look at her.

"What? Why are you sleeping in the hallway?"

She could see his shoulders tense in the darkness.

He sighed. "I wanted to be sure you were okay, but then I didn't want to wake you up. My energy is all fucked up, so I sat down before I lost my balance completely. I fell asleep sitting there."

Miranda's heart sped up as she tried to swallow the lump in her throat.

I've unbalanced his energy. I've made such a mess of my life, it's hurting my circle. Guilty tears burned her eyes.

"Matthew—"

He shook his head, running a hand through his hair in nervous frustration. "Good night."

"Please don't go," she choked out, tears running down her face as she stared at his back.

"I'm sorry this happened, Randa. I'm sorry about Larry," he

murmured, at a loss for better words. "Please. I can't handle the tears. My energy feels like it's raking nails against my brain as it is. If you keep crying, I'm going to kill him. I think I mean that literally. Prison wouldn't do well with me as an inmate."

Another sob broke loose.

"Miranda," he groaned, shoulders slumping forward.

"I really need a hug," she whimpered. "I know I've made a mess of everything, and you have every right to be mad at me. But—"

Her head was buried against Matthew's chest with his arms wrapped around her before she could finish her rambling.

A sound that might have been a moan under other circumstances escaped Miranda as her energy cycled and balanced with Matthew's touch.

Oh. That's what it wanted. Huh. I wanted this, too. That works out.

"Shh. I'm not mad at you, Miranda. It's not your fault," he gasped, panting for air. "I'm so sorry. I'm so sorry I've made such a mess of things. It's my fault."

"Are you okay? Do you need to sit?" she asked, trying to make sense of his words through his labored breathing.

"I'm fine. Just sorry. Very sorry, Miranda."

She began laughing through her tears. "How exactly is this your fault? You didn't marry him!"

Matthew nodded, not really reacting to her words. He seemed to be holding onto her to keep himself upright.

"Are you sure you're okay?"

He nodded. "Good. Better. The energy is better."

"Huh. Me, too. The energy was seriously pissed off at me earlier. It's never been mad at me before."

He hugged her tightly again, shaking with wheezy laughter.

"Your energy makes you short of breath? Is that a chaos thing?"

"No, Randa. I'm fine, almost back to normal."

"What—?"

"Did Ethan make you breakfast? He makes great eggs. He's the brother to live with in a bind. Good choice," he breathily praised, hoping to distract her.

Is he trying to distract me?

"Are you doing that thing?" she asked.

"What thing?"

"That thing," Miranda said, her tone obstinate.

"What thing?"

"Where you try to distract me from things you don't want to talk about?"

"Of course, I am. Why would I want to talk about Larry?" he asked, all innocence.

"That's not what I mean. You don't want to talk about why you're breathing hard."

"Remember that blue sweater you had? With the V-neck? Do you still have that sweater? It was the same color as your eyes. I loved that sweater on you."

"Matthew!"

"What?"

"Breathing!"

"I'm still doing it," he replied, tone sensible.

"Why do you do this? You know it makes me nuts."

He grinned down at her.

"I'm going to kick you!"

"I'll stop hugging you. Then where will we be?"

She sighed, falling silent.

His mouth opened and closed twice before words made their way out. "It hurts. The energy builds up painfully when it doesn't cycle properly."

She nodded when he paused. "That happens to me when I don't do my morning routine."

He smiled. "Tell me about the morning routine."

"Tell me about the breathing," she retorted.

Matthew's teeth clacked together in the darkness. "I don't have a way to cycle it without risking chaos or madness."

She waited silently.

"I lost my shit tonight," he finally whispered. "My energy unraveled. It's just settling down now. The pain is gone. I'm catching my breath from the sudden absence of pain."

"I caused you pain." The words fell heavily out of her mouth.

Matthew scrunched up his face. "I caused me pain."

She rolled her eyes. "How is this your fault?"

"It just is." He grinned.

"Again, you didn't marry him."

"No, but it's my fault. I should have done things differently in college," he admitted.

"Matthew," she groaned, bumping her forehead against his heaving chest. "Don't be that guy."

"What guy?"

"That guy that blames himself for everything, even when it's ridiculous. I married him, knowing what he was. It was my bad decision. I'll own it, thank you very much."

Matthew's breathing was the only sound for a moment. It was leveling off.

"You regret college? Specifically, what part of college?" she whispered, looking up at his face in the darkness.

Oh, God. Please don't regret becoming friends with me. My heart can't take that right now.

Matthew huffed out a laugh, wiping the tears from her face. "You know which part."

No. No, no, no, nononono…

"Or maybe you don't?" he asked. "What's wrong?"

She pressed her forehead into his chest, hiding her face again. Her words came out muffled. "Please don't say you regret being friends. My heart can't take that right now. It would be worse than Lawrence taking a swing at me."

Matthew pulled her away from his chest and scowled at her. "Randa! Why would you think that?"

Another sob escaped her mouth, this one more like a squeak of relief. "I don't know. I'm sorry. Everything went so wrong at the end of that semester. I made a fool of myself, and then you were just gone. You told me to move on, said you wanted better for me, wished me well, and then…gone.

"That first time I had dinner with your family, when you wandered into the big room, I thought you were a figment of my imagination. Like my brain was conjuring forth the closest friend I ever had to comfort me in my humiliation."

She felt him flinch before his arms tightened around her again.

"I'm—" she started.

"Miranda, if you say you're sorry, we're going to have words." He cut her off, his tone flat.

She went silent.

"I don't regret being friends with you. I regret the end of college. I regretted that last night as it was happening. I knew it was wrong, and I knew it was going to suck. I thought it would just suck for me, though. Not for you. I didn't want my fucked-up energy to hurt you. I wanted you to find someone better."

"That's stupid!" she yelled, forgetting to be quiet. After the words were out, she covered her big mouth with her hand. "Oops."

"There's good soundproofing in the house." He chuckled. "Apparently, self-sacrifice is a Trellis man thing. I'm in good company. Will and Adrian had the same outlook on life for a while."

"It's just energy, Matthew."

Matthew closed his eyes, yawning, resting his head on top of hers. "I'm sorry. I should have handled that night better. I regret hurting you like that."

She yawned in response to his yawn. "You're still not at fault for Larry. That one's on me."

He yawned again. "Fair."

"Okay," she said, voice mellow as she leaned into him.

"Now I really am going." He smiled into her hair.

"You can stay," she whispered to his chest, cheeks flushing in the darkness. "I don't want you to hurt."

He shook his head. "It's balanced out again. How about you?"

She nodded. "The energy feels better."

"Night, Randa," he whispered, kissing her forehead before closing the door behind himself.

As usual, Adaline woke as the sun peeked over the horizon on Monday morning. Sam was still fast asleep alongside her, his hand resting on her midriff.

"Shh," she soothed as Sam stirred in his sleep. She slipped out of bed. Usually, he would wake with her, and they'd walk together. It was a sign of his fatigue that he still slept.

Their puppy jumped into her warm spot in the bed, curling up next to Sam.

"Good boy," Addy murmured, rubbing his ears.

Of all the luxuries to enter her life over the last couple of months, indoor plumbing was Adaline's favorite. After a quick bathroom stop, she pulled on stretchy pants and a sweater before heading out of the bedroom.

They'd leave the lake house soon. Their home on the cornfield lot was in the final phases of construction in the western suburbs of Chicago. While they remained, Adaline would enjoy the lake view and beautiful colors of the changing leaves.

She started the coffee for their guests before heading out to the yard. The puppies, gathered from various houses the night before, trailed behind her.

"Be good," she whispered. "No barking. They're still sleeping."

Roving around her, the puppies were glad to be playing together again. They had been separated from each other for a few weeks. Strong and healthy, the dogs lived with their families now.

Adaline had moved on to nursing a litter of abandoned kittens Sam found in an alley behind the Trellis skyscraper.

"Please don't leave the wards," Micah said, walking toward her from the shore.

She frowned. "You did not sleep."

It wasn't a question, but he shook his head anyway.

"We are safe here, Micah. The wards are reinforced."

"Yes, but they only work if you stay within them. You walk through them every morning with Samuel."

She tilted her head, surprised that he knew that.

"I can feel the energy, Adaline. You and Sam walk the same paths every day. I can feel that just as I felt a third walker. Please, believe me. I know James and Evelyn think I am wrong. I know what I felt." Micah's voice was full of quiet intensity, urging her to believe his words.

She nodded. "I believe you."

"Does he?"

"Sam has known we are out of balance since July, Micah. If you are concerned about him not believing you, you are wasting your energy. He has been upset about the lack of balance for months."

Micah exhaled in relief.

"What did James and Evelyn say about the ward last night?"

"They don't believe me," Micah muttered. "Evelyn walked the ward line and returned what energy she could to those within it. James could sense some aspect of time but said something about it not being 'all of time.' I don't know what that means."

Adaline nodded. "Sam says there is a time embedded within a place. When I look for it, I can see it, too. But I don't like to see it. It's confusing."

Micah's jaw clenched. "Mistress, do not show or tell anyone how much you and the Walker share. As much as possible, keep that to yourself."

"Why?" she asked. "That's why you talked over me last night? About Walking?"

Micah nodded. "That's why I talked over you. I don't believe James or Evelyn would harm you, but time walkers are not known for being well balanced, and there were other people in that room."

"But I believe they already know, Micah. Most of them, at least."

"That's unfortunate."

She stared at him, waiting for an explanation.

"Does it cause you pain to harm living things?" he asked.

She nodded.

"Excruciating pain?"

She nodded again. "Unbearable."

"Then I would have you keep your additional abilities to yourself in the event you need to escape harm. It's difficult for a Mistress to defend herself. If they don't know you can Walk without Samuel, they will not think to counteract it. Keep it to yourself."

She pulled a face at him. "I don't think anyone means me harm, Micah. It was Sam that Jared wanted to speak with, not me."

"We don't know that," he disagreed. "We don't know what he wanted or how he was involved. I did not touch him that day at your parents' restaurant in Dallas. But I knew he did not belong there. He did not share the same bright energy that flowed from everyone else in that room. There is danger coming. I would have you leverage every advantage at your disposal, Mistress."

Taking his hand, she walked toward the water. "Walk with me?"

He nodded, gently squeezing her hand, accepting the peace and comfort she offered.

"You fear for us?" Adaline asked after a few moments.

"I do."

"Because of the third walker?"

Micah shook his head. "You are gentle creatures. Both you and Sam are good. There is no hate at all in you and very little in him. I fear James and Evelyn have let you grow powerful only to watch you suffer in your roles, ill-equipped to handle the responsibilities."

"We have each other. We will balance each other."

"You don't understand, Adaline. You don't understand what the energy will do to him over time."

83

"Samuel? You worry the energy will harm Sam?"

"They spoke of indifference last night. I don't think you under-stand what—"

"Micah, I know exactly what the indifference is." Adaline's voice was flat.

"Then it's already happening. He's already—"

"He has done nothing to harm me." She stopped walking, staring out over the water.

Micah waited.

She sighed, looking up at him. "He has not harmed me. I don't believe he would intentionally harm me under any circumstances. He does not touch the indifference; it holds no sway over him."

He watched her in silence, still waiting.

She dropped her eyes. "It came to me when we took the names. I tried to take his power through our accordance. I came close to strip-ping all of the energy from him."

Micah staggered back in surprise, dropping down to sit on the ground next to her. Suddenly, his smile burst free as he exploded with laughter. "That might be the most amazing thing I've ever heard. That brings me comfort, Mistress!"

She glared at him.

He grinned up at her. "You have the instinct to protect life as well as control power, Adaline. That balance was missing from every Mistress I have met before now, including Evelyn."

"She tried to drain James," Adaline replied without expression. "She has a survival instinct."

"She would have given up without Madrid. They needed each other to face off against a young, stupid Walker. Samuel is young, but I doubt he has ever been stupid."

Adaline's voice was emotionless when she eventually responded. "Samuel is kind. Gentle. After things were balanced between us again, he offered it to me freely. The indifference is within my reach in our binding. I could take it from him and kill every living thing on this planet without suffering for my actions. You've no cause to fear him. You should fear me."

Micah's smile remained in place. "I fear you both, but I am delighted as well. You are a pair equally matched. There is plenty to fear in him, Adaline. I've seen him coast through time. I've seen him melt a man's brain with a touch. I felt him shake the earth with lightning last night."

Adaline nodded at the truth of his statement then sat quietly next to him.

"You will stay with us? Help us learn?" she asked.

He nodded. "I will teach you. I may not stay, but I will visit to teach you."

"But you will not take your name?"

Micah's eyes were downcast. "I don't know what name you would have me take, Mistress. I am no longer Hate."

She nodded.

"I turned from this path—turned my back on it. I knew there was no going back when I did it, but I could not stay as I was."

She nodded again.

"I cannot stand your circle," he said, voice muffled with sorrow.

"Nonsense," she replied immediately. "You will stand with us tonight, named or not."

Micah blinked.

"It is Monday. Our circle stands tonight. You insist we are in trouble. You will come to watch over us."

Micah swallowed. "I cannot."

"Why?"

"Adaline, I am unable to stand your type of circle since breaking with my own. Your circle will not hold with me in it."

Her brow furrowed in confusion. "It will hold. You stood Jake's circle last night until you forced yourself out of it."

He shook his head.

"You don't want to be in a circle?"

After a pause, he responded. "I do not want to feel the rejection of your circle. It would be a harsh reminder of the choices I made, a reminder of where I am not welcome."

"But I'm inviting you. It will hold," she replied, voice confident.

"I will accompany you this evening as you requested, but I will not attempt the circle, Mistress."

"James and Evelyn invited you to their circle. You did not refuse them in this way," Adaline objected.

"They hold a different type of circle now. It is unlike yours. I am not welcome in a circle of ascendance."

"You are welcome in my circle, Micah. You will stand my circle," she replied stubbornly, lips pursed in anger at his rejection.

Micah sighed, shaking his head.

Adaline frowned. "I dislike that you do not trust me. I will tell Sam. He will tell you."

"THAT'S BULLSHIT." William laughed, sitting at the kitchen table with Micah and Noah. "Of course it will hold. Shut up and eat your corn flakes."

Noah grinned at the disbelieving expression on Micah's face. "Somebody at this table is not used to being laughed at."

Micah glared at Noah.

"I wasn't talking about you," Noah said quickly. "I was talking about the cranky, badass loner behind you."

William banged his hand on the table. "I love this. I love that we get to fuck with you now!"

Micah glared at him.

"You're really going to hang out for a while?" Will asked, laughing.

Micah nodded. "Maybe visit rather than stay. But you must learn. James and Evelyn don't seem inclined to teach you. I like this circle. I think the world needs this energy, and I've never seen so many uncorrupted pillars and so strong a pair. It makes me wonder what comes next. I would rather not lose any of you to ignorance. How is Loyalty this morning?"

The humor dropped from Will's face. "Beth said he's fine. She's unwell, though."

Micah nodded.

"Have you known all the pillars and pairs throughout your lifetime?" Noah asked, trying to change the subject.

Micah shook his head. "No. I stumble across them occasionally. I met a pair in the seventies that scared the ever-living fuck out of me. I am glad James and Evelyn didn't offer the names. Before that, I ran into a handful of pillars that found each other in the nineteenth century. They had no pair but had figured out enough to be dangerous."

"What happened?" William asked.

"I drained them. They were not smart. It was easy." Micah said the words without inflection or remorse. "I won't tolerate a circle looking for domination."

Will nodded, unsurprised. "That's what happened with your circle? Why you left?"

Micah shrugged, climbing to his feet and rinsing his bowl in the sink before putting it in the dishwasher.

"Can I get an actual answer on that?" Will asked.

"I was Hate," Micah muttered, voice low. "When I was told to push hate that would cause world war and mass destruction, I refused. When my circle tried to force it, I gave up my name. Any other questions?"

"So many." Noah sighed.

"Can we be done for now, asshat?" Micah rolled his eyes.

"I guess." Noah nodded.

"Tell me again why you can't stand a circle," Will suggested.

"The energy won't accept me."

"That's such a load of horse shit," Will disagreed.

Micah lifted his eyebrows.

"You've not stood a circle in two thousand years?"

Micah sighed. "I have not stood your type of circle in two thousand, four hundred, thirty-two years, and fifteen days."

"Not that you're counting or anything." Noah laughed.

"I'm not sure why you're laughing at me. You wussed out on being Lust." Micah grinned. "It's one of the most fun names, and you biffed it."

"I was hoping you didn't catch that."

"I did. I was saving it for an opportune time. I don't want to overuse it. Where is your Lady?" Micah asked.

"Hanging out with Adaline," Noah replied, shrugging.

William grinned. "Did Tali call her parents yet? She didn't go home last night."

"Fuck. I was trying not to think about that, William!" Noah bitched.

Will and Micah chortled together.

"Her dad hates him," William choked out between laughs. "Fucking hilarious. Last week, he was all, 'Go back to the other one!' You missed the love triangle, man. She and Luke dated for like a minute, and then she and Noah hooked up."

Micah's grin swallowed his face. "Peace and Water? They had to be so boring together!"

"I don't want to talk about it," Luke grumped, walking into the room.

"She kept falling asleep!" Will cackled.

"I stole his girl—" Noah crowed before banging his head on the table, unconscious.

"Oh man." Micah dropped his own head to the table, shaking with laughter.

William glared at Lucas.

"What? I'll take shit from you two. I'm not taking shit from him," Luke said with a shrug. "He's a moron."

"Tali!" William yelled. "He did it again!"

Luke's eyes went to slits. "Really? You're going to snitch on me?"

"Would you rather I beat you?"

"Maybe," Luke grumbled, not making eye contact as Talise and Adaline walked into the room.

"Lucas," Talise snapped. "Stop doing that. You'll give him a complex."

"Holy fuck," Micah howled as tears of mirth dripped down his face.

Luke rolled his eyes. "Give me a minute, Tali. The toast is almost toasted. I'll get out of here. I don't want to listen to him whine."

"Have you checked on Matthew yet this morning?" William asked.

"I stuck my head in his room a little bit ago. He was sound asleep. I think we'd know if he woke up on his own. I'm going to go see if I can get him moving," Luke replied, heading for the hallway toward Matthew's room with a pile of buttered toast and a pair of water bottles.

"Sam?" William asked Adaline.

"Sleeping peacefully with McFly," she answered.

Will rolled his eyes, biting back the smile that always came with the mention of Sam's puppy. "I can't believe you let him name that dog."

She grinned. "I still haven't watched the movies."

"McFly?" Micah asked.

Will let him think about it for a moment, knowing he'd catch up on his own.

Micah grinned again. "*Back to the Future*. I really do like this circle."

Noah stirred as Tali played with his hair. "Mmm, hi," he slurred.

"Time to wake up, sleeping beauty." Tali smirked.

Bleary eyes traveled the room, taking in the laughing expressions. "Luke's a jerk."

"Were you needling him?" Talise asked. "What did I say about trolling him?"

"I wasn't! I didn't even get the words out!" Noah objected over Micah's laughter.

"YOU SEEM SURPRISINGLY FINE," Luke noted, handing Matthew a bottle of water as he sat on the bed.

Matthew nodded, running a hand through his bedhead. He chugged the first bottle of water without pause. Luke immediately handed him a second bottle.

"Want to talk about it?"

Matthew glared.

"I'm going to make you talk about it before the energy goes nuts again," Luke warned.

"I'm fine, Luke. It's balanced," Matthew croaked, still waking up.

"Toast yet?"

Matthew shook his head, taking down another half of a bottle of water. "The water bottles are so wasteful."

"Well, I don't have the skills to hide six glasses of water without anyone noticing. So you'll need to either start sharing your oddness with the group or deal with things that make my life easier. Will, Noah, and Micah are in the kitchen."

Luke pulled two additional bottles of cold water out of his sweat-pants pockets. "I would have taken a lot of shit if my pants fell down. You know that, right?"

Matthew sighed. "I hate this."

"I'll recycle the bottles, Matthew," Luke replied, deadpan. "Time to talk!"

"Bleh. I'm fine. The energy is fine," Matthew said again.

"How'd that happen? Sleep doesn't cycle your shit. Did you wander off in the middle of the night and unleash madness in the middle of Lake Michigan? Is there a Kraken out there somewhere?"

"Nope, but I'm fine." Matthew polished off the second bottle of water and grabbed the third.

Luke stared at him. "You're not taking the water down as hard as usual. Your eyes are even focused. What am I missing?"

Matthew didn't respond.

"I know you're not telling me something. Out with it."

"I don't need to tell you everything."

Luke waited.

"Did you knock Noah out again?" Matthew grinned. "I felt the spike of your energy from the kitchen."

Luke's eyes narrowed impatiently.

"You're a pain in the ass. You know that, right?"

There was no response.

Matthew sighed. "I woke up around two in the morning. The energy was tearing my mind apart. I stumbled out of bed and chugged about two gallons of water. It didn't help. The energy was freaking out—"

"You should have woken me up!"

"So I was going to go talk to her, make sure she was holding up okay. But then I got to the door of her room—"

"How did you know which room she was in? You weren't awake for room assignments last night."

Matthew glared at his younger brother again. "We've discussed this. Do you want me to tell this story or not?"

"Sorry, go ahead."

"I didn't know what to say when I got to her door. Everything is so fucked up. But the energy calmed down just being closer to her, so I sat down for a bit."

Luke grinned. "Did you sleep outside her door? Matthew, that's adorable and pathetic all at the same time."

"You couldn't watch an R-rated movie with your ideal woman, and she's now dating your most annoying brother. You don't get to judge me."

"Touché."

"I zonked out, right up until she opened her door and I fell backward into her room."

"Busted!" Luke laughed.

"Yeah. We talked a little bit. She needed a hug. The energy settled down."

"I mean this in the kindest, most supportive way imaginable," Luke began. "But what the fuck are you doing sleeping in here? Why didn't you stay with her last night?"

"Um, she's *married*."

Luke glowered at him.

"She is!"

Luke made chicken noises at Matthew.

"Seriously? Less than a week ago, her husband took a couple swings at her. You want me to jump into her bed while her mind is still reeling?"

Luke considered it for a minute. "Not necessarily. I want an indication that you will jump into her bed when the time is right. You fucked it up in college, and we both know it."

"I don't think she has any idea what that energy cycling between us means," Matthew admitted.

"What do you mean?" Luke asked.

"Last night, she said her energy was mad at her, and that it had never happened before. I don't think she knows how badly I fucked up both our lives."

Luke snorted. "You didn't marry shit-bag Larry. Give credit where credit is due."

Matthew smiled. "She said the same thing."

"So, you explained last night?"

"Nope! Totally chickened out."

Luke winced then made more chicken sounds.

"I deserve that," Matthew acknowledged, folding a piece of toast and shoving it into his mouth.

7

———————

"*A*unt Lucy?" Ree's tiny voice whispered. "Adrian?"

"Right here, buddy," Adrian said, awake immediately. "What's wrong?"

"Where are we?" Ree asked, rubbing his eyes. "I don't remember. I feel weird."

Lucy covered his forehead with her hand. "Feel weird, how? You don't have a fever. Are you sick? Adrian, he's sick!"

"No, not sick," Ree said immediately. "I'm okay, I just feel tingly. Where are we? Why am I in bed with you?"

"We're at the lake house, Ree. We're at the house where Uncle Sam and Aunt Addy live," Adrian explained.

"Oh, I thought we were going to Grandma Darla's house for dinner." His little brow furrowed in confusion.

"We were. We did," Lucy stammered, unsure how to explain. "Then you fell asleep, and we came here to be together this morning."

"Are Mia and Meg here?" Ree's face lit with excitement. Jess's girls were his best friends.

"Yes, the girls are here," Adrian said slowly, watching Lucy.

Ree started wiggling to scoot out of the foot of the bed.

"Ree, stop. Wait a minute. We need to talk to you," Adrian said. "Before you go out to the house, we need to talk to you, okay?"

"Are you going to have a baby?" Ree asked, wiggling with excitement as he climbed back to the bed's center to face Lucy and Adrian.

Lucy swallowed wrong, coughing with her surprise as Adrian laughed.

"No, buddy. At least, I don't think so. Grandma Darla would have told us." Adrian chuckled at Lucy's outraged expression. "I'm not kidding. She has a weird gift. Ask Emma."

"Are you getting married?" Ree asked, singing the word cheerfully.

Lucy smiled. "No."

"Oh. Why not?" Ree asked, disappointed.

"Yeah, Lucy. Why not?" Adrian grinned as her cheeks turned pink.

"You're not helping right now," Lucy muttered to Adrian.

Ree's face lost its joy. "Adrian, are you leaving?"

"No, buddy. I'm not leaving. I promise." Adrian's face fell serious, still regretting the time he spent away from Lucy and Ree over the summer.

Ree frowned again, quiet for a moment.

"I promise, Ree. I'm not leaving," Adrian repeated.

"Am I dying?" Ree whispered. "I'm not going for treatment anymore, but I don't feel bad. Just tingly."

Tears immediately filled Lucy's eyes, spilling down her cheeks. "No, Henry. You're not dying. We think you're all better. No. This is good news. We have happy news."

"Okay." Ree's voice was low and uncertain.

Lucy looked at Adrian before taking a deep breath and turning back to Ree.

"Your mom came home last night, baby. She's here with us. She's healing, but she's with us again."

Henry watched his aunt with no expression on his face.

"She's sleeping in the next room. We can go see her when you're ready," Lucy offered.

The little boy sat silent and still, staring at Lucy.

Unsure what to do, Lucy looked at Adrian again before she continued. "We're all here, okay? All of your uncles and aunts, Grandma Darla and Grandpa Hank. Grandma Ava and Grandpa Clyde. Jess and Blake and the girls. We're all here. Everyone's safe. And your mom's here, too."

Ree shifted his gaze from Lucy to Adrian.

"She didn't want to be away from you, Henry," Adrian explained, worry in his voice. "Your mom was running from bad people and wanted you to be safe with Aunt Lucy."

Ree's tiny face lit with anger so profound, it slapped at Adrian's senses.

"Ree?" Adrian breathed, shocked. Ree had never shown genuine anger before.

"Aunt Lucy ran from bad people, too! But she didn't leave me. She took me with her because Aunt Lucy loves me!" Ree yelled.

Adrian rocked back, nodding in acceptance of the point.

"I do love you, Henry. I love you more than life itself. Never ever doubt that," Lucy said, hugging the tiny warrior boy. "Your mom left you with me because she knew you'd be safer with me than with her. She loves you enough to want what's best, even when it's not what she'd prefer."

"Aunt Lucy," Ree wailed, breaking down into sobs. "Please don't make me go. I don't want to go away from you—"

"NO! Ree, no," Lucy gasped, finally understanding. "You're not going away from me. You're staying with Adrian and me. Don't think that. That's not happening. Your mom will be with us, too. You'll be able to see your mom, too. But you're not leaving us. Understand?"

"You won't make me leave?" Ree cried.

"No, Henry. You stay with me," Lucy said, determination in her voice as she glanced at Adrian. "Your mom won't take you from me."

Ree took a heaving breath, wiping the tears from his face. "You promise?"

"I do," Lucy replied.

"Do you want to say hi to her?" Adrian asked after Ree settled down.

Panic flashed across his face. "Do I have to?"

"Not right away. Not if you don't want to," Lucy said immediately.

"Ca-can I go see Mia and Meg? Are they in the bunk room?"

"They're in the bunk room," Adrian confirmed. "If you're going to bounce around on the trampoline floor, you need to get dressed and put on your bike helmet."

"Adrian," Ree complained, smiling. "The entire room is padded. Why do we have to wear helmets?"

"Because I caught you jumping off one of the top shelf bunk beds after I told you not to do it." Adrian smiled back, glad to see Ree calming down.

Ree paused, getting out of the bed. "She's not going to come in the room, right?"

"No," Lucy assured him. "I'll tell her you're not ready to see her yet."

"I love you, Aunt Lucy."

"I love you more, Ree."

TEN MINUTES LATER, Lucy stood outside the door of Linda's bedroom, debating what to do and say. When last they spoke, Linda was dropping Ree off for a weekend visit.

Three years, Lucy thought. *We haven't spoken in three years. She was in that cage for two of those years.*

She knocked on the door, swallowing the lump in her throat.

The door flew open. "I wondered how long you were going to stand there," Linda said. "You look terrible."

Lucy snorted, wiping tears from her face. "You look like you haven't eaten a good meal in two years."

"I had pizza last night." Linda grinned. "It was even warm. Amazing. He doesn't want to see me."

It wasn't a question. Lucy didn't respond.

"I wouldn't want to see me, either," Linda said, looking at her feet.

"Can I come in? Can we talk?" Lucy asked.

Linda huffed a laugh. "By all means, come into my suite. There's a goddamn seating area here and a private bathroom. Who the fuck are these people, Lou?"

Lucy shook with silent laughter, closing the door behind herself. "It's been a strange couple of months. Are you hungry?"

"Are you going to ring for the butler if I say yes?"

"No, I'd open the door and yell for someone to bring us food. Chances are it'd be delivered by a billionaire. Wanna try it?"

Linda grinned. "You are so full of shit."

"So, Noah," Lucy began as the tray of pancakes and sausages was laid on the table before the women. "If you were to classify your personal level of wealth, what category would it fall into?"

Noah looked suspiciously between Lucy and Linda. "Is this a bet? What's the bet? Linda, this probably wasn't a good bet."

"It's just a question, Noah," Lucy replied with a charming smile.

"It feels like I'm being set up as the butt of a joke. I'd like to avoid that."

"Too late." Lucy grinned. "It's already funny. Play along."

Noah sighed. "Hank told me last week that I'm worth about four billion dollars."

"Son of a bitch!" Linda shouted.

Noah flinched, looking around. "Don't say that! My mother is a very nice woman, not a bitch. Pick a different curse."

"What the fuck?" Linda laughed. "Your mom was the little middle-aged woman at the head of the table last night, right? Darma?"

"Darla," Lucy and Noah said together, looking around anxiously.

"Lou, you too?" Linda grinned.

"She's delightful," Lucy hedged. "She runs this family with an iron fist, though. We do as we are told. Speaking of—bye, Noah. Girl talk time."

"Can't I stay here?" he whined.

"Why? What's wrong?" Lucy asked, curious. She and Noah were not particularly close.

"Tali's hanging with Adaline, and they don't talk with words. Luke made me sleep again. Micah and Will are making fun of me. No one else is awake yet."

"The kids are awake. Go jump around the bunk room with them," Lucy offered.

Noah's face lit with a smile before dropping into a suspicious scowl. "Is Adrian in there?"

"He is."

"I'm not wearing the bicycle helmet! He can't make me," Noah insisted.

"You just go right ahead and tell him that," Lucy said, nodding along.

"He's going to make me wear the helmet, isn't he?"

"Only because the kids are in there," Lucy agreed.

"He's no fun at all. Your boyfriend sucks, Lucy."

"I know," she said, escorting Noah to the door. Turning back to Linda, she grinned. "He sucks in all the right places."

Linda's mouth dropped open in shock. "Did you just make a sex joke? YOU? You made a joke about sex being fun?"

"Hey, by the way, it turns out that sex *is* fun!" Lucy laughed.

Linda's answering smile turned sad. "You have a boyfriend. You're in an actual relationship. I've missed so much."

"Well," Lucy sighed, "to be fair, most of it was awful. Things only got fun in the last few months. Ree found Adrian in June. And it's not like you had a choice."

"*Ree* found the tall, muscle-bound doctor?" Linda asked.

Lucy nodded. "His bloodwork indicated that he had cancer. We did chemo through Medicaid three times. It didn't work—"

"Because he didn't have cancer," Linda murmured. "It was the binding—whatever they were doing to the binding?"

Lucy nodded again.

"He went through chemo because of me," Linda mumbled, eyes filling with tears. "I kept trying to break it, but it came back. Over and over, it just kept coming back. I didn't know how to make it stop."

"Let me tell the story!" Lucy interrupted the morose thoughts, trying to smile.

"Sorry."

"So Medicaid told me to go pound sand, that the treatment wasn't working and they wouldn't pay for anymore—"

"Oh, I bet that went well for them." Linda laughed, knowing Lucy's determination had no bounds.

"I was arguing with a bitchy woman in a billing department at a hospital on the north side when Ree comes into the office, holding Adrian's hand. I thought he was scamming. I wasn't nice."

"Lucy," Linda mock-scolded. "Such trust issues."

Lucy snorted. "Says the woman who spent the last two years in a cage."

"Touché."

"So I was working in this terrible job, we were living in this terrible apartment..."

"I'M NOT sure how I feel about you hooking up with Rage. I mean, I don't fully understand the name thing, but Rage doesn't sound like fun," Linda said skeptically.

"He's the guy that makes the kids wear helmets when jumping around the trampoline room, Linda," Lucy said, deadpan. "You'll see."

"He helped me last night. I don't remember a whole lot before getting hit with the water in the shower, but he helped me. My aunt was there, too."

Lucy nodded. "She's probably here now. I haven't been out in the living room yet."

"I don't remember coming here. I don't remember the car ride."

"I'm pretty sure Sam brought us. No car necessary."

"Sam. The time guy?"

"That's him," Lucy said, eyes welling with unexpected tears.

"Lucy?" Linda asked, touching Lucy's arm.

"H-he came through for me last night. I've never been nice to him, never given him a reason to like me. He scares me a little bit without meaning to do so. But he came through for me. His money saved Ree, he gave me a house, he's never been anything but kind to me. I... haven't been particularly grateful or respectful in return."

They were quiet for a moment.

"I don't know what to say to him now."

"Okay." Linda shrugged. "If it's awkward, we'll just blame it on you being overwhelmed by my august presence."

Lucy didn't acknowledge the words. "Lucy?"

"David is dead."

Linda shook her head. "He heals like me. I don't think he can be killed. I saw Jared break his neck a few weeks ago, and he just hopped right back up. John wasn't like that, but David heals. He's not dead, Lou."

"He's dead, Linda. I promise. I slammed lightning through him, then Sam damned him to hell. I watched it happen."

"Damned him to hell? I think they were talking about that last night." Linda shook her head. "I don't know. It's fuzzy. I was so tired. Even now, so tired."

"We can talk later," Lucy offered. "Still hungry?"

Linda dropped her eyes to her hands. "I know he doesn't want to see me, Lou. Do you maybe have some pictures? He's really okay now?"

"He's good. Great. Just frightened. He thought you were going to take him from me."

Linda didn't respond.

"He doesn't know you," Lucy continued after a few heartbeats. "You can't take him. I won't allow it."

Linda's head snapped up, hurt on her face. "Where the fuck would I take him, Lucy? I have nothing. Nowhere to go. He's better off with you and the billionaires."

Lucy pulled a little smile. "Just being clear. He stays with me. Fortunately, you're staying with me, too. So there's that."

"Really?" Linda choked out, eyes going glassy. "You'll let me stay around for a little bit?"

"Of course. What the fuck did you think was going to happen?" Lucy asked in an annoyed tone.

"I didn't think that far ahead, Lou. I've only been awake for about an hour. Sorry," Linda muttered, bending to accept the hug Lucy offered. "I think my aunt would help me, though, if you don't want me around. She helped me last night when I couldn't even shower on my own."

"We'll figure it out. Give Ree some time. I'll go get my phone. I have a ton of pictures."

"IT'S FINE, REE. I PROMISE."

Ethan could hear Adrian whispering in the hallway outside of his open bedroom door.

"Adrian, would you go check? Please?" Ree whispered back.

Oh. Poor Ree, Ethan thought, rolling out of bed. *Poor Linda. What a mess.*

"Ree, she's in her room. Aunt Lucy is with her." Adrian's voice was thick with sympathy. "Let's have breakfast, buddy. It's time to eat."

"I'm not hungry," Ree responded. "Maybe we could just go back to the bunk room?"

"You said you were hungry."

"I was, but now I'm not. Let's go back, Adrian."

When Ethan pulled his door all the way open, Ree was trying to pull Adrian the opposite way down the hallway.

The poor kid just jumped a mile. I should have said something before opening the door, Ethan berated himself, sharing a look with Adrian. *Oh man, Adrian's freaking out.*

"Uncle Ethan!" Ree ran full out, throwing himself into Ethan's arms.

"Hey, buddy. It's going to be okay," Ethan soothed, scooping the little boy up off his feet and into a hug. Arms and legs wrapped crushingly tight around Ethan, Ree began sobbing. "I didn't mean to scare you, Henry. I'm sorry."

The sobs were coming so fast and hard, Ree had trouble taking a breath. Adrian nodded as Ethan backed into the bedroom with Ree, closing the door behind them.

"Okay, Ree, it's going to be okay, buddy." Ethan ran a comforting hand up and down Ree's back. "I know. It's scary. I know. But Aunt Lucy and Adrian will make it okay."

"He was scared that Linda would take him from us," Adrian muttered, causing Ree's sobs to redouble. Adrian winced.

"No, honey," Ethan murmured. "No one's taking you anywhere. Do you think we'd let that happen? No, we wouldn't let that happen. You're not leaving us. Your mom's just going to join us. She'll be part of our fun."

"No," Ree cried. "She can't come back now."

"Ree," Ethan chided. "Why? Why can't she be part of our fun?"

"Uncle Ethan, no. Everything is just right like this," Ree sobbed.

"It'll be even better with your mom," Ethan said confidently.

"It might be worse. No, she can't be here!" Ree yelled as the sobs slowed.

I have never been so glad for the soundproofing in this house, Ethan thought, glad there was no risk of Linda overhearing her son's words.

"I don't see how she'd make it worse. What would she do that makes it worse?" Ethan asked reasonably.

Maybe Linda did something terrible to him before she split?

"I don't know. But we're good now. Aunt Lucy doesn't cry, and now we have Adrian and you and everyone else. I don't want to make it bad again."

"Ree, did your mom make your life bad before?"

Henry considered the question seriously as Ethan sat him down in one of the sitting area chairs then sat down on the bed so he wouldn't hover over Ree. Adrian stood at the foot of the bed, behind Ethan, looking lost.

"No. I don't think so. I don't remember much. We used to eat cereal and do puzzles. And she used to read to me," Ree eventually mumbled.

"See? If life wasn't bad with her before, why would life be bad with her now? She did the best she could to keep you safe."

Ethan winced as Adrian leaned toward him and squeezed his upper arm in warning. *Okay, I won't say that. Thanks for the bruise, Adrian.* He glared over his shoulder toward his older brother, noticing the panicked expression.

"You know, you are awfully panicked for someone trained to deal with life and death," Ethan muttered. "You're not helping. Either calm down or go away."

Adrian frowned. "Sorry."

Ree's tears started again. "Don't be mad at Adrian!"

Oh, for fuck's sake.

"I'm not mad at him, Henry. Calm down. Sometimes brothers complain at each other. We do this all the time. You know we do this."

"No, you don't! You complain at Uncle Sam or Uncle Jake. You don't complain at Adrian!"

Touché.

"Ree, let's stay on point here. If your mom didn't make life bad before, why would she make life bad now?" Ethan questioned.

Ree stared at Ethan, completely still and silent.

What is going on in his brain?

"Henry, you can say anything you want to me right now. I won't be upset."

"Promise?" The question was a whisper.

"Of course."

"What if she doesn't like me, Uncle Ethan? What if I do something wrong? Is she going to leave again?"

Adrian gasped before Ethan turned and scowled at him.

Rather than offer reassurances, Ethan decided to answer the question as it was asked.

He shrugged. "If she doesn't like you, that's her problem. If she leaves again, oh well. We'll be fine, just the way we are now. She can't take that from us."

Ree's eyes were huge in his face as he watched Ethan.

"You're wonderful, just as you are. You can't do something 'wrong' to change that. If she doesn't see how awesome you are, that's her problem. Understand? We don't change who we are to suit others."

Ethan paused, waiting for Ree to nod in acknowledgment.

"That said, she already knows how wonderful you are. She is so anxious to see you, to know you're okay. She was really hurt last night, but all she could do was ask about you. She loves you with her whole heart, just like Aunt Lucy loves you. I know you're scared. But believe me. She's *even more* scared that you won't like her."

"You think so?" Ree asked, eyes darting between Adrian and Ethan.

"Yes, Henry. Absolutely," Adrian murmured. "Your mom was so tired last night, she could barely stand. But she had to see you before she went to sleep. She cried her eyes out at the sight of you. She was *that* relieved that you are okay."

Ethan and Adrian let Ree think on his own for a moment. When there was no more questions forthcoming, Ethan stood up from where he was sitting on the bed.

"I'm going to go get some coffee. Are you and Adrian staying in here or coming with me?"

After an extended pause of consideration, Ree frowned. "I'm kinda hungry."

Ethan smiled at him. "There's my brave Henry. Let's go find some breakfast."

LINDA FIDGETED, pulling her borrowed shirt straight.

"You look fine," Darla reassured her. "It's going to be fine."

Linda fidgeted again. "Thank you. I don't know why you're nice to me, but thank you."

Darla and Nora sighed together.

"It's going to be good," Nora murmured, taking Linda's hand. "He's a great kid. The best-behaved five-year-old I've ever known."

"Okay," Linda muttered, looking at the floor. "This is surreal. At this time yesterday, I was trying to will myself to die."

Nora swallowed hard, squeezing the hand she held. "Let's not say that in front of Ree."

Linda burst out laughing. "Yeah, good call."

"Are you ready?" Darla asked.

"He's out there? He's willing to see me?" Linda asked.

Nora and Darla nodded together.

"Are you sure? He didn't want to see me a couple of hours ago. If he's not ready, don't rush—"

"He asked," Darla assured her.

"Maybe I should stay in here until all the bruising is gone? I don't want to scare him."

"They told him you were hurt," Nora said calmly. "He knows you're bruised. It's fine."

"But by tomorrow, it'll be gone. Then he won't have to see me like this." Linda's voice became more panicked.

"Do you want to stay in this bedroom?" Nora asked.

"No. Not really."

"Then what are we doing right now?" Darla asked.

Linda paused, considering. "He's good. Happy. I don't want to risk that. He's been through so much."

Darla's eyebrows shot up. "So have you."

Linda nodded, taking a deep breath. "Okay."

"Okay," Darla agreed.

"Ready?" Nora asked.

Without another word, Linda pulled open the bedroom door and looked each way down the hall.

"It's to the left," Darla murmured.

Linda turned resolutely down the hall, taking even, determined steps toward the son she'd fought so long to protect.

Fought and failed to protect, she thought. *Lucy saved him. Not me. I owe Lucy everything.*

The hallway opened into a giant open space that made up an oversized living room, kitchen, and dining space in one. The entire southern wall of the room was made of glass, overlooking Lake Michigan in the fall.

Linda surveyed the room quickly without looking directly at any of the faces inside it. There was a large collection of people on the patio outside, pointedly not looking into the room.

Okay. Here goes.

Her eyes dropped to look at Lucy first. Linda smiled at her sister. Lucy smiled back, her expression filled with sympathy.

God damn, I love you, little sister.

Adrian sat at the other end of the couch. They were each holding a hand of a little boy. Her little boy.

Holy shit. Holy shit. Holy shit.

Linda's head swam, making her wonder if she was going to blackout.

"Breathe," Nora whispered from behind her.

"Hi, Ree," Linda rasped out, staring at her son.

Ree's eyes were fixed on her, staring, wide with wonder and shock.

He's not ready for this. They pushed too hard. They should have let him be. Oh man, he's not—

"Momma," Ree whimpered as his little face scrunched up into tears. "You're here!"

Linda sat on the floor, body wrapped around her son, rocking him as they cried together.

In the coming years, Linda would wonder if she ran to Ree or if Ree ran toward her. She had no memory of the journey to him that day. Her brain stopped gathering input somewhere between saying hello to her child and hugging him tightly.

In the end, the only memory she retained was the sensation of that hug.

8

"Good grief, I can't even look at that kid right now. I'm going to be a sobbing mess again," Noah bitched.

"Shuddup," Ethan murmured, pointedly not looking at Ree, who stood, holding hands, between Linda and Lucy, with Adrian behind him.

It took Lucy a minute to realize that everyone was trying to *not* face them. "You big sissies!"

"Shut up, Lou!" Hennessy scolded. "That was a kick to the junk!"

Lucy whomped him on the head. "You know what a bigger kick to the brain is? Seeing someone you care about—"

"WE'RE NOT TALKING ABOUT IT," Beth roared.

The room went silent as everyone tried to not-look at Beth's tears while not-looking at Ree between Linda and Lucy.

"We will never joke about last night. Do you all understand?" Beth growled, glaring around the room as she wiped tears from her cheeks.

Jake stared at his feet. "I have no idea where to look right now. There are no safe places."

"Down is best," Hank agreed.

"Holy fuck," Micah murmured, quietly amused by the rampant mushy feelings in the room.

Darla glared daggers at him. "There are little ears in this room."

Micah's head tilted in a look of confusion.

"Oh, this is better." Ethan chuckled. "Let's laugh at the new guy."

"He doesn't like that," Noah stage-whispered.

Micah turned a glare on Noah.

Noah pulled a face. "How come Ethan didn't get the glare?"

"Please explain," Micah said to Darla, ignoring Noah.

"No foul language in front of the children. It's not that hard, Micah," Darla sighed. "Just common sense. I don't want them to learn a new vocabulary. But my boys have trouble with this concept. So, if you violate the little ears policy, you will be doing chores."

Micah grinned. "Chores? You're going to make me do chores?"

"Usually dishes." Darla nodded.

Linda shrugged. "That sounds reasonable."

Lucy snorted. "Just wait. They can't help it. It's ridiculous."

"I never should have tolerated the language when they were teenagers. I should have put my foot down," Darla lamented.

"Can we get back on course?" Hank asked. "What's the plan? We can't stay here forever."

"Why?" Micah asked, serious again.

"We have work—" Hank began.

"You are wealthy beyond imagining. None of you need to work," Micah disagreed.

"We can't just disappear," William said.

"Why?" Micah asked.

"We don't even know what we're running from," William argued. "Chill out, man. What happened to 'this is a whole lot of fun...?' Remember saying that a couple of months back?"

"This is different."

"Why?" William asked.

Micah ground his teeth together. "Hunters capture and drain. They are terrible people in general. But there's a name and a face and someone to fight. So defeating hunters is fun. I'll gladly pit my will and strength against just about any hunter on the planet with confidence that I can successfully redeem or avenge those lost.

"That ward in Ohio was evil. I don't know how else to describe it. An area of effect ward like that can't be fought. There is no saving anyone from its effects. It drained time from every last person who crossed it, old and young. Even those who are typically safe from hunters."

"I get that you're afraid. I can feel the terror coming off you. That's concerning. I just don't know how to run from an unknown. It's not that I don't believe you, Micah. It's that I don't think we can do anything until we know more," Will explained.

"You need to learn how to protect yourselves and how to work together. All of you. That will take longer and be harder to do if you're insisting on business as usual," Micah argued.

Sam cleared his throat, stopping the discussion and cutting off Hank before he could speak. "I agree with Micah. And I agree with what Dad was about to say.

"I've been looking. I still can't find where we are in time exactly. I've never been lost like this. Again, I would think we were in the wrong time if we weren't all here together. It's all skewed right now. There's no way to figure out where we're supposed to be because the center of it is out of balance."

"Does anyone know what he's talking about?" William muttered, frustrated. "I hate it when he does this."

Sam sighed. "I don't have words for it. I can't describe it. I'm sorry. I really am. I just know this is wrong. Where we are—when we are—is wrong. It's not supposed to be like this."

His eyes circled the room, touching on each member of his family, including Ava, Jess, Clyde, Blake, Nora, Ben, and Gregg, before finally landing on Micah.

"We need to be smart about this. But we also need to do enough with the business to ensure there is no global economic tailspin. We'll balance work and learning. We've been taking turns being in the office. We'll continue that and space the days out a little more so we have even more time away. That shouldn't unbalance anything economically."

Micah nodded in acceptance. "Until you know enough to keep yourselves safe, you should live here, behind these wards. They're strong wards. Someone that hasn't been here wouldn't be able to find this place. Has Jared been here?"

Sam thought for a moment. "No. We moved here after Dallas. I don't think we ever mentioned this house to him. But we're not staying here."

"Why?" Micah growled. "Why are you insisting on making this difficult?"

"Because I agree with William, too," Sam said, unperturbed. "We can't run and hide. We don't even know what he wants. If he wants to talk, let him talk to me."

"Sam, that's foolish. Jared could have called Nora, Ben, or me to get a hold of you in the last couple of months. He could have sat down for a conversation with you very quickly and easily. You wouldn't have refused to talk to him. He knows that as well as I do," Greggory corrected. "It wasn't a conversation he wanted. It was a power play. He wanted you to know he has powers you weren't aware of."

The crowd of family and friends shared wary glances.

"You are in danger. What part of this is unclear?" Micah asked before gesturing to Linda. "She was held in a cage for years so someone could spy on Wind. What is happening to keep tabs on the rest of you?"

"You're blowing this out of proportion," Hennessy disagreed. "There is security around them, even when they don't know it. They're rarely without protection."

"What?" Jake asked, glancing at Hennessy. "That's just Lucy."

"No," Hennessy disagreed. "It's not."

"How would that protection have helped you last night?" Micah asked Hennessy.

"It was stupid to fire on him last night. I acknowledge that," Hennessy replied. "I'm not claiming otherwise. That doesn't change the fact that even if the security couldn't help them, the security can keep tabs and call for help when needed."

"And did the security keep tabs on you all last night, when you disappeared from Hank and Darla's house?" Micah asked.

When Hennessy didn't respond, Micah continued. "They stockpiled that energy for years, Hennessy. It takes a tremendous amount of energy to make yourself impervious to something like gunfire. To stop a bullet cold and reflect it back correctly? I have no idea how he managed that.

"If you shot me now, the bullets would pierce me, damage me. Then I would heal. Even with all the energy I have gathered, I could not bounce the rounds back at you.

"If Samuel is correct, the man you shot continued to heal after lightning roasted his body. That level of heat can disintegrate a body. Yet he was recovering from it. Lightning is what eventually destroyed the Father from my circle. I've not heard of someone healing from that type of damage before.

"Whoever he was, whoever 'Jared' is, they've been preparing for a battle for a long time. Probably longer than any of you have been alive. I don't know how else to make this clear to you. You are all in genuine danger. Greggory was correct. Last night was not about a discussion. Or it was not only about a discussion. He wanted you to understand he has more power than you initially thought."

"I don't mean to minimize the threat," Lucas chimed in. "But we've been scattered for months since Texas. If they've been gathering energy for years with the intent to hurt us or hurt Sam, they could have done whatever it is they wanted to do before now."

"There's no indication that Jared intended harm to Sam. I have trouble believing he's capable of keeping someone in a cage for years. Maybe he's fallen in with a group of hunters that are affecting his mind. I don't know. But I've known him for most of a decade, and I can't imagine him wanting to hurt anyone."

Greggory sighed. "I feel the same way, Luke. But that doesn't change the fact that they pulled Linda out of a cage last night. And it doesn't change the fact that Ree has been sick for years."

"Ben?" Nora asked. "What do you think?"

Ben shook his head. "His mind was unbalanced when we were in Dallas in July. He was fine on the flight down but decidedly not fine the night they took the names. He wouldn't talk to me and intentionally kept his thoughts shut down. I want to believe he's not capable of doing horrible things, too. But before that day, I would have insisted that he would never hide his mind from me. Luke's point is valid, though. If they intended to harm, there would be no reason to warn you ahead of time."

Talise cleared her throat. "He was waiting for you. In the basement last night, he was waiting for you. He wanted to talk to you, Sam. He was excited when you showed up."

Sam nodded. "I could feel it radiating from him. He wanted to monologue. He has something to say, something he wants me to hear. Something he wants to school me about. There will be a discussion before the danger gets serious."

Sam paused, considering options, while everyone stared at him. "We'll ward everything we can, Micah. And I'll see if we can get more of the cornfield houses done quicker. Sometimes money and more people make construction move faster. Sometimes more people just get in the way. I'm not sure which phase we're in right now."

"What are the cornfield houses?" Micah asked, obviously unhappy with the decision.

MICAH STOOD in the center of the street outside of Jess and Blake's house, looking at the work in progress on multiple homes. Most of the Trellis family stood on the sidewalk, watching him. Ava and Clyde had taken the children inside with Linda, Darla and Hank, Gregg, Nora, and Ben.

"Why didn't you tell us you had security on us?" Jake asked Hennessy again.

Hennessy glared at Jake.

"Seriously. I had no idea. I feel kinda violated."

Hennessy rolled his eyes, an unusual expression for him. "Jen at the office has a panic button and is armed when in the office. Does that make you feel violated?"

"She is?" Jake and Noah said together.

"She is." Will nodded. "When she took the executive administrative role, she agreed to additional training. If a threat ever makes it past security and onto the forty-third floor, she's the first person in sight. We can't have her be a sitting duck up there. Her primary directive is to hit the panic button to summon help and get safe. But she also knows how to handle a firearm to protect herself if the need arises."

Noah and Jake shared a look.

"Badass!" Noah laughed. "I'm going to give her so much crap tomorrow!"

"Not too much crap. She'll shoot your ass." Jake laughed.

"I can't believe she never told me that!" Noah continued to laugh.

"If you never knew the security was there, there's nothing to feel violated about. They don't follow you or enter into your space. But most of you have retired military as neighbors for a reason."

Ethan glared at Sam. "How come they get away with retired military neighbors, but I live in a secured fortress?"

"I like you more than I like everyone else," Sam replied, a grin breaking across his face as his siblings groaned.

"Picking favorites is total bullshit. You know that, right?" Jake bitched.

Sam's small smile returned, causing everyone around him to smile a bit. "I didn't have anything to do with their security, Ethan. I didn't know it was there, either."

"Well, you pay for it," Hennessy corrected.

Sam shrugged. "That's as it should be. I'm glad the additional security is there. But Micah's point about it being inadequate is well taken."

William and Hennessy nodded in agreement.

"How did you find this place?" Micah called. "Do you understand what this is, Sam? Power sinks are incredibly rare."

"Mom told him." Jess smiled. "I had a similar expression when I finally felt it."

"How did you *miss it?*" Micah asked, appalled. "Your restaurant was on a tiny power sink as well. I assume that it was not an accident."

Jess nodded. "It was intentional. My parents bought that restaurant because of the sink. This one has gotten stronger since we moved in. It wasn't this obvious at first. Now I feel weird when we're away from it for too long."

Micah nodded slowly, not looking at Jess. "This is a good place for you to be, Madam Sight, if you're going to hang out with this crowd. It will help you."

"I mean, I could move back to Texas and leave them be. Addy certainly doesn't need me anymore," Jess said. "But I think I need them at this point."

Micah kept nodding. "You are a target of whatever is coming. Madam Sight is a different type of power and not always on the side of righteousness. You should stay where they can protect you. Your children would be in danger away from here. They reek of energy and have no defenses."

Jess stared at Micah then glanced at Blake. "My children are in danger?"

"You are all in danger. I don't know how else to make this clear. They will come for the weakest among you first—your children, Hank, Darla, Clyde. Anyone that can't defend themselves will be leverage. You must take this seriously."

The group was quiet for a few heartbeats.

"Sam, how did you come to own this land? Who told you it was here?" Micah asked, breaking up the loaded silence.

Sam started, returning to reality after being lost in his thoughts. "No one told me it was here. We were driving by one day. I told William to pull over and offered the farmer a lot of money for the land."

"Who was with you on that day? Who knows you own this?" Micah asked.

"Dad and William were in the car with me. A lot of people know I own it. I had to get permission to build houses here."

"There are ten houses in progress and two standing. Explain them to me," Micah requested.

"Ava and Clyde live in the ranch. Jess, Blake, and the girls live in the other one. Addy and I will live in the home you're facing. Hank and Darla will be next to us—"

"All of you. You're all moving here?" Micah exhaled in relief. "These are your houses? All of them?"

"Yes, all of them. This is our land. Not Nora, Gregg, and Ben. Not Claire and Tom. But all of our family. We could put houses here for them…" Sam's voice trailed off as he thought about it. "No. That's not the purpose of the extra lots."

"Extra lots?" Micah asked, eying the empty space across the street.

"The space is zoned for two more houses. I don't know who they're for, but not Gregg and Nora. Not Ben."

Micah shook his head. "They are friends and confidants, but not pieces on the game board. You would not sacrifice the world for them. They are not of your timeless circle."

"The organic circle welcomes them," Sam disagreed.

"The organic circle seems to welcome everyone you care about, including me. Don't include me in it." Micah glared at Jake, ignoring Sam and Adaline's collective sigh.

"Anyway, these are the cornfield houses. Three of them will be done in the next couple of weeks. The rest of them will be done before the end of November. I'll see if more resources can make that happen faster without drawing attention to it," Sam said into the awkward silence.

"We weren't going to move out here right now, though, Sam," Matty muttered. "We got the house started because you insisted, but I wasn't going to move here until after the wedding. We have to do this now?"

Sam stared at her.

Matilda stared back.

"Please, Matty?" Sam asked eventually. "I think Micah is right, and the danger is real. I can't do a great job warding a high-rise condo with several thousand people living in the building. I think we have some time before the danger grows. But we should use it to plan, not pretend like it doesn't exist."

"I'm not arguing any of this, Sam. I was a fan of the cornfield houses from the beginning," Will hedged. "Let's lock it up tight with traditional and extra-special security to keep everyone safe. But we have to live our lives. We can't be secluded from the rest of the world. And we don't even know what we're running from yet."

Sam frowned. "I'm not running from anything, Will."

"Then what are we doing here?"

"I thought you would understand."

"I don't," Will said, shaking his head.

"I'm fortifying our defenses and gathering our power. We need to be ready to answer whatever is coming for us. We won't be ready if we're sprinkled all over the place."

William's mouth dropped open.

"I don't know what the fuck I'm doing," Sam admitted. "I was hoping you or Hennessy would start leading this effort. I don't know combat and tactics like you do."

William stared at his middle brother, mouth agape.

"William, Jared *wants* something. And it's probably not something we want to just surrender," Sam clarified.

After a glance around the crowd, Sam looked at Micah. "I don't think they understand. I don't think they get that we're in the calm before the storm."

"They're coming for your wife, Terror. They'll come for your wife and children. Will you accept anything less than the best possible protection for them?" Micah asked, knowing he finally found the right words to get his point across. Micah watched the resolve settle upon William's shoulders.

"You're moving, Carrots. Deal with it."

9

"The sun will set in twenty minutes," Micah interrupted the conversation around Ava's living room.

Everyone stared at him.

"And?" William asked.

"Don't you close a circle tonight? Have you decided against that?" Micah asked, confused by the baffled stares.

"Yeah, we'll leave here in about a half-hour and still be an hour early. The farmhouse is only about ten minutes from here," Will explained.

Micah's eyes traveled the room. "I don't understand."

"What don't you understand?" Sam asked.

"You don't close the circle at sunset? Why?"

"Um, why would we?" Sam asked, looking to Gregg and Nora for more information. They shook their heads.

Micah blinked, looking at the gathered crowd. "The energy cycles better as the sun rises and sets upon your circle. You don't time your circles?"

"We base them on when people get to the farmhouse from work.

Usually around seven-thirty in the evening," Nora explained. "I've never known of or noticed a difference. Gregg?"

Greggory shook his head. "Never."

"Well, you wouldn't," Micah grumped. "But almost everyone else in this room would. It's easier to release the energy and to share it out with the sun's cycle."

"Huh, we should do that next week." Will grinned. "See, you're teaching us shit already."

Micah glared at him before turning to Adaline. "You're still insistent that I attempt to stand your circle?"

She raised her eyebrows, responding with a single, decided head nod.

"Let's try now, then. I would rather your circle fall without your entire crowd of usual participants watching," Micah suggested after thinking about it for a minute.

"The circle will not fall." Adaline's voice echoed with power, showing her annoyance. "Stop this."

"Mistress, circles of ascendance do not welcome traitors. It will fall."

"Traitor?" Jess started, genuinely surprised. "You do not have the colors of a traitor, Micah. You don't see yourself clearly. Sam has the right of it. You are no risk to us."

"I'm not saying I betrayed *you*. I'm saying I betrayed the energy. A circle of ascendance, full of growth and humanity, will not welcome a traitor. It will not stand with me in it," Micah vowed.

"Micah, you will stop this now. You belong to me, to growth, and you are the most human of us, even more than William. You are welcome in my circle. You will not speak this nonsense again." Power radiated from Adaline, causing the air to vibrate with raw energy.

"We will do as you ask and close a circle now, here, in the center of this power sink. After it is closed, you will *never* speak words of such nonsense to me again. You will not doubt me again. I understand your head tells you it is impossible, but we both know your body and soul don't believe it. Stop lying to yourself."

The room was silent as gazes flicked between a seriously pissed-off Mistress and a baffled Micah.

"See," Noah muttered to Matthew, "I told you. I told you she does it, too! It's worse than when Sam does it because we don't expect it from her."

"I mean, I believed you," Matthew murmured back. "But I missed her bossing Tali around yesterday. It's freaky to see."

"There are too many people around. Too many construction workers, Addy," Sam whispered. "We should go to the farmhouse to close a circle."

Adaline turned a glare on Sam.

"Okay, you can glare at me," Sam allowed meekly. "But we should still go to the farmhouse. Once construction is done, we can do all the circles here. If someone sees us doing this now, there will be questions to answer."

"I'm not pleased with you," Adaline growled at Sam.

"I know."

"But you're probably right," she allowed. Her rampant energy started to dissipate from the room.

Noah scratched his head. "The ladies are scarier than we ever thought of being."

Talise, Miranda, and Adaline snorted in unison.

"Noah, you have no idea what goes on in my head. Don't make assumptions," Matthew advised.

William and Adrian chuffed in agreement.

"AUNT REBECCA'S FARM?" Linda asked, eyes wide as she got out of the car with Adrian, Lucy, and Ree at the farmhouse.

"Of course." Nora nodded from behind them. "I know you and Lucy were here. I gave Lucy a bit of a scare a few months ago when she said she knew this place."

"She died not long after we visited. I've wondered..." Linda's voice trailed off, hoping she didn't have to ask the question out loud.

Nora nodded again. "She was drained not long after you were here. Sam said you did not lead the hunters to this place. It's not your fault."

"Aunt Nora, my mom...?"

"Her, too," Nora murmured.

Linda nodded, tears dripping down her cheeks again. "I'm sorry about your sisters. I don't remember Mom, but Aunt Becky was always kind to me."

"You should come home with me, sweetheart," Nora replied, not acknowledging the misplaced apology. "You'll need help getting a life together. I'd like to help. I don't know how you ended up in foster care as a kid, but you are welcome with me."

Linda's face froze as she shuffled her feet uncomfortably. "It was supposed to be a temporary thing. My dad wasn't well. He had been so adamant about breaking ties with you—"

"I know. I'm not blaming you, Linda. That's not what I meant at all. I'm sorry that it happened, though," Nora clarified, surprised by her niece's reaction.

Linda shook her head, clearing her thoughts as she walked with Nora and Gregg, following Adrian, Lucy, and Ree. "Anyway, Lucy said I'm also welcome with her. I don't know what Ree is comfortable with. Can I let you know after I talk with him?"

Nora nodded for the third time. "Of course. You're always welcome. We stand the circles behind the farmhouse. Have you ever been in a proper circle before?"

"A few times." Linda nodded. "There were also a few circles that were wanna-be circles. They just felt wrong. But not since...well, not since I've been away."

"Hmm, I wonder how that worked," Nora mused. "If you're a named pillar, you have too much energy to be without a circle. I wonder how they managed—"

Gregg cleared his throat. "There are other ways of removing energy from people."

Nora's eyebrows shot up. "You think they drained her in slow stages?"

"You think they did something else? People that have collected enough power to withstand lightning aren't going to let a single drop of energy go to waste," Gregg replied, looking ill.

Nora swallowed, squeezing her niece's hand. "This is different. Our circle with the larger group later tonight will be different than your other experiences, but more akin to them than what's about to happen."

"What's about to happen?" Linda's eyebrows shot up.

Gregg grinned. "Who knows? The last time we did a circle without the larger group to dilute and distribute the power, we blew up a lot of energy. This might be different because they're better balanced than they were in Texas, but Micah will add some flair."

"You think the circle will hold?" Nora asked, curious. "He seems insistent that it won't, and I don't think he's been wrong yet."

"I would not bet against Adaline."

"Fair enough." Nora's lips quirked up at the mention of betting. The Trellis family's silly habit of random ten-dollar bets was catchy.

I AM ABOUT to be burned by the circle, forcefully cast out, and unmasked as a traitor, Micah internally lamented. *These people have no idea, no fucking clue at all. I cannot do what they ask of me.*

Still, he walked toward the field with the Mistress on one side of him and the Walker on the other. Even after two millennia on his own, he would not go against a righteous Mistress.

He flinched in surprise as she grabbed his hand and gave it a squeeze. She didn't share energy; it was a gesture of companionship.

"No fear, Micah," she murmured. "There is no hate left in you for the circle to exploit, and you are not evil."

"Mistress, if this circle holds, it will wake the hate that lives within me. There is no hiding it from a circle like this. I am about to be unmasked as a villain, and they will not trust me to teach them after this. Please, reconsider," Micah quietly pleaded.

"If you stood as Hate, you would be no more a villain than William or Adrian, Micah. Rage and terror are not evil, nor is hate. It is part of being human, part of living."

"Adaline, you have never known pure hatred. No good can come from it. Nothing."

Adaline's lips twitched into a small smile. "I know you don't mean that to be funny, but it is. When the weight of hatred is lifted, enlightenment takes shape. You cannot have awareness and enlightenment without recognizing the absence of understanding first."

Micah glowered at her in frustration. "You sound like a fortune cookie."

"You are no longer Hate, Micah. You gave up that name," she reminded him, smiling faintly.

Their conversation ended as the group trickled into the field, and people took up their positions around the circle.

Micah's brow furrowed in confusion. "Why are you building an elemental circle?"

His words were met with the now-familiar looks of confusion.

Oh, for fuck's sake.

"What exactly have you learned from James and Evelyn?" Micah demanded from Sam.

Sam raised his eyebrows. "James taught me how to pull energy from the organic circle and how to pack a meaningful threat into as few words as possible."

"Fucking useless pair," Micah swore. "Your elements are standing the corners of the circle."

"They always do." Sam nodded. "When Talise was out of position, the circle was...disorienting."

Micah glared at him.

"What did I do? I don't know why you're mad." Sam sighed.

"A circle of ascendance is considered 'elemental' when two of the four corners are elements. Again, this is the first circle I've known to have all four elements."

Sam nodded along. "Makes sense."

"The energy builds and disperses differently when the circle is elemental. You don't send out as much life energy into the world. Are you trying to combat global warming like this? I'm not sure you can do that quickly."

"We release life energy," Sam said, looking confused again.

"I'm sure you do, but not as much as you could. The corners of a circle dictate how the energy stacks and builds. You're building elemental energy. That's not the same as life energy," Micah explained.

"I know, but we build up a lot of energy, then Jake makes it life energy, then Addy sends it out."

Micah's mouth dropped open in shock as he turned to stare at Jake.

Jake shrugged. "It gets too hot in the circle otherwise."

This is fucking terrifying. They're like children playing with unsecured nuclear warheads.

William snorted as if he could hear Micah's thoughts. "Whatever, man. You should know by now that we do things our own way. Get your ass in the circle. Let's do this."

"I-I have no idea where to stand with you positioned like this," Micah admitted, eyes still wide.

"Pick a spot, any spot," Sam directed. "I'm not sure where you go yet."

"Where I go?" Micah asked.

"Yeah," Sam said, shrugging. "Where you stand in the circle. We'll figure it out."

"The circle rotates, Sam. Right? You all move around? Based on your goals?" Micah asked, looking around at the confused faces.

"What goals?" Noah whispered to Talise.

She shrugged.

When no one responded and Micah didn't move, Will broke out in a full grin. "Just come here, man. Stand between Lucy and me. It's fine."

Micah shook his head in disbelief then headed toward William for lack of a better option.

"You're really going to stand directly in front of me like this?" Micah asked Sam with a sigh.

Sam smiled his little smile. "I am."

"Can you back off just a little bit?" Micah asked. "You're so close our toes are almost touching."

"I know."

"Why are you so close?"

"Because you'll need help," Sam said, unperturbed.

"Mistress, the circle will not hold with me. He even says so!" Micah yelled to Adaline, who was walking her way around the circle.

She chose not to respond.

"Sam, you have to stop her. Stop this. Someone's going to get hurt," Micah whispered. "She's so intent on this—"

"I'm not telling her *anything* when she's in this mood." Sam laughed. "It's fine, Micah. She's almost back to the start."

This is going to hurt her, hurt them. They have to stop this!

"It's almost closed. It's almost over," Sam said, his voice soothing. "Look at me, Micah."

Micah's eyes snapped to Sam's, wild with panic and fear.

"It's almost over now," Samuel said, voice echoing with power. "Hang on just a little bit longer."

"Walker, please. I don't want anyone to get—" Micah's pleas abruptly stopped when the circle snapped closed.

As the air whooshed out of his chest, Micah felt his heart stop beating.

It's almost over now, Micah thought, recognizing the truth of Sam's words. Oddly, he did not welcome his own death with as much relish as he anticipated. Vision going black around the edges, Micah toppled forward straight into Sam's waiting arms.

"Holy crap! He's heavier than I thought!" Sam bitched, lowering him to the ground.

If Micah had breath, he would have laughed. Still, a shadow of his usual grin spread across his face. There was noise around him, but he couldn't make out the words.

Preparing himself for the slide into unconsciousness, Micah started when his heart thundered back into motion and his lungs sucked in oxygen. Two millennia of displaced energy exploded out of him, relieving pressure so pervasive and familiar, Micah forgot what life was like before it existed.

"Stop fighting the circle," Adaline chided through their mental connection. "Let go. Let the energy pass through."

Pushing himself back up to a sitting position, Micah looked around as he gasped for air.

Samuel stood before him, eyes glowing and power at the ready. "Micah, look at me."

Micah's eyes snapped back to Samuel's face as he felt the Walker's energy wash directly against his mind.

"Good. Good. You're yourself."

"Who else would I be?" Micah wheezed.

Sam shrugged. "Doesn't matter. Addy says to let go."

"I let it go. The energy went. It's gone. What does she mean?"

There was a throaty sigh of annoyance from behind Sam.

"Oh," Sam said, stepping to the side. He pulled a sheepish look across his face then smiled at Adaline. "Hi, honey."

She glared at him.

"I know, you told me," Sam admitted with a nod. "I had to be sure, though."

She continued to glare.

"It's fine," Sam said with a shrug.

Her eyes narrowed further.

"Okay, I'll just go wait over there."

Still gasping for breath, Micah's grin bloomed with his chuckle as

Sam wandered back to the middle of the circle. "You excel at bullying him."

Adaline's glare turned on Micah.

"*What did I tell you to do?*" she asked through their mental link, obviously annoyed.

"Mistress, the energy exploded out, it's—"

"No, Micah!"

"I don't know what else you want me to do."

"What did I tell you? What were my words?"

"You told me to let the energy go."

"No, I didn't," she corrected. "I told *you* to let go. I told you to let the energy pass through. Look down, Micah. Look at the line of the circle."

He shook his head. "I can't see it."

"Yes, you can. You choose not to see it. Get up, Micah, on your feet."

Micah groaned as he climbed upright. "You're mad because I laughed at you this morning, right? It wasn't a mean laugh, Addy. It was a surprised chuckle of delight. Don't be mad about it."

Amusement flashed in her eyes, but her scowl remained. "Look for the circle, Micah. It's visible. Just look for it."

"Oh, holy hell," he breathed, catching sight of the energy for the first time. It flowed around him as water flows around a rock in the river. "Oh."

"You keep yourself apart from it. Let go. The circle will welcome you. Surely you understand that now. Welcome it in return, let it pass through you. It's time to share energy and life with the world again," Adaline murmured, tone now gentle. She surprised him with a hug before turning back toward the center of the circle.

Micah watched her walk away, his sight going blurry with tears.

"YOU LOOK RIDICULOUS RIGHT NOW, just so you know." William laughed.

Micah started again, turning toward Will.

"You do. You've got tough guy man tears going on, which is fine. Whatever. But you look utterly baffled and uncertain. It's not a good look on you. I prefer condescending, cocky Micah. Let's go back to that version of you."

"Oh, shut up!" Ethan yelled. "I like this!"

William laughed. "Hey, you only like assholes, little brother. He's not your type. He's going to be battle buddies with Hennessy and me."

Ethan's cheeks flamed red, visible even in the fading light.

"I guess I missed the part where we decided he couldn't be both?" Matilda looked around, confused. "Did we decide that over cereal while I was sleeping in? I don't like that decision. I want him to be Ethan's honey-bunny and Will's battle buddy. We can't do that?"

Sam's eyes lit up. "I want that, too! I didn't know that was up for discussion. How did we decide that already?"

"I was not included in that decision." Darla scowled at William.

"I thought Ethan and Eric were going to be a thing? What happened to that?" William asked, turning to Ethan.

"They were boring together. Too busy trying to out-polite each other. It was like when Luke kept making Tali fall asleep. Most boring double date ever!" Jake cackled.

"Oy!" Tali yelled.

At the same time, Luke yelled, "Hey!"

"So, no Eric?" Will called over the laughter. "I missed that update. But see! You don't like nice ones!"

"Really? We have to talk about this now? You people can't tease me about this later? In private?" Ethan asked, voice flat.

"This is private," Hank said, looking around. "It's just us."

Hennessy grinned. "This is even better than when we gathered up Lou. Look at him. He's so confused!"

The entire circle turned to stare at Micah.

"I don't understand what's happening."

Ava sighed, swallowing her own laughter. "This happened the first time they closed a circle, too. The circle that blew up and brought you to Dallas was like this. When it's just them standing the circle, the social filters drop. They're probably going to start throwing energy at each other soon."

"Micah!" Adaline barked from the center. "We're waiting for you."

"Addy, I don't know how—"

"You know you're getting me in a lot of trouble, right?" Sam complained. "Join the circle, Micah. Offer up your energy, and let's do this!"

"It already took energy," Micah disagreed.

"It took that. You didn't offer it," Sam said with an eye-roll.

"Oh." Micah's brow furrowed in concentration.

"It's not that hard, man." Will laughed again. "You look constipated."

"Fuck you," Micah muttered. "I haven't done this in a long time."

"It's like having sex. Wait. That's right, you don't do that, either."

"I'm going to fucking punch you, man. Shut up!" Micah yelled, laughing.

"Yeah, I'm fucking terrified of you and your man tears," Will cackled back.

Micah's lips pursed to hide a grin as he tried to look affronted. "You're going to be sobbing uncontrollably when you hold those babies, *Lord Terror*. Shut the fuck up."

"Fuck you."

"No, fuck you!"

"No, fuck you!"

"What the fuck?" Micah asked, throwing his head back in joyful laughter.

Without warning, the circle erupted in the shimmering, pale pink pearlescence of joy.

Will grinned. "Ta-da!"

"Joy," Micah breathed in a tone of wonder. "This is joy."

"Yup." Will nodded. "It's like your power hymen grew back after centuries of disuse, though. I'm surprised your nose is not bleeding. Gotta work on better control, man. We can't bicker and swear at each other in front of the larger circle."

"But this came from me," Micah murmured, still looking around with wide eyes.

"And?" Jake asked. "All sorts of shit comes out of me. Literally and figuratively."

The boys in the circle laughed, though Darla scowled when Hank snorted.

Still serious, Micah focused on Samuel and Adaline in the center of the circle. "Thank you for allowing this. Thank you for this gift."

Adaline and Sam shared a look, not understanding.

Micah shook his head. "I've never shared anything but hate within a circle."

"What? What the hell?" Adrian asked, shocked. "We dump every emotion you can think of into the circle."

"That's because they allow it to be so," Micah muttered into the now silent clearing. Tears dripped down his cheeks again. "They allow you to be so open. It is a gift. Cherish it."

"I can't imagine a circle being any other way than this, Micah," Greggory said, concerned. "How is this different?"

Micah shook his head, not sure how to answer. "They are different. You are all different. I'm glad for it."

"The others will start arriving soon. We should close this circle and head back to the farmhouse," Beth said, wholly unmoved by the experience. Sam's eyes darted to her in concern.

"I'm fine," she muttered in response to his unasked question.

10

"You're grounded," Talise's dad, Mike, yelled as she walked into the farmhouse.

Tali sighed. "I called."

"You called this morning!" Mike yelled. "Too late!"

"Things got a little weird last night, Dad. I'm fine, I promise," Talise explained.

"Of course you're fine. But you scared your mother half to death," he howled.

"No, you didn't." Monica laughed. "I knew who you were with, if not exactly where you were. I was fine. Your father was pacing like a ninny, though."

"She could have been lost or hurt!" Mike complained, voice lower as the gathering crowd laughed at his expense.

"Mmm." Monica scrunched up her face. "Admit it. You were worried about an unplanned pregnancy."

Mike nodded. "It's true. I do. But that's not why I was upset."

"Noah's family is happy, loving, and rich, honey. It ain't gonna get better than this. Let's hope for lots of babies." Monica laughed, heading over to chitchat with Darla, Ava, and Jess.

"You're still grounded." Mike scowled at Talise.

"No, I'm not." She rolled her eyes. "I'm sorry I didn't call last night. We ended up at the lake house in Michigan. It was a whole thing. We were all together the whole time. No unplanned pregnancies. I promise."

"You're grounded," Mike insisted again.

"No," Tali said, shaking her head. "I'm a grown woman, Dad."

"I don't care. You live in my house. You'll live by my rules."

"Oh! Oh!" Noah yelled, excited. "See, that's what I told her. She should move in—"

"NOAH!" Talise shouted over him. "Not helpful."

Mike shook with disbelieving laughter. "I'm going to rip his head off."

"What's going on?" Luke asked, joining the fray. "What's wrong, Mike?"

Mike threw his hands up. "She didn't come home—"

"Oh yeah." Luke nodded. "There was a thing. We gathered up more people for the circle. You'll see. Anyway, we were at the lake house last night to be safe."

"You were there, too?" Mike asked, instantly calming down.

"Yeah." Luke continued to nod. "We all were. My parents and Ava and Clyde, too. Gregg, Ben, Nora. Yeah."

"I just said that," Talise muttered to her dad.

"Yeah, but…"

"It couldn't be helped," Luke said with a shrug. "I'm sorry if we worried you. The Walker said we had to go to the lake house, so we went to the lake house. By the time we got there, it was late. A call would have woken you up. But you could have called her. Or Noah. Or me. Or my parents. We were all there."

"Oh. I didn't think about that."

Talise's eyes narrowed. Faintly, only because she was looking for it, she sensed the tingle of energy that went with Luke's peace. Luke was soothing her father. She glared at him.

His lips quirked up at the corners as he met her eyes.

"Tell me again why you can't date this one instead of that one," Mike demanded of his daughter, gesturing between Luke and Noah.

Talise rolled her eyes again. "That one makes me sleepy," she replied, pointing at Luke.

"Yeah, but the other one makes you...not sleepy. Can you just not date the sexy one?" Mike bitched, not for the first time.

"Your dad thinks I'm sexy," Noah muttered, making Talise and Luke both choke back unexpected laughter.

"Dad, I like this one. You like this one, too. He's funny. I felt you locking down that laughter."

"He's dumb!"

The group turned to look at Noah.

He shrugged. "Only about some things. Other things, I know a lot about."

Luke put a staying hand on Noah's arm, warning him against cracking another joke.

"You're not moving out! You've been on three dates," Mike declared.

"I'm not moving out," Talise agreed. "I'm not grounded, either."

"Fine," Mike said.

"Fine," Talise answered, kissing her dad's cheek.

"Where'd your mother go? Is there beer in the fridge?" Mike stomped away, still unhappy, but more at peace with the happenings.

Talise turned to Luke with her eyebrows raised.

"I'm sorry about this morning," he muttered to Tali and Noah. "I overreacted. I'll get used to it. But seriously, man. You're dumb. No survival instinct whatsoever."

Noah grinned at his little brother. "I stole Luke's girlfriend..."

Talise smacked him upside the head. "Stop it. It's not funny anymore. It was only funny for the first eight hundred times."

"He's dumb." Luke laughed, hugging Talise. "Good luck."

"I'm not really that dumb," Noah whispered to Talise as Luke walked away.

"I know." She laughed.

"So tell me again why we can't live together. This would be so much easier! I'm convinced your dad would like me more."

"Nah. It would piss him off. Quit looking for shortcuts. I want to be wooed properly!" Talise grinned up at Noah.

"There's a lot more dancing in my future, isn't there?" he asked, grinning back.

"I'll never admit it if you tell him this, but you're a better dancer than Luke."

Noah smiled, briefly kissing her lips. "Excellent. Something new to bait him with."

"It's time. I'm tired of the stolen girlfriend thing. It makes me sound fickle."

AFTER SAM INTRODUCED Linda and Micah, Adaline closed the larger group circle.

"Wait," Gregg called before Sam and Adaline could release energy. "Before we begin in earnest, but while the circle is closed, something must be spoken and felt to be understood."

Sam quirked his eyebrows up.

"Hear me now, friends and family," Greggory called, voice loud with the power he rarely displayed. "Jared is no longer a part of Harbor, part of this circle. And we have reason to believe he means us harm.

"He fled from the Walker's wrath last night. It is clear Jared has stolen power from others and has taken lives. I warn you all, keep your distance from him. If he reaches out, do not return the call. Do not meet him for lunch. Do not welcome him into your home or your energy. Doing such things may cost you dearly.

"This circle protects you from random attack. Most hunters can't touch your energy because your energy is moored here, safely within this group. But he also had energy tied here. He was a part of this circle for most of his life. I'm unsure how the power would react if he chose to attack. Be cautious, please."

The silent gathering stared at Gregg in shock.

"You can feel the truth of my words. You know I speak with honesty. I don't know what he's gotten himself into, but he is no longer a friend. You must guard yourselves well. If you like, Nora and I will help with warding your homes."

After thirty seconds of uncomfortable, silent shuffling, Gregg nodded. "I'm done, Addy, Sam. Sorry. It needed to be said, though. Ignorance puts us all at risk."

"Thank you," Sam said, meaning it. "I didn't know it was possible to do that. To infuse your words like that."

Gregg's eyebrows shot up. "You empower your words often."

"I guess I never thought to empower them with truth," Sam admitted.

"No, Sam. Not truth. Honesty. Integrity. Belief. Trust, even. But not truth. Truth is a power in its own right, separate from life and time. Even time cannot hide from the truth. You have no sway over it."

After considering Greggory's words, Sam nodded in acceptance. "That makes sense."

"*They are terrified,*" Addy mentally shared with Sam. "*Can you feel it?*"

Looking around the circle, Sam nodded in response. "*William looks ill.*"

"*I am not sure how to make it better,*" she admitted.

"You are afraid," Sam said aloud. "I can feel it. How can we help?"

The circle shifted uncomfortably around them, but no one spoke for a moment.

"Greggory," a middle-aged woman called in a flat, emotionless voice from the circle's far side. "Jared was of this circle. Did he take my son from me?"

Nora gasped, her eyes filling with tears.

Gregg rocked back in surprise. "I had not thought of that."

Sam's eyebrows raised in a question. He didn't know the woman who asked the question and hadn't heard her son's story.

Ben sighed. "We lost two college kids to hunters this spring. Autopsies showed an aneurism in one and a heart attack in the other, but they were both completely drained. You could feel it within fifteen feet."

Sam nodded quickly, trying to cut additional description short. He understood the foul feeling of a hunter's actions. The woman didn't need to rehash details of her son's demise.

"W-we could feel the circle fighting for Seth, Anne's son," Nora explained. "He fought his attacker, but then the circle just gave out. We thought it was losing strength. With Karen, the other one, she was just gone from the circle—suddenly gone. No struggle of any kind. If we couldn't feel the hunter, we would have accepted she died of natural causes."

"I don't know, Anne," Greggory answered the woman. "I wouldn't think him capable of it. I don't think he could have hidden such a thing from our circles. But he's proven me wrong several times in the past few days. I don't know. If it comes to light that he did it, he'll answer for it."

Anne nodded. "I'll hold you to that."

Turning back to Sam, Greggory spoke again. "Start the circle, Sam. The fear is well-founded and wise. Soothing it is not in anyone's best interest. It will help us remain cautious."

Without another word, Sam released sadness and determination. At the same time, Adaline offered pure life energy, leading off a subdued and tentative circle building.

This is how the circle used to be all the time before they knew me, Sam realized. It was only then that he noticed it had changed over the last few months. The members of Harbor no longer feared him. They didn't socialize much, didn't try to engage him. But there was no fear.

When the circle got around to Linda, she unloaded blindingly bright joy and hope to celebrate her freedom. Her energy was radiant enough on its own to change the entire atmosphere of the group. Whispers and questions full of curiosity started immediately.

At Lucy's turn, she released the usual elemental energy she shared.

Then, against her will, the circle yanked joy, shame, sorrow, and grati-tude from her.

Baffled, Sam knew some of the emotions were targeted toward him but couldn't figure out how they fit together. He made a mental note to talk with Lucy.

Maybe she was ashamed of the death last night? he wondered.

After Lucy, the circle went as expected right up until Beth's turn. Usually a source of hope, joy, and peace, the entire circle gasped as one when she released pure red rage.

Sam felt ill.

My fault. I shouldn't have allowed Hennessy to go with us last night. I should have known. I should have seen that. My fault he was hurt. My fault he almost died. My fault she's suffering, Sam berated himself.

"Your actions that saved his life," Adaline reminded him through their mental link.

"I'm failing this circle. I'm failing to keep them safe," Sam responded.

"As am I," Adaline acknowledged.

When the circle continued to stare at her, Beth quirked a small smile, lacking amusement. "I'll be having a word with Jared when the opportunity arises."

"Well, that's terrifying," Noah muttered.

A startled round of muffled laughter broke out around the circle.

"Laugh all you want," Noah said, serious. "When the mood strikes, she's more vicious than all the rest of us combined. If he wasn't such a dick, I'd almost feel bad for Jared. Almost."

Out of sequence, the circle pulled a feeling of satisfaction from the grieving mother, Anne. She shared a glance of understanding with Beth before the energy of the circle moved on.

"Lucy?" Sam asked, heading toward her after the circle closed.

She flinched before turning to meet his gaze.

"I'm sorry," Sam said immediately. "I'm sorry that had to happen last night. I'm sorry. I don't want you to be ashamed. I did it. It was my decision, and I did it, not you. Okay? It wasn't your fault."

She blinked. "Sam, what are you talking about?"

"Um. About the guy. David? That was his name, right?" Sam asked, looking around to make sure no one was listening. "I finished it. Not you. It was my doing. Please don't regret it."

Utterly baffled, Lucy's mouth dropped open. "You think I regret what happened to him?

"Well, the circle... Shame? I don't want—"

Lucy broke out into genuine laughter that startled Sam. "I hope he rots in hell for all eternity. He was evil. He took joy in torturing others. I'm sorry you got to do the honors. I'm sorry he didn't suffer any longer. I'm not sorry he's gone. I don't regret it, Sam. I don't feel shame about it."

"But then what? What's wrong?"

Lucy stared at the ground, trying to think of the right words.

Adrian sighed next to her. "She feels like she hasn't been kind enough to you, that she's been too reserved with you, too afraid. She's ashamed of that now."

Lucy glared at him.

Adrian gave a small smile. "Yeah, I know I'm in trouble. I'm just moving this along because I know he won't leave it alone, and you won't spit the words out. So now it's done."

"I'm not cooking for a week. You're dealing with takeout," she threatened before turning back toward Sam.

"Sam, I—" Her words cut off as Sam folded her in a firm hug.

"No," he said simply. "No shame or regret because of me. No sorrow."

"But—"

"No," he said again. "No. It's over. We move on from here, okay?"

Lucy was surprised to be choking back a sob as he squeezed her tighter. "Sam."

"Love you, Lou. It's over and done, okay? No more."

Letting her go, he turned and walked away without another word, heading toward where Adaline waited across the field.

"RANDA!" Matthew called, running to catch up to Miranda and Ethan after the circle.

Ethan smiled without looking at her. "I'll meet you at the farmhouse."

He was gone before Matthew caught up with Miranda.

"Holy cow, you two hauled ass out of the circle." Matthew laughed. "I was talking to Jess and then turned around, and you were already gone. How are you? I haven't had a chance to talk to you all day."

"I'm fine. Good," Miranda murmured, now anxious about their whispered conversation in the middle of the night. She'd spent most of the day trying to puzzle out what Matthew regretted about that last day in college.

Not wanting to read too much into his comment, she also desperately wanted his words to mean he regretted not being with her. He had said he regretted hurting her, which was different than regretting not being together. So he probably didn't mean what she wanted him to mean.

But then he also said the thing about self-sacrifice, she acknowledged to herself.

Matthew touched her arm, startling her out of her relentlessly circling thoughts.

Matthew tried to study her downturned face. "You're sure?"

"Yep."

"One hundred percent sure?"

"Of course."

"Because you're not looking at me when you say that. I can't tell if you're embarrassed about something or if you're really not okay."

Miranda smiled despite her anxiety. Of course, he'd read her body language like that.

She looked up into his eyes. "I'm fine, Matthew, just out of sorts. How are you feeling?"

His face scrunched up. "Surprisingly fine. Pretty sure Darla's going to make me replace the big room window, though. She'll make me do that shit myself, not just hire someone to do it."

She held her smile in place.

"What's wrong, Miranda? I can feel your nervous energy," Matthew admitted. "It's radiating off you."

Miranda dropped her eyes again before peeking back up at him, debating how to answer.

Do I say it? Do I ask? He asked. I should ask. I'm going to ask, she decided.

Opening her mouth, she took a deep breath just as someone bumped into her.

"Oh, sorry," the man murmured. "Are you okay? This is a terrible place to stop and talk."

"Sorry," she mumbled, looking around.

Surrounded by people trying to make their way back to the farmhouse, Miranda realized she and Matthew were standing in the middle of the main walkway. There was a wide gap of room around Matthew.

Ugh, this is so not the place for this conversation.

"We should go inside. We're blocking traffic," she said.

Matthew's lips quirked a little bit before his eyes dropped. "No one wants to bump Captain Fucking Chaos, but they'll trample Lady Earth no problem."

They started walking with the crowd back toward the house, naturally in step.

"What are you thinking?" Matthew asked.

"I'm thinking that it's nice to walk with you. I've spent a couple of years walking behind Larry. I'm so used to looking at the back of his head." She said the words lightly, meaning them as a joke, but she could feel Matthew's energy surge with anger. "Sorry."

"He's a fucking moron," Matthew breathed, trying to force the energy down.

Hesitantly, Miranda grabbed his hand, hoping it would help the energy cycle. Matthew started at her touch but then gently squeezed her fingers in thanks.

"You can come home with me if you want," Matthew blurted.

What? What does that mean? Does he mean stay with him or "stay with him?" I'm still married. Can I do that? People do that, but can I do that? What the fuck am I thinking? Of course I can do that! It's Matthew! Miranda internally babbled.

"I have empty bedrooms. If you don't want to stay with Ethan, come to stay with me. I'm not going to lie. He makes better eggs. But you know me better."

Of course. Of course he doesn't mean that how I want him to mean it.

"Ethan and I have fun together. Thank you, but I'm good where I'm at. His apartment is not far from my lawyer's office anyway," she mumbled, somehow fighting off tears.

Matthew nodded, not speaking again.

OCTOBER

ednesday evening, the Trellis family regrouped at the farmhouse for "training" with Micah.

"Do we need a circle?" Luke asked, unsure what to expect.

"You have a circle," Micah countered. "You're always in the organic circle when you're together. You need to learn how to use it, and Jake needs to learn to manage it."

"For fuck's sake." Jake sighed. "I told you. It's not something I *do*. It just happens."

"That's crap," Micah disagreed. You'll see. Fear, come here. We get to punch each other now."

"Ha!" William laughed, approaching Micah. "Let's do it. I'm sad you're not wearing the three-piece suit, though."

Micah grinned then slammed a fist into Will's face without warning.

"Really?" Will asked, unperturbed as he cracked his nose back into place.

"You think someone trying to hurt your wife is going to ask if you're ready first?" Micah asked, still grinning as he watched the rage flash across William's face.

They were grappling on the ground within a second.

"Quit pushing that fucking button, you asshole!" William yelled as he dislocated Micah's right knee.

Micah laughed. "Quit letting me push it, you moron. Dislocating is good. Better than breaking. All but the worst breaks start to heal on their own. A dislocation doesn't heal well until the joint is at least somewhat pushed back together. You buy yourself a few seconds when sparring with someone like me."

Micah flipped William airborne, tossing him about ten feet away. "Getting some distance from your opponent also gives you a chance to regain your feet and pop joints back together."

"This is disgusting," Beth murmured, watching as William charged Micah again, doing something that crushed Micah's left rib cage.

Gasping for breath, Micah continued his lecture, unfazed. "Obstructing air flow is helpful. If you can manage it, cutting off oxygen to the brain will render someone like us unconscious. But it is not an effective way to kill one of us. Beheading and then reducing to ashes is the best way to destroy a fully empowered pillar that regenerates. If the pillar is tightly bound to their pair, do not trust that beheading alone will get the job done."

Grappling on the ground again, Micah somehow ended up on top of William's back as Will tried to twist his way free. Micah paused to let his ribs pop back into place.

"Pumping fear into someone that controls hate isn't going to help you, Will. Find something else in your circle to move me," Micah taunted.

"What the fuck are you babbling about?" Will grunted, frustrated.

"Pull a different emotion from your circle. Many emotions are lurking here that would affect me. You know me well enough. Use something other than fear."

After about fifteen seconds of waiting, Micah sighed. "Fine. You're not ready to do that yet. You're trapped, yes? You can't dislodge me?"

William stopped thrashing, silently admitting the truth without words.

"Great. I'm going to hurt you now. If you don't use your circle, you'll remain injured until the Mistress helps you."

"Fuck you!" William swore.

Micah sighed. "Okay, class. Broken bones slow me very little. Dislocated joints are better. Damage to airflow is better still. Damage to sensory nerve centers is the next step up. It is disorientating, excruciating, and time-consuming to heal without help. For someone like me, without a circle, this could be deadly."

"What are you going to do?" Adrian asked, morbidly curious.

"William, do you understand? You have to find the energy from Adaline and use it. You have access to it. Your Walker and Mistress might be the most giving pair to ever exist. Learn to use it," Micah coached. "Do you understand what I'm saying?"

"Just do whatever the fuck you're going to do, man, before Hennessy loses his shit," William grunted, trying to throw Micah off his back again.

Micah grimaced then reached around and damaged William's eyes, eliciting a roar of raw pain from him.

Matilda bent over then fell to the ground. "I'm going to be sick," she muttered as the entire family shifted uncomfortably.

"Stay!" Micah barked at Hennessy. "He is not permanently damaged, Jessup. He needs to learn to do this. He will be fine, Emma. Stop crying. You'll distract him from what he needs to do if you don't calm down."

Once Hennessy acknowledged the words, and Emma turned away, sobbing into Sam's chest, Micah spoke. "William."

William continued to scream in pain and rage. "I'm going to fucking kill you!"

"WILLIAM!" Micah yelled over the babbling, roared words. "Find the binding to Adaline and fix it. You can do this. Pull the power to kill the pain and heal the injury."

"Let him up, Micah," Adrian demanded, his anger palpable in the field.

"Not until he does this," Micah replied, not bothering to take his eyes off William.

"Micah," Adrian growled, turning red in the face.

A glare of cold indifference turned on Adrian. When Micah spoke, the words were soft. "You saw how easily I immobilized him, even with all his training. Do you think you'd do better against me, Dr. Trellis? You all must learn—"

Something intangible shifted in the field, cutting off the lecture as Jake dropped to his knees, holding his head.

"Good," Micah said simply. "Again."

"The pain is gone, but I can't find the energy to heal the damage," William muttered. "Jake?"

"Vertigo," Jake groaned as he retched into the grass.

Micah's head tilted in curiosity. "Do you feel the energy, Jake? Can you push it toward him?"

Jake shook his head.

"Look for it," Adaline murmured. "You were able to correct it when you looked with Jess. Look for it. I taught you how to use that type of sight. You can do that."

"I don't think I can," Jake replied, trying and failing to regain his feet.

Micah sighed.

"Jacob," Adaline said, drawing his focus. "Look for it."

The group was silent for a moment, no one moving except William as he shifted under Micah's weight.

"It doesn't look weird," Jake said. "I don't know what to do."

"See the binding to William?" Adaline asked.

Jake made the approximation of a head nod.

"Pull his binding to mine," she explained. "It's what I do to heal someone. I bind their energy to mine."

"I got it. I feel it," William called. "Enough, Jake."

Micah smiled as he felt William pull the power to himself. "Very good. Good. Now pull energy to toss my ass off you. I can force enough energy into my body mass to pin you for a moment, but you have access to more energy than me. Use it. You shouldn't be stuck like this."

"Hmm," William murmured, seemingly unbothered by having his eyes gouged out a minute ago. "Physical strength?"

Micah smiled. "You make a good student for this—willing to learn despite the pain."

"Yeah, well…" Will's voice trailed off for a second. "Pip? You okay?"

"You're asking if *I'm* okay right now?" Emma wailed. "Are you fucking kidding me?"

"She doesn't swear like that often, man. You owe my wife an apology," Will said, shifting in place again.

Micah nodded. "We should have left her inside with your parents, Ava, and Jess. Love never battles like this. I'm sorry I didn't think of it, Emma.

"Back to the problem at hand. Fear is one of the best sources of strength, but fear, hate, and rage are pretty evenly matched in a heads-up match. I suggest you need to play with gravity more than strength against me."

Miranda, pale and queasy, gave a little squeak. "That's me, Will. I can do that."

Matthew's eyebrows shot up. "You can? Like zero gravity? I want to do that!"

"Can we do this first?" Will called, entertained despite his predicament.

"It's not all about you," Matthew retorted, trying to ease the tension in the field.

Some of Adrian's rage eased away with the banter. Emma gave a snotty snort of surprised laughter.

"Okay, Randa," Will called. "I think I found your binding. How do you do this?"

"Oh, like, on purpose?" she asked, surprised.

Micah sighed again.

"Usually, I just think about being lighter. I've never tried to make anything else lighter. But I made Larry heavier when I shoved him," Miranda mumbled, knowing she sounded stupid.

"Micah? Tips?" Will asked.

"I've never done it before," Micah admitted.

"Okay. We're going to wing it," Will replied, launching Micah airborne on the word "wing." Flying more than fifteen feet in the air, Micah cackled like a kid on a trampoline before he landed on the ground, leaving an indentation.

"Hey, look at that. You're right, Miranda. You can make people lighter and then *a lot* heavier." Will laughed, walking over to where Micah lay, stunned and crumpled. "That's a neat trick."

"Quick learner," Micah muttered, forcing his rib cage back into position again. "I'm really fucking hungry. Let's eat. Pull some water out of the ground to wash your face so Darla doesn't hate me."

Matthew grinned at Miranda. "Would you make it so I can jump back to the house like the Incredible Hulk? I've always wanted to do that!"

"He wanted to go to space camp when we were kids, too." Luke smiled.

MATTHEW SCOWLED as Miranda and Ethan entered the big room on Sunday evening.

"That is a sad mockery of the blue sweater," he complained.

Miranda paused, looking down at herself. "This is the exact same blue sweater."

Matthew frowned.

"It's not how you remember it?" she asked, trying not to be disappointed by his obvious disappointment.

"I guess not. It looked different before. Not as loose."

"I was twenty-five pounds heavier then," Miranda reminded him.

Matthew's frown deepened. "Yeah, remember when you ate food

and you didn't look like a skeleton surrounded by skin? Those days were fun."

"Stop that, right now," Darla scolded. "You will not pick on her! What is wrong with you? I raised you better than—"

"I'm not picking on her!" Matthew objected.

"Sounded like you were picking on her," Ethan disagreed.

"It's okay," Miranda muttered, looking at the floor as her eyes filled with unshed tears.

"Gah! She's going to cry. You're an asshole!" Jake yelled at Matthew then flinched, catching his own lousy language. "Sorry."

"That one gets by on a technicality of truth," Darla declared, still glaring at Matthew.

"I'm not picking on her! Miranda, I'm sorry. I didn't mean to pick on you. It just came out. You look so different now, though. I have not yet adjusted to this version of you—so timid and fragile. I can't believe it's the same sweater. Still, I shouldn't have said it. The words were out before I thought about it," Matthew apologized.

"I know," she muttered, trying to hide that she was wiping at tears. "I always liked this sweater, too. And I miss grilled cheese sandwiches."

"Grilled cheese?" Matty asked.

"Yeah. On a good sourdough, where the bread is toasted on the outside and buttery wonderful on the inside. You know? Grilled cheese?" Miranda asked, distracted.

"Butter inside? What?" Adrian asked, brow furrowed.

Miranda looked around the confused faces eyeing her. "Butter on the inside of the sandwich."

"I've never pitied you before this moment," Luke replied, straight-faced. "Butter on the outside for toasting, Miranda."

"Oh no," she said, her voice more firm than usual. "Very light layer of mayonnaise on the *outside* facing side of the bread. A very light layer of butter on the *inside* facing side of the bread. The mayonnaise does something amazing while toasting and doesn't leave a mayo flavor at all. The sandwich crisps better and still has a wonderful butter flavor."

The family stared at her in shocked silence before turning in unison to Darla.

"I've never tried it," Darla admitted somewhat apologetically.

"I'm with Miranda on this," Emma said. "Once you go mayo, there's no going back."

Will jerked in surprise. "How could you not tell me this before now?"

Emma's mouth dropped open before she started shaking with laughter. "It's a secret passed down from generation to generation. If you weren't in the know, it wasn't my place…"

William's lips twitched. "Okay, I didn't mean for that to come out so accusatory. But this seems like something we should come to a consensus on before the kids arrive."

"What is the appropriate type of cheese for a grilled cheese sandwich?" Emma asked, eyes narrowed in suspicion.

"That's a trick question!" Will yelled, startling laughs out of Lucy and Linda next to him. "There is no wrong type of cheese. Ever."

Emma smiled at Miranda. "At least he's got that part right."

"Grilled cheese and tomato soup next week?" Darla asked the room at large, noting the agreeable head nods all around.

Hank's eyes lit with joy. "Reubens?"

"I'm not pickling beef for corned beef, and we used the end of the sauerkraut. If you'll be happy with store-bought beef and kraut, sure."

"Never mind," he murmured, deflating a bit.

Darla's lips twitched when she met Ava's smiling eyes across the room.

"You need to stop spoiling them." Ava laughed.

Darla rolled her eyes. "After everyone's moved, we're going to start rotating where family dinner is held."

"That is an empty threat." Hank laughed. "You love this. You plan all week for this."

Darla grinned at him. "Shh."

"Why can't you have grilled cheese?" Jake asked Miranda, going back to the original topic.

"Because." Miranda shuffled uncomfortably.

"Is this the weight thing?" Jake demanded. "Seriously. Larry is not a svelte guy. He doesn't get to decide what you eat. And he's a lying, cheating asshole. Fuck him. Eat the grilled cheese!"

Darla cleared her throat.

"It slipped out. I'll be quiet," Jake agreed immediately.

"Kids?" Darla asked.

"We don't talk like Uncle Jake," Ree, Mia, and Meg recited as one.

Ethan sighed, rolling his eyes at Jake before turning to Miranda. "Are you happy with the way you look and feel? Jake is right about this. No one else gets a say unless you're a danger to yourself."

Miranda shifted uncomfortably again, knowing all the eyes were focused on her. The room was silent.

"I really am sorry, Randa. I didn't think before I spoke," Matthew apologized again. "Ethan's absolutely right. If you're happy, great. You're beautiful at any weight you're happy with."

Miranda blew out a sigh as her cheeks blazed red with the compliment. Unwilling to make eye contact with anyone, her gaze landed on the floor. She could feel the looks of concern and affection pointed at her and didn't want to trigger more tears. "I don't know what I am. It's difficult to stay this thin. My body doesn't like it, and I'm tired all the time. I'll think about it, okay?"

"That sounds good," Ethan murmured, hugging her.

Matty scooted over to make room for Miranda on the couch next to her. "You know what's better than being thin?"

"Hmm?" Miranda asked, ready to be done with the conversation, but not wanting to disappoint Matilda.

"Being strong. Limber and strong beats thin any day. I bet I outweigh you and you're a half foot taller than me."

"Mmm," Miranda said, nodding.

"Let's join a gym. We can work on it together," Matty suggested, smiling when Miranda's eyes snapped to her face.

"Really?" Miranda asked, excitement creeping back into her voice.

Matty nodded. "I work out every day at home, but we can join the gym that's halfway between Jake's place and Ethan's place."

"Our place," Jake corrected.

Matilda grinned. "Our place. Fine. Better equipment, more room. Let's do it. We'll start packing you full of protein, too, so your hair stops falling out."

Miranda scrunched up her face. "How'd you know my hair is falling out? It's not noticeable."

"Sometimes I know things," Matilda said, trying to pull off an all-knowing older sibling voice.

"I'm sad we don't live closer," Lucy muttered. "I'd absolutely get in on the girl power thing. Boxing with Adrian is getting old."

Sam shrugged, walking into the big room with Adaline. "We'll all be living on the same block before long. We'll put a gym in someone's basement."

"Oh." Matilda sighed. "Maybe no gym memberships since we're moving the week after next. But you should come work out with me!"

Miranda nodded in agreement. "It's a date."

"Did you move into the cornfield house yet?" Luke asked. "You're the first one to move into the new houses, right?"

"Tuesday. Furniture is delivered tomorrow," Sam answered. "Technically, Ava, Clyde, Blake, and Jess moved in first, but I know what you mean."

Luke turned to his dad.

"Movers come for our stuff on Thursday. Next week's dinner is in the new house." Hank smiled. "Spoiler alert if you haven't been there: the new house is exactly like this house, but with different paint, a bigger big room, a bigger dining room, and different kitchen fixtures."

"Exciting!" Emma clapped.

"There's even more exciting news..." Hank said, turning to Darla.

Darla's lips quirked. "You couldn't wait?"

"No, I couldn't," Hank admitted. "I had a tough time keeping it to myself on Friday."

She smiled fondly at her husband, knowing his excitement came with profound relief. "None of you should be surprised by this. But it's official. My cancer is in complete remission. It's gone as far as anyone can tell. I'll go for regular scans for a while, but it seems like it is behind us for now."

The room was still and silent for a minute as the family absorbed the news. Finally, Adrian blew out a gusty sigh of relief and charged his mom with a hug, breaking the spell and triggering a widespread cheer of happiness and victory.

Between the kisses, hugs, and celebratory joking, it took the family a minute to realize Hank was silently sobbing, hugging Sam and Adaline as one.

After the majority of tears had passed and the group sat quietly collecting itself, Micah cleared his throat. "I've never had a grilled cheese sandwich. I have no idea what you're talking about."

Ethan gasped into the stunned silence. "Lack of grilled cheese is almost as bad as being alone for hundreds of years. Poor you!"

Micah nodded, knowing he must be missing out on something special. "Poor me."

1 2

*M*iranda started in surprise early Monday afternoon when there was a knock on Ethan's apartment door. Security had not called about a visitor. After glancing at the security system screen that showed the hallway, she rushed to open the door.

"Hi!" she said.

"Hi," Matthew replied, smiling. "I come bearing gifts to beg forgiveness."

"Oh. Um, I'm not upset with you."

"Maybe not, but I'm upset with me. You have enough crap on your mind without me being a jackass."

Miranda smiled. "What did you bring me?"

"What else? The fixings for grilled cheese. Have you given up on getting dressed every day?"

She looked down at herself, only then realizing she was wearing Ethan's rumpled t-shirt that she had slept in and stretchy pants that had a hole in them. Miranda wasn't entirely sure if she'd brushed her hair that morning. Or her teeth.

"Gah!"

Matthew grinned. "Bored and lonely?"

"Perpetually," she admitted, grinning back. "Can I go get cleaned up really quick?"

"I'll start lunch."

"You have to try it with the mayo," she said, grin falling.

"Already have. There's no going back."

"When did you try it?" Miranda laughed.

"I had a late-night snack when I got home last night."

Ten minutes later, Miranda walked into the living room freshly showered, complete with styled hair, perfect makeup, and neat clothing. It was the fastest shower of her life.

Matthew's lips twitched as he bit back laughter. "From one extreme to the other?"

"You caught me by surprise. You didn't have school today?"

His face dropped into his "I'm not happy" expression as he sighed.

"Matthew?"

"After much discussion, I've taken a leave of absence from school."

"Why?" Miranda asked, shocked. Matthew loved teaching.

"Sam and Micah feel that my being at school, unaware and untrained, may put the kids at risk if danger comes knocking. Luke doesn't have a fixed schedule; he'd be hard to ambush. Beth is almost always with Hennessy. Pretty much everyone else works at the company and is together. I'm usually alone and surrounded by vulnerable kids."

"I'm so sorry, Matthew," she whispered.

"We've agreed that I'll go back once I have a better handle on the energy and how to use it. I won't allow fear to rule how I live my life. But I won't risk the kids, either. Micah and I will train most days. He wants me to be both physically stronger and more in control of the energy. I'm hoping to go back to school after the holidays. How are you?"

"Fine," she said immediately as he put a sandwich and soup bowl down in front of her. "That's not tomato soup."

"No, it's not," he agreed. "Upgrade. Lasagna soup."

"It's delicious. I shudder to think of all the fat and carbs in this meal."

"Then don't think about it," he suggested, tone subdued.

They were quiet for a moment while they ate.

"What happened, Miranda? How did you end up with him?" Matthew burst out.

"Oh. Um..." She hesitated, surprised by the abrupt question.

"I'm sorry. We don't have to talk about it if you don't want to," he offered, shifting uncomfortably. "It's just...four years ago, you were dead set on not living like your mom."

"Ah, yes, I was," Miranda sighed.

The silence between them grew weighty.

"I don't know where to start explaining this," she said, sinking into the familiar emotions of shame and remorse.

"Okay," Matthew said, squeezing her hand across the table. "How about at the beginning?"

Miranda's eyes closed at his touch. She wasn't sure if her heart beat unsteadily because of the energy cycling between them or because it was Matthew touching her.

"I'm not a strong person," she began after collecting her thoughts.

"What? That's bullshit. Stop that," Matthew scolded immediately. "Stop talking and thinking of yourself like that. It's not healthy. I don't know when you started that, but you should stop it."

"Not healthy, but true. Someone has always taken care of me. I've always been somewhat of a debutante. My father was furious after he met you."

"Charles didn't exactly hide that disapproval." Matthew laughed.

"I'm sure he would have handled it differently if he knew about Sam. Funny how you failed to mention that, by the way."

"It wasn't something I shared with anyone. I told you about my family, just not the money."

"True, but it was a pretty big thing to leave out of the conversation. You didn't trust me?"

Matthew exhaled. "Now you're doing that thing."

"What thing?"

"That thing I do when I don't want to talk about something. Stop distracting me." Matthew's smiled. "I trusted you. I just wasn't in the habit of talking about it. There was no reason to bring it up before your parents surfaced that weekend, and it seemed like it was too late after that. Back to the shit-bag!"

Miranda smiled back, rolling her eyes at being caught so easily. "I was supposed to go to school, meet some aspiring business prodigy, fall madly in love with him, get married, and make babies. I wasn't supposed to be hanging out with some liberal arts brainiac that argued philosophy with my dad."

Matthew grinned.

"By the start of my junior year, it was apparent I was not doing the appropriate husband-hunting. I didn't stay on campus over the weekend. I didn't attend the socialite stuff. There were a lot of stretchy pants and sweaters and books, not unlike right now. My brother was getting married. I met Lawrence at his wedding. They work together.

"He was nice in the beginning, not particularly interesting or interested in me. But my dad was ecstatic when we chatted together and then danced at the wedding. The next weekend I was home, Lawrence was at Sunday brunch. It was the first time in my life I can remember Sunday brunch not being a nightmare."

"Sunday brunch?"

Miranda snorted a cute little sarcastic laugh. "It's like the *Twilight Zone* version of your Sunday family dinner. Everyone tosses everyone else under the bus—"

"We do that!" Matthew objected, laughing.

"You do that to distract, not to judge," she corrected.

"True. Sorry to interrupt."

"My grandfather hosts it and spends the entire meal scowling at us, letting us know how unworthy we all are. But my grandfather likes Lawrence. I suspect he still likes Lawrence, even after the cheating and the punching. He's never had much use for me."

Miranda paused, considering how to continue.

"So Lawrence was there, and Grandfather left me alone. Lawrence showed up to the next brunch, too, and it was actually a good family interaction. We don't have many of those. Mom and I get along well. Dad and I do okay, too. But in his mind, a woman's place is to find a man to take care of her, get married, and make babies. I was not following his guide for a happy life.

"In Lawrence, I think they all saw the opportunity for me to have what my dad wanted for me and what my mom had, not realizing it wasn't what *I* wanted. Lawrence and I dated, off and on at first, not serious. He seemed harmless enough, and everyone else liked him.

"We saw each other more frequently. My family was so happy. I was 'finding my way,' to use Mom's words.

"I guess I just got used to people liking me better because I was with him. Then I ended up in this mindset where I couldn't disrupt the balance. I needed to stay with stupid Larry to keep things calm.

"After we got engaged, it occurred to me that Lawrence didn't actually like me. Sunday brunch was so much worse because he joined in picking on me, pointing out everything I did wrong. That's really where the eating and food thing started. He'd complain if I ate something he didn't approve of or overate something. Then I'd get nervous and be too upset to eat.

"But we were so far along by that point. I was just finishing school, and we were most of the way through planning the wedding. I figured he'd get bored and leave eventually, then I'd be free of him and my family couldn't blame me for kicking him to the curb. I could do what I wanted to do. I just thought it'd last longer than it did. Now I have nothing to show for it but a lawyer bill and a bunch of wasted time."

Silence fell between them as she picked at her food, no longer hungry.

"That's it. That's how I ended up with Larry."

Matthew's voice lacked inflection when he finally spoke. "What did you expect to have when it ended? How could it have ended too soon but also been a waste of time?"

"Ah. Ethan suggested that I never say this to Sam. So promise you won't tell?"

"I'm really going to hate this, aren't I?"

"Probably," she muttered, cheeks flushing.

"Tell me."

"My grandfather gave us a lump sum for a down payment on our house. My parents also gave us a lot of 'getting started' money. I knew they were going to do it. I figured Lawrence and I would make it at least a year and have some assets to split between us."

Miranda could hear Matthew's jaw crack. "You stayed for money?"

"I stayed because I had nowhere else to go, Matthew. Literally. When I found out he was cheating, I talked to my family. The general consensus was 'get over it.' I don't have friends. At least, I didn't after you and before Matilda. I was financially dependent on Lawrence. He wouldn't let me work. I was stuck until there was something to split between us.

"I could have left when Sam offered in August. I could have accepted his help and left. I didn't. I thought we'd make it a year, then we could split without me having to take a hand out. I don't like being dependent on others after all this.

"I understand now that my family, outside of Matty, isn't going to like me. It's just not part of how we interact. My parents love me, but I don't think either of them understands or likes me. I don't think my mom likes herself, either. I wanted to break free and be independent, not break away and live off of Sam."

"You didn't call me. After he hit you, you called Ethan."

"Yes."

"Why? I would have been there. You have to know that."

"I didn't doubt it," Miranda said with a sigh. "I was ashamed. I didn't want you to see me like that. And I was afraid you might do something to Lawrence you later regretted."

"You're wrong about that. I would have damaged him and not regretted it at all," Matthew muttered. "I still want to punch him in the head."

"Matthew! You're not a violent person. Stop that!"

He snorted. "I'll happily make an exception."

"What about you?" she asked.

"What about me?"

"No girlfriend? No relationships?" Her eyebrows quirked up.

Matthew gave an exaggerated sigh, stretching his arms in front of himself and cracking his knuckles. "Jane Austen is overrated and unduly praised because she was one of the few accomplished women authors in the period."

Miranda slapped her hand on the table. "How dare you! You take that back!" she yelled, completely distracted by his nonsense statement about her favorite author.

Matthew smiled to himself, wanting so desperately to hug and comfort her after poking the bitter memories that went with talking about Lawrence.

He stayed on his side of the table, though, content to watch her eyes light with the passionate spirit he'd longed to see in her since reconnecting.

"YOU'RE UP, Rage. Let's do this," Micah called the following Wednesday, standing in the field behind the farmhouse.

Adrian snorted, shaking his head.

"Come on," Micah taunted. "You were all ready to jump in the ring last week. Let's do this."

"No. I get the point." Adrian shook his head. "I can feel the circle now. I'm not playing."

Micah's head tipped to the side in confusion. "Scared of the pain?"

William outright laughed. "His pain tolerance is probably higher than mine. There's no fear coming off him."

"Come on, Rage. Time for school." Micah clapped his hands. "Be brave. Be bold. Take one for the team. They all learn when they watch this."

"No," Adrian said again. "Sorry."

"What's your problem?"

Adrian sighed. "I don't want my family to watch you beat the shit out of me. They had a hard time after Will and I threw down a few months ago. They don't need that again. They got the point last week, and I did, too. I'm not hurting you for no reason. I'm not causing them stress and displeasure for no reason."

"That's commendable," Micah said with a nod. "Now get your ass over here and let's do this."

Adrian glared at him.

"You need to know how to do this, man. I know it's not your nature to use the rage, and I know you think you have a handle on the organic circle. But you won't really know until you're fucked up, fighting for your life. Do you really want the first time you try to do this for real to be your *first time* doing it?" Micah asked, serious and focused.

"I'm not doing it today. No. Give them some time before you physically maim someone again," Adrian replied.

"Adrian—" Will started, sighing at the set of his little brother's shoulders.

"I'll do it."

Every pair of eyes in the field turned to Matthew.

"I'll do it," he said again. "It doesn't have to be Adrian. I heal, too."

Adrian gasped. "Matthew, that wasn't my point. I—"

"I know. Your point is valid. So I'll do it."

"Watching you get pummeled is worse than watching me get pummeled. I'll do it," Adrian said.

"No, it's fine, Adrian. I agree with you. I'll do it."

Micah rolled his eyes. "Come on, Chaos. Let's do this. I haven't thrown down against your type of energy in a long time. It's always an interesting fight."

Matthew stepped to the center of the field, recognizing the uneasy shifts around him.

"I'll let you initiate," Micah offered.

"Great," Matthew said with a smile. "Perfect."

"Whenever you…" Micah's words trailed off as his eyes went wide. "Stop it."

"Okay," Matthew said. "Let's do this instead."

Micah let out a keening whimper, dropping to his knees. His eyes were wide and unseeing, searching the field for something that wasn't there. Tears leaked down his cheeks as his arms folded over his head.

"Are we done?" Matthew mumbled, staring at the ground in front of him in shame.

At Micah's nod, Matthew turned and walked back to his spot next to Ethan.

"What did you do?" William asked, amazed. Micah remained crumpled in the middle of the field, trying to pull himself together. Then Adaline was there, touching the back of his neck gently, offering comfort.

"He said it last time, Will. There are plenty of emotions here that would affect him. And they did. Pumping someone full of joy and hope when they're used to having neither is its own sort of torture. Then ripping them away causes another form of pain," Matthew explained, gesturing to Micah, still on the ground. "Plenty of time to escape. No physical harm to anyone. Lesson learned, right?"

The group was silent. Shocked, appalled gazes moved between Matthew and Micah.

"You did that well. I wasn't sure anyone was listening when I said it," Micah eventually said, voice monotone.

"I was. I figured they should see that, too," Matthew said quietly. "I'm sorry. I pulled it away as soon as I felt the madness pull at you. I didn't expect it to happen that quickly."

Micah nodded in acceptance. "I expected you to come with chaos and madness. I was prepared for that. I was not prepared for happiness."

Matthew nodded.

"You can all do that," Micah called, voice booming in the open space. "You are all bound to the center of your circle and bound to each other to some degree. You can pull from those around you, given that your companions will allow it. You can use and deny each other energy in a fight to secure victory."

The field was silent for a full minute.

"I could have healed the gunshots," Hennessy said. It wasn't a question.

Micah nodded. "I'm certain William or Samuel would have shared that energy with you. If they had known it was possible, they could have pushed it to you if you were incapable of pulling it to yourself."

"I thought using all the types of energy was my thing?" Jake asked, confused. "If everyone can do that, what the fuck is my purpose?"

Micah threw his head back, laughing. "Jake, you still don't get it. I don't know how to make it clearer for you. You'll see in time, I think. In the meantime, figure out how to manage your natural circle. That belongs to you, and it's more powerful than you realize. You have to learn how to actively manage it."

"How the fuck do I do that?" Jake asked, annoyed at being laughed at.

"Practice," Micah suggested, eyes going back to Matthew. "Well done. Remind me that I don't want to face off against you again. If you throw the other energies around like that, I am afraid to see what you do with chaos when you mean harm."

Matthew nodded, shifting uncomfortably. "Sorry."

"Don't be," Micah said. "You should use chaos like that and let them see it."

Matthew's lips quirked. "I guess. But my name isn't Chaos, Micah."

"It's close to it. I can see and feel it," Micah disagreed.

"Close." Matthew nodded. "But not the same."

ETHAN'S APARTMENT door opened on Thursday morning as
Matthew knocked. Miranda walked right into his arms, offering a hug
of comfort and understanding.

Oh my God. I love you, he chanted over and over in his head. *I have
always loved you. I will always love you. I fucked up our lives in epic fashion,* he
continued his mental confession.

Matthew spent the previous night tossing and turning as he warred
with his energy and remorse.

"Hi," he muttered into her dark brown hair, tone muffled.

She smells like strawberry shampoo and mint toothpaste. Matthew sighed.
His arms wrapped around her of their own accord.

"You okay? I tried to catch up to you and Luke last night after what
happened with Micah, but you hauled ass out of there."

Matthew stood in the apartment hallway, wallowing in the feel of
her, unwilling to move. "Better now. I didn't want to discuss it with
everyone. I'm sorry, I knew you were trying to catch up. I didn't wait."

*I couldn't look at you after doing that. I couldn't look at you after intention-
ally hurting someone like that,* he thought, not wanting to admit the
words out loud.

"S'okay," she mumbled. "I get not wanting to rehash it with the
whole group."

They stood together for a few more seconds, wrapped together.
Miranda's arms loosened as she stepped back from him.

Matthew exhaled, shifting his gaze down to meet her sweet blue
eyes. She was so close, just a few inches between them. If he dipped
his head down to her, they'd be kissing.

She wouldn't pull away. I know she wouldn't. I could kiss her, he thought.
*Fucking shit-bag Larry. She's not even a month out of that relationship, still
reeling.*

"Matthew?" she asked.

Is she staring at my mouth? Should I kiss her?

Miranda sighed. "Shakespeare was a better storyteller than
Homer."

Matthew gasped in outrage, opening his mouth to argue before he'd even followed her all the way into the apartment.

They were still yelling at each other, arguing and laughing when Ethan walked in the door at lunchtime.

"I heard you two arguing while I was still in the elevator," Ethan laughed. "The neighbors are going to complain."

That gave Matthew pause. "You have neighbors now? Other people live on this floor? When did that happen?"

Ethan snorted. "Yeah, right. I was kidding. Sam would lose his damn mind."

13

Friday night, most of the Trellis family was gathered behind the farmhouse for Micah's training again.

"We could have just asked Ethan," Will pointed out, trying not to laugh.

"It would have killed all the fun." Emma grinned.

"I can—" Sam started.

"NO! Shut it. You don't get to bet," Adrian yelled as Lucy broke into giggles.

"I don't think Matthew and Miranda are together yet," Emma offered. "They didn't seem together on Wednesday."

"Boo!" Noah yelled. "You're supposed to want the lovey-dovey stuff, *Lady Love!*"

"I do!" Emma laughed. "I just don't think it's happening yet. But why didn't Matthew ride with you and Luke like usual?"

"Boo!" Noah yelled again for good measure. "We left the city earlier to pick up Tali and stop at the cornfield houses before coming here. He didn't want in on the tour of the greater Chicago area cornfields. Also, five of us wouldn't fit in the car comfortably. He didn't ride with us because they're together."

"Time will tell. Pretty sure you're going to owe me ten bucks," Adrian taunted.

Noah made a rude gesture at Adrian. "Luke, what name did Matthew take? Just tell me! It's killing me to not know!"

"I didn't ask, Noah. He'll tell us when he's ready. Let it go."

"UGH! That's boring!" Noah bitched, laughing.

"You people are ridiculous." Micah sighed.

"Whatever, man. You keep saying that, but it's not coming across as a complaint." Will grinned at Micah.

"I'm not complaining. I love this about you. But it makes it hard to take you seriously," Micah replied, no longer hiding his grin.

"I don't know. Matthew took you down pretty fast on Wednesday. Maybe take us a little more seriously?" Beth suggested without a trace of humor.

The family went quiet, all humor gone as they stared at Beth.

"What? It's true."

Hennessy whispered something to her.

"I won't stop it, Jessup. Screw him," Beth said, not bothering to lower her voice, openly scowling.

Shock registered on Micah's face. "Have I done something to offend you, Lady Hope?"

"Yeah, you fucking idiot, you have—"

"It's fine. Beth, we talked about this. I thought you were okay with this?" Hennessy interrupted.

"I decided I'm not fine with it. It's my turn in the ring tonight," she said, voice loaded with a taunting challenge.

The Trellis men shuffled uncomfortably, unwilling to make eye contact with Micah.

"Beth, Hope doesn't fight in the way—" he started.

She snorted. "That's what you think. I have some rage to work through, Micah. Be a good sport. They have to learn, after all. *Anything* to ensure we're prepared, right?"

"I wouldn't do it, man," Noah stage-whispered into the uncomfortable silence. "She's vicious. Broke my arm *twice* while we were kids. I'm more than four years older than her, too."

Micah rolled his eyes at Noah. "You probably deserved it."

"I'm not claiming otherwise. But she's capable of breaking bones. Don't discount her."

"I'm not foolish enough to discount anyone that glares at me with that much rage. Not hate, though, Beth?" Micah asked, eyebrows raised. "Few can manage that type of anger without it crossing into hate. I can't feel hate coming from you, though."

Beth smirked at him. "I'm remarkable in a lot of ways."

"Just so we're clear on this—" Will started.

"Oh, I recognize I'm about to take a beating, William. There's no way I'll take a swing at her." Micah almost laughed. "I'm just not that stupid. If you didn't manage to gut me, Samuel would roast my brain."

William nodded, unashamed.

Sam hesitated, gaze traveling between Beth and Micah. "She fights her own battles, Micah. You do her a disservice if you pander to William's sensitivities."

Beth grinned at Sam. "You're my favorite brother."

"Oh, fuck you!" William yelled. "I'll beat Sam's ass if you say that again."

"Why do I get the beating?" Sam frowned.

William glared at him. "I'm not hurting my princess. But I can make you bleed no problem."

"Well, you can try," Sam said, starting to smile. "You'd have to catch me first."

Emma snorted, shaking with real laughter. "This is the most asinine conversation we've had in a while."

"But it's interesting," Adrian said. "Sam, you wouldn't object to Beth getting punched in front of you?"

"Well, I wouldn't go that far," Sam said, offended. "If someone was truly out to hurt her, or anyone else for that matter, I'd have a problem with it. But for training? For her own chosen battles? She's capable of fighting them without my interference."

"What if it was Matty?" Jake asked.

"Matty is more than capable of taking care of herself."

"Damn straight," Matilda murmured.

William and Jake shared a disbelieving look.

"He didn't interfere with my fight when we got Linda out of Ohio," Lucy offered from her place between Adrian and her sister. "He didn't get involved until it was pretty much done."

Sam shrugged and nodded. "It was your fight."

"Would you watch someone beat the shit out of me?" Noah asked.

"I have watched several people beat the shit out of you. I watched Will slug you on Wednesday night after you made that joke about Emma's boobs getting bigger." Sam laughed.

"Oh, true." Noah grinned, winking at Emma.

"The whole point of this is for us to figure out how to defend ourselves. You shouldn't need help," Sam said reasonably.

"I agree," Micah said, nodding. "Still, it's nice to know I'm not going to end up eating lightning if Beth breaks a nail busting up my face."

"Ethan?" Jake asked Sam, knowing this was a more difficult question.

Sam froze in place, thinking.

"Yeah, thought not," Jake muttered. "There's no way you could watch Ethan take a punch."

"It's not that he can't..." Sam's voice trailed off.

"Usually, Love commands that sort of defense, not Joy," Micah said, surprised.

Emma laughed. "I can kick ass all on my own, belly full of babies or not, thank you very much. Also, William would chew up anyone that tried to touch me."

"True," Will said, nodding. "On both fronts. She dropped a stalker that managed to break into her place and pull a knife on her last year."

"I forgot about that!" Matty yelled. "I remember reading that!"

Car doors slammed in the distance.

"Final call for bets!" Emma yelled, back to laughing. "Is Miranda arriving with Ethan or with Matthew?"

"Feel better?" Hennessy asked, watching Beth scrub dried blood from her face. Rinsing the washcloth, she picked at the skin wedged under her nails.

"I really do." She smiled, causing her lip to split again. "I feel like Micah and I have a better relationship now."

"Did you have to crush his knee? It made me a little sick to hear the joint snap like that," Emma mumbled, handing Beth a fresh face towel.

"Yeah, I did. He'll heal. It's fine."

"What exactly were you trying to prove?" Will's tone was terse.

Beth cleared her throat then used the mirror to stare at her eldest brother, standing in the doorway. "He doesn't get to rip your fucking eyes out a few days after I watched Hennessy impersonate Swiss cheese. Hard no on that. And I think we both understand each other better now."

Will snorted.

"He was oh-so-worried about you trying to protect *me*. It never occurred to him that I might take exception to him hurting you," Beth clarified.

"We have to learn, Beth," Will said, still meeting her gaze. "I am best equipped to be the practice dummy. Let's not make a habit of beating the ever-living fuck out of the guy trying to help us."

"Will—"

"No, Princess. I understand. The timing was terrible. I didn't think about it before training last week. I should have. I'm sorry. I knew I was going to be screaming before I made it out of that fight. I should have sent you and Pip inside. But, to Sam's point, that does you both a disservice. He's trying to help us, and that means teaching us how to fight and manage pain. He doesn't deserve your rage."

"I disagree. He doesn't deserve my hate. I don't hate him. He knows that. But he deserved my rage."

"Beth—" Will started.

"No, Will. Who else would you have me direct that pain and anger at? Hennessy? He chose to go into that basement with you. You? You stood there and watched him get shot, but I know that destroyed you almost as much as it did me. The guy that Sam and Lucy roasted? He's gone. Lucy, for wanting to protect Ree? Linda, for needing saving? There is no perfect way to deal with it. I was working through it as best I could, and then he gouged your eyes out. There's a price for that, training or not.

"Micah caught my rage. I don't think he'll hold it against me. God help Jared if I get to lay hands on him, though. I'll fucking kill him."

Will shook his head, walking away. "You owe him an apology, Bethany."

Beth shrugged, smiling at Emma again. "That was a given. I have no problem with that. I'll talk to him just as soon as Addy finishes putting his psyche back together."

BETH WAS WAITING in the entryway of Hank and Darla's new house on Sunday afternoon. She threw the door open before Micah could ring the doorbell.

"Why don't you just walk in like everyone else?" she asked abruptly, knowing she surprised Micah.

"It's not my house. It would be rude to just walk in," he replied, lips upturned into a small smile. "Feeling better?"

"I am." Beth nodded, unsure how to start her apology.

"I'm not mad. I wasn't upset," Micah offered.

"Oh, good. Will gave me a serious guilt trip."

Micah shook his head. "It's strange to think of anyone trying to stand up for me. I haven't adjusted to that concept. Even when I had a circle, I didn't have that type of support."

"That's a shame. I hate that you've been alone for so long." Beth squirmed uncomfortably, realizing she beat the crap out of someone that had never had friends or defenders. She mentally sighed at her poor judgment.

He nodded, acknowledging her words but not addressing them.

After a moment, he continued. "Guilt would be misplaced. The purpose of training is to learn and practice. You did an admirable job of working with the energy at hand as well as doing damage. Are you still angry with me?"

"No," she said immediately. "Now, I just feel like a jerk. I took a lot of anger out on you."

Micah grinned. "You did it well."

"I was pissed."

"You're a force to be reckoned with when you're angry."

"Well, duh." She grinned back at him. "Hennessy and William both take delight in teaching me how to defend and attack."

Micah threw an arm around Beth's shoulders, offering comfort in a way she'd understand, as they walked toward the big room. "I can't believe you let him call you 'princess.' Can I call you princess?"

"Only if I get to beat the shit out of you regularly."

"Pass." Micah laughed. "I'm glad you can fight, Beth. I'm glad you can defend yourself. Hope is a force unto itself, but it's destroyed easily without defense. You are masterful at avoidance. Only one in four of my jabs landed and I am quick."

"I'm quicker." She smiled, poking him in the ribs. "This shirt is very fetching on you, Micah. It brings out your beautiful eyes. Are you trying to look your best for any particular reason?"

His smile fell a bit, but his eyes remained bright.

"Hope is good. Hang onto it." Beth grinned, stretching to kiss his cheek before they took seats in the big room.

"WHY WON'T YOU TELL ME?" Noah yelled as Ethan and Miranda joined the family a few minutes later. "It's bad enough I lost ten bucks betting on you, you damn monk! You have to keep secrets, too?"

Ethan looked around, ignoring Noah. "You weren't kidding. This house is near identical to the other house."

Hank nodded, shooting side-eye at Sam. "We just built the other house. It was less than five years old. We didn't especially want to move again."

"I don't deserve that glare!" Sam objected. "Micah's the one that said we need to lock it down."

"I wasn't glaring," Hank said primly.

"You started construction on these houses well before I showed up," Micah objected.

"Well, I have no response to that. But it's still Micah's fault," Sam said with a straight face.

"How are you here before us?" Ethan asked, surprised that Sam and Adaline were already in the big room. They were typically the last to arrive for Sunday dinner.

"We live next door now. Poor form to make you all wait on us," Sam said, continuing his look of innocence.

Ethan was unmoved. "You had no commute even before the move. You instantaneously disappeared from one place and appeared in another. We still had to wait for you."

"That was then, this is now." Sam quirked his little smile. "I'm trying to be courteous."

"You seem good. Happy. Feel good?" Ethan asked, smiling at his younger brother. It made Ethan happy to see Sam happy after so much strain and sorrow.

Sam grinned back. "I like it here. I like being on the power sink more than I thought I would. Your house will be ready in three weeks. You'll move here, right? So we can all be together?"

Ethan rolled his eyes. "I'm guessing I don't have a choice. But I didn't pick that house, Sam. And I like being in the city."

"It's a good house—good space! I talked to it, and it shared with me. It's excited you're going to live in it. Don't make me a liar!"

"Huh?" Miranda asked, confused.

"Don't," Hank whispered. "Don't ask. Just let it go by."

The joy dropped from Sam's face. "Adaline got to tile your shower. It's beautiful."

Ethan's eyebrows shot up as he turned to Addy.

She grinned. "Your kitchen backsplash, too. It's lovely. Blake is going to teach me how to hang cabinets in Matthew's house."

"She has a gift for tile. It's gorgeous," Blake agreed. "Her hands are tiny enough that I think it makes it easier to line things up."

"I can help, too!" Sam offered.

No one humored him with a response.

"Why won't you tell me?" Noah demanded into the awkward silence.

Matthew sighed.

"Come on! It's been months."

"Noah, let it go. You've been on this, Sam-style, since Wednesday. Let. It. Go," Jake demanded.

"Oh, like you don't want to know!" Noah bitched.

"What? What's wrong?" Miranda asked.

Jake dropped his head into his hands. "He is obsessed with knowing the name that Matthew took. Functionally, it's Chaos. We all know it. But he won't leave it alone."

"Really?" Miranda asked, surprised. "None of you know?"

Head shakes all around the room caused her mouth to drop open. Her eyes paused on Luke.

"I haven't asked," Luke admitted. "He'll tell me when he's ready."

"Yeah, but..." Miranda said, breaking out into genuine laughter. "How do you *not* know this? Come on!"

Matthew grinned at her.

"I know what it is." She grinned back.

"I knew you would." He laughed, enjoying their little secret.

"COME ON!" Noah yelled.

Matthew rolled his eyes.

"You're not going to tell them?" Miranda asked. "I won't tell if you don't want them to know."

Matthew shrugged, still grinning as he stood to hug her. "I don't care. Go ahead."

"He studied ancient Greek mythology, Noah." Miranda laughed. "Spent years studying it."

"So?"

"Lord Pan, the god of the wild things. Also, shepherds, mountain wilds, and rustic music."

"A+." Matthew laughed, looking around the room at the shocked faces. "They're not smart."

"They're plenty smart. They just never had you for a teacher." Miranda grinned up at him. She enjoyed the feel of his arm around her waist and the happy zing of energy where their skin touched, his hand to her arm. "Though the mountain wilds belong to me, and rustic music is more of a Luke thing, isn't it?"

"It's fun overlap." Matthew grinned again, kissing the top of her head as he wandered out of the room. "Anyone else need a beer?"

"Pandemonium," Micah muttered, nodding. "It fits."

"Weren't you alive for Ancient Greek times? Shouldn't you have known that?" Noah asked, looking at Micah expectantly.

"Rome, Noah. I am from Rome," Micah corrected. "Knowledge wasn't as accessible at the time."

"It's the same thing, though, right?" Noah asked, confused. Talise winced. "Sorry, Micah."

"You are so fucking stupid," Jake choked out through his laughter. Darla glared.

"Sorry! Sorry, kids. I know. I owe you five bucks each. Start a tab," Jake offered, still laughing at Noah.

"You have to admit he has looks going for him, though. He's pretty, and it works for him." Talise grinned, patting Noah's arm.

The room erupted in laughter, spurred on by Noah's good-humored grin.

14

"*M*iranda, thank you for agreeing to meet with us directly," Lawrence's lawyer said cordially. "We appreciate the act of trust and goodwill. No one in this room wants to harm you."

Miranda nodded, unable to speak. Her mouth was dry and her hands were shaking. This was her first meeting with Lawrence since the night he took a swing at her.

It's been almost a month. I haven't seen him in nearly a month, she realized. *He looks terrible.*

Indeed, Lawrence looked as if he hadn't slept in days. His patchy facial hair had gone unshaved for at least a week. Dark circles rimmed his drooping eyes. He sat stiffly, clearly uncomfortable.

It was difficult to feel too bad for him, though, given the glare he had targeted on her.

"We would like to discuss the terms for dissolving the marriage, but we'd also like to discuss the criminal charges against my client," the lawyer continued.

"I've made our stance on that very clear," Miranda's lawyer, Mark, responded immediately. "We'll be leaving now if—"

Lawrence's lawyer was shaking his head before Miranda's lawyer could even finish talking. "No, Mark. I told you this would be a factual, cordial conversation when I asked for this meeting, and I'll end it myself if we veer from that tone."

"Then why are we here?" Mark asked. "I made our terms clear."

"We would like to extend a counteroffer. The couple has marital assets valued at one point four million dollars. However, their personal debt is closer to two point six million—"

"That's not accurate," Miranda said immediately. "The mortgage on the house is less than a million. There is less than ten thousand dollars in credit card debt."

Lawrence's lawyer shook his head. "There is the matter of the home equity line on the house and the personal loans."

"I don't know what you're talking about," Miranda murmured, looking at her lawyer. "There is very little equity in the house. How could we have an equity line? And I have no personal loans."

"The home equity line was extended and tapped out four months ago. Almost a million dollars in personal loans were paid out three months ago," the lawyer explained.

Holy hell, what is happening? What is this? What would he even do with all that money? Miranda panicked in her mind.

Mark shook his head. "We'll be contesting that in court. If my client wasn't a party to the loans, wasn't even aware of them, she is not responsible for them."

"They're obligations extended and accepted during the marriage with no premarital understanding documented. You might be able to convince a judge that she knew nothing about it. Maybe. But we have an offer that would make this easier."

Miranda's lawyer's face turned cold. "If you suggest we drop the criminal charges to relieve her of the debt, we'll be leaving. Ultimately, even if you manage to hang the debt around Miranda's neck, it won't impact her life. You know she has friends helping her."

"But it would be months of back and forth negotiations in court. She'll have to testify in the criminal case. My client tells a different story of what happened that night. Do you want to play he-said, she-said, Miranda? Do you want to deal with that stress and anxiety?"

Mark told me this man's name. I know he did. What is this lawyer's name? I wasn't listening. I should have listened more closely, she thought, distracted.

"Miranda?" the lawyer asked again. "Almost a month later, Lawrence is still suffering from his injuries that night. Stretching and using that side of his body is painful. Surely, you've noticed the change in his appearance. He was far more injured than you that evening. He's paid for whatever injury done to you in pain and discomfort. Is he to pay with his livelihood, too?"

"Mr. Suffolk," Miranda croaked, pleased that the name came back to her, even if her voice was unsteady, "Lawrence and I both know what happened that night. If he's chosen to fabricate a story to make himself look better, I will caution you both to review the police reports. We each made statements that night, and I don't believe he thought far enough ahead to lie at that point."

"You snide, selfish, little bitch—" Lawrence howled.

"Lawrence!" the lawyer barked.

Mark stood to gather his things. "Let's go, Miranda."

"I would like to know where the money went," Miranda said quickly, looking at Lawrence's lawyer. "What did he do with the loan payouts? I don't believe we spent that money together."

The lawyer dropped his gaze and didn't respond.

The girlfriend. He was supporting the girlfriend.

Miranda walked out of the office with her lawyer without another word.

"WHAT NOW?" Miranda asked her lawyer once they were back in his office, seated with coffee. She didn't look at Mark as she asked, instead focused on the view of the lake out of the high-rise window.

I wonder how much Mark charges per hour. I'm such a damn pampered princess, I don't even know. I went right from Daddy to the shit-bag and now to

Sam and Ethan. Matty's right. I need a life, Miranda admitted to herself, not for the first time.

She sighed, thinking about her prior plans, now beyond her reach.

"There's nothing on your credit report about personal loans or an equity line. I'm somewhat curious how he got that line without your signature on it, given the house is a joint asset," Mark replied.

"You didn't answer my question. I assume they will not accept our offer. Are we looking at a long divorce process?"

Mark nodded in acknowledgment. "Sorry, I wasn't trying to avoid the question. There's not much to drag out when it comes to the divorce. There are no assets if the debt numbers shared today are correct.

"We can allow him to accept all the debt, as they offered. You'd walk away from the marriage as soon as we can get in front of a judge, assuming he can buy you out of the house's mortgage. Or we can make them liquidate everything and drag it out. Those are your options."

Miranda nodded.

"Is there anything else that you want from the house?"

"No," Miranda said decisively. "Things that hold sentimental value either never moved to the house or have already been removed by a friend, along with my personal items."

"But you didn't take anything Lawrence would contest?" Mark asked.

"Not unless he wants my socks and underwear for some reason. It was just clothes and pictures, the birthday present from my sister, and a glass vase my grandmother made me."

Mark frowned. "Your grandmother was a well-known artist. Her work has increased in value over the last several years. Can you prove the vase was given to you before the marriage?"

"I have a picture of me holding it, standing with her when I was eleven." Miranda sighed. "I don't think Lawrence ever understood the significance. And I don't think he realizes her work has increased in value. He's only ever thought of her as my grandfather's wife, not a person in her own right."

Mark nodded.

"So, not much to the divorce. What about the criminal charges?"

"That's a better question for the district attorney," Mark hedged.

Miranda turned toward him, raising her eyebrows.

"If the DA moves forward with the charges, I expect the process will take a while. There is no history of a domestic disturbance between you, no permanent physical damage done to you. You've been seeing the counselor I suggested?"

"I have." Miranda nodded, going back to staring out the window. "She's very good."

Mark nodded in agreement. "The counseling will help the case. Again, I recommend we sue in civil court."

"He doesn't have anything for us to sue for." Miranda's eyes narrowed. "Why do you keep suggesting that?"

Mark sighed, rubbing his eyes. "Miranda, there's very little chance the criminal charges against him will stick. He has no prior record of violence, and he was seriously injured that night. The charges against him will be reduced. He'll likely be sent for counseling and maybe some community service. But I'm amazed the DA hasn't already agreed to reduced charges."

"He's going to just get away with it?" Miranda asked, thinking of Ethan's experience.

That man almost killed Ethan and walked away with not much more than community service. Of course Larry's going to get away with this. Why would I expect otherwise? she asked herself.

Mark watched her. When she met his eyes, he nodded again.

She blew out a frustrated sigh. "Well, at least he'll keep his securities license so he can pay off his massive pile of debt. He has to go for counseling. He takes all the debt and goes for at least a year of weekly counseling. Violence was out of character for him. He needs help."

"We have no way of enforcing the counseling. You know that, right?"

"Well, no legal way to enforce it. But, as you said, I have friends. I imagine Sam will ensure it's done to my satisfaction if I ask." Miranda smiled to herself. She'd been managing Sam's anger toward Larry carefully over the last few weeks. He'd be glad to have a way to help.

"May I ask how you know Mr. Trellis? I've asked around. To the best of my knowledge, the Trellis family has never gotten involved in someone else's life like this. The Beloved Foundation supports causes that would help you in these circumstances. Trellis Industries has programs to support their employees like this. But I've never heard of the family getting so personally involved."

"You sound decidedly uncomfortable, Mark," Miranda observed, a little smile playing across her face.

"I am," he replied, serious. "I just told you news you didn't want to hear. I'm quietly wondering if my career is about to end."

Miranda blinked. "He would never... Sam would never do such a thing, Mark. Never. He might destroy Lawrence's financial livelihood, but only if I let him. He can be savage about protecting the people he loves."

"And that includes you?" Mark asked, clearly fishing.

Miranda smiled. "My sister is engaged to Jake Trellis. I think I've become a de facto member of their family."

"Matilda Benton? Your sister is Matilda Benton?"

Miranda nodded, surprised that he was so informed to know Matty's name off the top of his head. Mark still looked stressed. "Sam would never get in the way of you doing your job. You can relax, Mark. I promise he's not going to take this personally."

Mark exhaled in relief. "I've never met him, and I'd really like to stay off his shit list."

"Don't take a swing at me and everything should be fine," Miranda muttered, back to staring out the window.

MIRANDA RANG her grandfather's doorbell the following Sunday morning. Standing on the stoop, she thought of the causal ease at which Ethan walked into Darla and Hank's house without knocking.

Miranda always knocked, even at her parents' house, her childhood home.

Always so careful. Polite. Can't offend anyone. Must ask permission. She mentally rolled her eyes at herself.

Her father opened the door, a pleasant smile on his face. "Baby girl, I'm so glad you came to your senses. Welcome home. Come in, we were just waiting for you."

An apology automatically sprang to her lips. She paused before speaking. "I'm not late."

Her father's eyebrows shot up. "That's all you have to say?"

Their eyes met as Miranda contemplated her words.

"Hi, Daddy, it's good to see you. I'm not late. Why would you be waiting for me?"

Charles frowned. "You're the last to arrive. That's all."

They watched each other for another moment before Miranda nodded.

"This attitude of yours leaves a lot to be desired, Miranda. I don't know what's gotten into you lately, but this new stubborn, confrontational streak is not becoming of a lady."

What would Matty say to that? Miranda wondered. Then she burst out laughing, realizing that her sister would tell Charles where to stick his lady-like behavior.

The frown deepened on Charles's face. "You will not treat me with disrespect, young lady! You need to check your attitude."

Miranda was oddly pleased that her father took her laughter to mean something she didn't intend. She wouldn't have otherwise had the gumption to laugh in his face at a time like that, but she didn't regret it.

"What are you two doing out here?" Megan's head poked around the corner to see into the entryway.

"Arguing," Charles said.

"Being scolded for existing," Miranda retorted without thinking.

She laughed to herself. *Matilda, Ethan, and Matthew are fabulous influences.*

Megan frowned. "Stop it. Both of you."

"Stop existing? No. I won't do that," Miranda said, grinning at the shocked looks on both of her parents' faces. Thinking briefly over her life, she couldn't remember ever being so cheeky.

"What has gotten into you?" Megan asked, mouth hanging open.

"I don't know. I just showed up for brunch, as expected. Daddy, I'm not going to take the subtle slights. I didn't 'come to my senses.' I let Lawrence off the hook. Get it right. And I'm not late. You weren't waiting for me. More accurately, I'm the last to arrive, which is different than making everyone wait for me."

Miranda's gaze traveled between her mother and father, taking in their blank looks of surprise. So, she caught it when her mother's lips turned up just a bit.

"Fine, Miranda. Fine." Charles sighed. "I didn't mean to imply you had inconvenienced us this morning. You haven't. The last few weeks with the threat of charges hanging over Lawrence was a rather large inconvenience, though. I suggest we avoid the topic unless you want an earful from your grandfather."

If I could think of something pithy to say to the old man, I'd yell it down the hallway right now, she thought, sure that her grandfather was listening. Miranda lamented her lack of imagination.

"Randa," Megan's voice was chiding. "Don't you dare. I haven't seen you in weeks. Get in here and tell me what you've been up to."

Dutifully following her parents into her grandfather's house, Miranda smiled. "Mom, Ethan went back to work that following week. You could have come to visit. He wasn't home to throw you out. Again."

Megan flipped a smile over her shoulder at her younger daughter. "You are cheeky today. I like this. This is good."

Charles snorted in disapproval.

"She's an adult, Charles. My sass doesn't bother you. Why does hers?" Megan asked.

They turned into the sitting room where her grandfather, brother, and sister-in-law sat in stiff silence.

"Good morning," Miranda said brightly. She bent to kiss her grandfather's cheek, as she'd done her entire life. He turned away from her. "Or not."

"There's the little turncoat," Benjamin growled. "You've had everything you ever wanted, and this is how you repay that generosity?"

Miranda sighed in time with Megan and Charles behind her.

"The man broke my face, Grandfather. He deserved every bit of pain and worry that he brought upon himself."

Always "grandfather." Never grandpa, pops, papa, or anything less formal. Miranda had a sudden tactile memory of her grandma, squeezing her hand in comfort. *Gram, why did you do this for so many years?*

"Your face is fine," he retorted. "Serves you right for disobeying your husband—"

"Dad!" Megan yelled, cutting him off. "That's wrong, and you know it. Mom would be rolling in her grave if she heard that!"

"Your mother is nothing but a box of rotting bones at this point. She doesn't care," Benjamin responded, unrepentant.

The tears sprung to Miranda's eyes without warning.

"There she goes, getting all weepy over a long-gone dead woman. What the hell is wrong with you?" Benjamin barked at Miranda. "You could have damaged the brokerage with that little stunt. Don't you have any family loyalty at all?"

Miranda looked around the room. Her mother was chewing her bottom lip in agitation. Her dad was standing beside her mom, rubbing his eyes, somehow sensing what was to come. Her brother sat on the other side of the room with his wife, doing his best to pretend like Miranda didn't exist.

"I guess I'd have more loyalty if this was more of a family," she finally responded. "The charges are dropped. I'm not sure what else you want from me at this point."

"You could apologize," her grandfather replied snidely, ignoring her comment about family.

"I could, but I haven't done anything wrong," Miranda said, remembering Ethan's words about when an apology was appropriate. "Do you intend to do this all through brunch? If so, I'll just leave now."

"That begs a bigger question," her grandfather replied. "Where would you go? You aren't staying here. I doubt your parents will take you back. You haven't worked a day in your life. What do you intend to do with yourself?"

Megan touched Miranda's arm in warning.

Mom didn't tell him where I've been staying? Wow.

"Where do you think I've been for the last month?" Miranda asked, curious.

"You've been with that family. The gay one. I know that. I had to hire a damn private investigator to make sure you wouldn't humiliate us further. But you can't stay there forever. What are you going to do? I'll be damned if I help you again."

Pretty sure you're already damned, Grandfather. But still. I don't want your help.

"Then why do you care?" Miranda asked.

"Call it a matter of curiosity. I want to know if I should publicly disown you at this point or not," Benjamin replied coldly.

Miranda sighed, thinking about what was ahead. She had formed a new plan that required Sam's cooperation to get started, but she was confident he'd go for it. Her grandfather would never offer her any sort of meaningful financial or emotional support.

Why did I come here? Sunday brunch is always like this. It's been like this my entire life. I don't need this.

Finally, Miranda shrugged. "I'll figure it out. Feel free to disown me if the open-ended nature of my answer bothers your sensibilities. But I'm not asking you for anything. I know better."

She turned to Megan and Charles. "I'm not going to stay for

brunch. This toxicity doesn't need to be a part of my life. Let me know when you'd like to have lunch or dinner."

Tears leaked down Megan's cheeks as she nodded. Her father nodded stoically as he touched the center of his chest.

Love you too, Dad.

"YOU LOOK TERRIBLE!" Darla exclaimed as she came around the corner from the big room later that day. Miranda stood in the entryway where Ethan scratched Roscoe's ear and rubbed Glinda's tummy.

"Hey! I do not look terrible! This is a new shirt," Ethan teased, kissing the top of Darla's head in greeting. "Go easy. It's been a rough day."

"What happened?" Darla demanded, squeezing Miranda into a hug.

"I went to my grandfather's house for brunch, knowing it was going to be terrible. It was terrible. I left," Miranda quickly summarized. "I vented many angry, frustrated tears on Ethan's old shirt, which is why he's wearing a new shirt."

Darla's gaze darted back and forth between the two of them. "I didn't like the old shirt anyway."

Miranda started laughing.

"Hey! You don't even know what shirt it was!" Ethan laughed.

"Doesn't matter. This one's nicer." Darla smiled at their laughter. "Come on. We're still missing Will and Emma, Jake and Matty, and Sam and Addy."

"Sam and Addy live next door. Literally. Sam was all about starting a new courteous streak. What happened to that?" Ethan groused. "Should I go get them?"

"They're not late yet. You're early," Darla pointed out.

"You know I always arrive at the perfect time. Anyone that arrives after me is late. It's my superpower as a gay man. We've discussed this," Ethan replied sanctimoniously.

Miranda snorted. This was a new exchange for her. She wondered if Ethan and Darla were making it up as they went just to make her laugh.

Darla rolled her eyes, grinning affectionately at Ethan. "Okay, Super Gay. Let's go sit down in the big room."

It's like two separate worlds, Miranda thought, comparing her morning and her evening entries into different houses. *I can't imagine what it must have been like growing up with Hank and Darla.*

"You okay?" Ethan asked, squeezing her hand. Miranda caught the little jolt of happy energy he shared.

"Sloppy. I caught that." She smiled.

"I wasn't trying to hide it," he said with a one-armed hug. "It's going to be fine. You'll see."

Miranda nodded, blinking quickly as she rounded the corner into the new and improved big room. Not paying attention to where she was going, she walked right into Matthew's solid chest and almost bounced off him.

"What happened?" he asked.

"I'm fine," Miranda said immediately in a remarkably good impersonation of Matilda.

Matthew waited.

"I tried to attend Sunday brunch. You know. Like this, but with my family instead of yours, so it's horrible. I left shortly after arriving. I really am fine. How are you?"

"I'd be more likely to believe that if you'd look at me when you said that," Matthew suggested.

"I am looking at you. And your chest. Have you been working out?" Miranda asked, feeling Ethan shake with laughter next to her.

"Awww, Matthew's blushing!" Ethan crowed.

"I've been kicking his, ahem, derriere, a lot," Micah called from the seating area. "He'd be every bit as strong and indestructible as Fear and Rage if he chose to work at it. He doesn't, so I choose to make him do it."

"Did you just use the word 'derriere?'" Ethan asked, laughing outright. "Did I hear that come out of your mouth?"

"Little ears," Micah murmured, looking away as his ears turned red.

"Nope, you're too 'tough guy' for that word," Ethan decided, still laughing. "Come up with something better."

Micah sighed.

"Come on, Micah. It'll be fun. Inoffensive synonyms for the word 'butt.' Go!"

There was another sigh as Micah glanced around the room, noticing all the laughing eyes on him.

"I'm not doing this," he muttered. "You people are ridiculous."

"Boo!" Ethan shouted, startling everyone. "Come on, Micah. Do it! I want the grin!"

Oh my goodness, is Ethan FLIRTING?!? I love this! This makes my day better! Miranda resisted the urge to bounce in place. She squeezed Ethan's hand in encouragement.

"Please?" Ethan said, his smile faltering when Micah didn't play along.

That did it.

"Backside. Tush, posterior, heinie, tuchis, buttocks, booty, buns, seat, cheeks, keister, fanny—"

The room exploded in laughter.

"Now I lost it." Micah laughed, grinning despite himself.

"Rump roast," Noah yelled.

"Be-Hind!" Lucy laughed, elongating the first syllable, grinning at Ree then Jess's girls across the seating area.

"Caboose," Ree added, looking at Linda.

Sensing the challenge from her son, Linda smirked and added, "Patootie," before turning to Adrian.

"Really?" Adrian asked. "I'm a doctor. I'm not playing."

"Boo!" the room yelled.

"Rear-end." Adrian sighed, earning a round of laughter.

"Can't believe I missed that one," Micah admitted. "You people are still ridiculous."

Darting a quick look at Ethan, Micah grinned again before turning away.

Yeeeeeee! I need to move out of Ethan's place! I love this! Giving up all pretenses, Miranda bounced with happiness.

"Is that a boob bounce?" Matthew asked, suspicious.

"Nope, it's a best friend bounce!" Miranda grinned.

"What's a boob bounce?" Jess's daughter, Mia, asked, eliciting a sigh from the adults in the room.

15

*W*alking along Lake Michigan on Friday morning, Miranda tried to cycle energy with the earth. It was challenging to do while walking in shoes. But it was mid-October in Chicago, and the breeze was cool. People would stare if she took her shoes off and stood in the cold sand.

She missed her little yard. Even more, she missed the garden and fruit trees she tended with her grandmother. They'd be busy making apple butter and canning the end of the fall harvest at this time of year.

After her grandmother died, their garden and trees were torn out and paved over. Her grandfather's yard now had a pointless water feature. Miranda wanted to put fish in the cement pond to make it less ridiculous. Her grandfather wouldn't allow it. So it was a water feature that did nothing but evaporate water.

Miranda sighed at the thought. *So wasteful. So disrespectful to our natural resources.*

Maybe she'd feel better about it if someone actually *enjoyed* the fountain. But no. Her grandfather didn't go into the yard at all. For a long time, she believed he didn't go out there because it reminded him of her grandmother.

That was foolishly naive of me. Immature, naive, and coddled—that's me.

When Lawrence's cheating first came to light, her grandfather had prattled on about how all men need more than one woman. Apparently, Benjamin supported something akin to a personal harem of women until age took the fun out of things.

"Why be married if that's what you wanted?" Miranda had asked.

"Why not?" her grandfather replied. "Someone had to produce my heirs. Your grandmother's family had money. They helped launch the brokerage. So I married her. Never promised anything more than I gave her: children and a home."

Ah, Gram. So many things we didn't talk about.

"Are you okay?" a voice said from behind her.

Miranda turned. He was tall, musclebound, and shirtless, dark brown hair, rich brown eyes, and obviously just finishing a run. His bronzed skin was glistening with sweat in the weak fall sun.

Miranda stared.

"Um, I've been walking behind you—back toward my place, not following you," he quickly clarified. "You keep sighing. Are you okay?"

Miranda blinked, still staring at his chest.

"Should I get help?" he asked, concerned.

"Oh! Oh, I'm sorry." Miranda flushed red with embarrassment. "I'm fine, thank you. I was just thinking. Thank you for your concern. I'm fine."

She turned her back to him, mortified. *I just ogled a total stranger. A shirtless, hairy-chested, delicious stranger!* She gave herself a mental head slap.

"Are you sure?" he asked tentatively. "You seem upset."

"Well, I am," she said, walking fast. "But I'm fine."

"You don't want to talk about it?"

"N-no, thank you," she stammered, looking at him over her shoulder. "Are you following me now?"

"Um. I don't know. Yeah. Maybe. I'm sorry. I didn't mean to scare you." He stopped, looking sheepish.

Miranda stopped, too, turning to look at him again. "You didn't scare me. I just...never mind."

Oh, holy cannoli. The muscles. The pecs. I can't stop staring. Look at his eyes, Miranda. His face. Not nipples. Oh, holy cow, I can see his nipples. Hairy man nipples. They're over the muscles. Pecs. Wow.

"Did I lose you again?" he asked.

"I'm sorry." She laughed, turning even redder. "I can't stop staring at your chest. I don't know what's wrong with me. Well, I do know what's wrong with me. I'm married to not-svelte Larry. That's what's wrong. I'm sorry."

His face shut down into a mild-mannered, polite expression that reminded her of Sam. "Well, Larry's a lucky guy. I hope your day gets better."

"Oh! Oh," Miranda burst out laughing in earnest. "Larry's an idiot. I'm in the middle of a divorce. It's part of my sighing. Sorry. I don't know how many times I've said 'sorry.' Too many. Sorry."

He grinned.

"I did it again." She nodded. "I'm working on it."

"Fair enough."

"I do apologize for staring at your chest, though. That's not right."

"Are you kidding? It boosted my ego like fifteen points!" He struck a pose. "Wait, wait. I'll flex properly for you."

Ohmigod! Don't look!

Miranda smiled awkwardly, pointedly not looking at his chest. "Sorry, I ramble a lot when I'm nervous. Sorry."

"Wow. I get why you're working on the 'sorry' thing. That's time well spent." He smiled. "I'm Kareem."

"I'm Miranda," she muttered, wincing over her flood of apologies in the last two minutes.

"It's nice to meet you. I'd offer a handshake, but eww. I'm sweaty," he said with a bright white grin. "But if I flex again, will you look this time? I need that admiration in my life."

She burst out into another fit of giggles. "I'm—"

"Don't say it! You're working on it." He laughed.

"I was going to say I'm terrible at meeting new people."

Kareem kept grinning. "For future reference, it's adorable."

He's flirting! The muscles are flirting with me! What do I do? She smiled, dropping her gaze to her feet.

"I'm all kinds of gross from running," he continued after a few seconds of silence. "But there's a great little breakfast cafe not far from here. It's right down the street from my place. Can I interest you in an omelet if I take a quick shower and meet you back at the cafe?"

"Um…" She hesitated.

"Say, yes!" he demanded. "I want to count the number of apologies that come out of your mouth over an hour."

Her smile fell as her cheeks flushed red again.

"I was teasing," Kareem apologized. "It just seems like you could use a friendly conversation."

"You don't have to get to work?" Miranda asked.

"Nope, my license transfer hasn't gone through yet, so I have no appointments. Have breakfast with me," he encouraged her.

"Appointments?"

"I'm a psychologist. I promise to only psychoanalyze you and your need to apologize a little bit." He smiled. "I just moved here from North Carolina to be with a long-distance girlfriend. She dumped me three days after I got here. We can commiserate over our failed relationships."

She didn't respond.

"It's just omelets, Miranda," he said, still smiling at her.

MATILDA'S EYEBROWS LIFTED. "You had breakfast with some strange dude you met while walking on the beach? Is this a sappy Hallmark movie?"

"I don't think you understand about the muscles." Miranda laughed, still cooling down from working out with her sister.

"And nipples. Yeah, I get it. Lucy would understand, too." Matilda chuckled.

"Lucy?"

"Yeah, you wouldn't know it from the way he dresses, but Adrian is extremely ripped. Like, as ripped as William, but not as bulky. He's a boxer."

"No shit?" Miranda exhaled. "I didn't realize muscles were such a thing for me until I was staring at his lovely golden, ripped chest. I felt like a total pervert."

"Are you going to see him again?" Matty asked.

"We're having dinner tomorrow. It was a good breakfast. He told me about living in North Carolina and his ex-girlfriend. I told him a little bit about my bungled marriage and stupid Larry. It was relaxed." Miranda smiled at the memory.

Matilda keeled over in a fit of giggles. "I can't believe you pulled out the 'not-svelte Larry' thing. Jake will be so happy."

"Hello, ladies. What will I be happy about?" Jake grinned, walking into the apartment door at that moment.

"Miranda met a hot dude running on the beach this morning and had breakfast with him. She went full-on spaz-ramble and told the guy that she was married to 'not-svelte' Larry," Matilda summarized.

Jake's face fell.

"What's wrong?" Matilda asked, still laughing.

"Was the hot running dude named Matthew?" Jake asked, tone flat.

After a moment, Miranda sighed. "He doesn't want that with me, Jake. When we were in college, I tried and tried. I outright threw myself at him. He told me he wasn't interested, wished me well, and then avoided me. For years." Miranda's voice was small and sad.

"Don't pull out the pouting," Jake barked, unmoved. "I don't care what happened in college. And I think you know his perspective on life has changed since then. He thought he was poisonous, Miranda. No hot dudes running on the beach!"

"Excuse me?" Matilda's voice crackled with outrage.

"You heard me!"

"Who the fuck do you think you are to dictate what she does with her time? Miranda, has Matthew indicated in *any* way that he wants something other than friendship with you?"

Miranda didn't respond, looking back and forth between her sister and Jake.

"Randa?" Matty demanded.

"No. Not really. He said he regretted the way things ended in college, but that could mean many things."

"No, it can't!" Jake objected.

"Yes, it can," Matilda argued. "He could regret that he didn't talk to her afterward, regret that he didn't let her down easier, or regret that she made a pass at all!"

"What exactly did he say he regretted, Miranda?" Jake demanded.

"Um. I don't think I want to be a part of this argument."

Matilda and Jake both turned to her, offering near-identical scowls of anger.

"Enough with the cowering!" Matilda yelled at her little sister. "I know you're plenty feisty deep down in there. Confrontation is uncomfortable, not bad! Don't be a doormat, Miranda!"

"I'm not a doormat!" Miranda squeaked.

"Yes, you are!" Jake yelled at her. "Who the fuck am I to tell you what to do? You're a grown-ass woman! Do what you want. Tell me to fuck off and mind my own business!"

"Fine," Miranda tentatively replied, fidgeting with the buttons on her shirt. "Fuck off and mind your own damn business!"

The foul language sounded ridiculous coming out of Miranda's mouth with her timid voice.

Jake grinned. "I'm telling Darla you swore."

"No little ears," Miranda objected, cheeks flushed.

"Matilda's ears are plenty little."

"Oh, fuck you!" Matilda yelled, throwing a couch pillow at his head, laughing.

"Okay, but seriously. No running dudes on the beach!" Jake objected again.

"Jake—" Matty started.

"He's never brought anyone home for dinner, Matty," Jake interrupted. "Never talked about anyone. Never shown interest in any sort of relationship with anyone.

"That first time you showed up for dinner, Miranda, we all thought he was going to snap Larry's mind into pieces. He didn't want to stop hugging you. We could all see it."

Miranda didn't respond, lost for words.

"Before you get hot and heavy with someone else, talk to him?" Jake asked.

"Jake, I'm still married to not-svelte Larry. I'm not hopping into bed with the hairy chest. I was just admiring it," Miranda muttered, cheeks flushing deeper with embarrassment.

"Promise?"

"She doesn't owe you any fucking promises, Jacob!" Matilda yelled.

"I know," Jake said defensively. "I just want them to be happy, Matty."

"I don't even know how I would broach the subject with him, Jake. We're friends. That's it," Miranda said, her voice somber. "I agree with you. I would rather be with him than anyone else. But he doesn't want that."

Jake groaned. "Yes, he does!"

"No, he doesn't. He has not indicated that at any time in the past, though I have made my thoughts and feelings clear."

"I'm going to talk to him," Jake declared.

"No," Miranda gasped. "That's too awkward and strange, Jake! Leave it alone. He's a grown man. Let him live his life."

Jake groaned. "He's fucking it up!"

"Bella," Matilda fake sneezed.

"I dislike this." Jake smiled at Matilda despite himself.

"We're going to argue about you trying to boss my little sister around," Matty promised.

"I dislike that even more." He pouted.

"Wow, Lawrence sounds like a piece of work," Kareem said about halfway through dinner on Saturday night. "Why is he like that?"

"What do you mean?" Miranda asked, cutting the next section of her chicken entree into tiny squares.

"Why is he so focused on the money? Why is he so opportunistic? Did he lack something in his childhood?"

Miranda blinked before her lips turned up into a small smile. "You're not psychoanalyzing me! You're analyzing him!"

Kareem sat back away from the table. "I guess I am. I just like to understand people."

"His parents are a lovely couple, not wealthy, but he didn't starve," she answered.

"Hmm. So, what will you do now? Continue living with your friend?"

"Until everything is settled, yes. Ethan has asked me to stay, so I will. I don't have anywhere else to go right now, anyway."

"You're fortunate to have such friends," he replied, sounding wistful.

"I am." She nodded in agreement.

"And after it's all settled? What will you do with yourself, Miranda?"

She squirmed in her seat for a moment. "Promise not to laugh?"

"Of course."

"I want to start a non-profit that teaches underprivileged kids how to economically grow healthy food for their families," she said, almost in a whisper. Admitting her long-term dream out loud for the first time was daunting and freeing all at once. "I'm going to start a plant nursery so I have the income to support the non-profit. I have a green thumb. I can grow anything."

He threw his head back in laughter.

Miranda's face fell as her gaze dropped to her plate.

"I am not laughing at you, Miranda. I am laughing at the absolute perfection of it. I've never felt such an elemental earth power! It's absolutely perfect!" His grin was bright with enthusiasm.

Miranda went utterly still, her eyes searching his face. "Excuse me?"

His head tilted in confusion. "I just meant that your energy is so strong and so clearly earth driven. It is an ideal way for you to spend your day."

She stared at him.

"My energy is not as focused as yours, but don't you feel it?"

Closing her eyes, Miranda took a deep breath, focusing on the person across the table from her.

Kindness. Understanding. Compassion. There is energy within him. I missed it. She sighed, disappointed in herself. *I used to think I was good at spotting this kind of thing.*

"I'm usually better at sensing the energy in others. I wasn't paying attention," she admitted.

"Your mind was elsewhere, in the land of sighs." He smiled again.

After a few moments of awkward silence, he picked up the conversation again.

"You seemed like you could use a friend. And I don't know anyone at all here since Sarah ended things. You were struggling to cycle energy. I thought perhaps we could begin a circle?"

"I have a circle," she said automatically before considering her words.

His heavy brows furrowed into a frown. "Why were you struggling alone yesterday morning?"

Miranda squirmed again. "I have a morning process that's a little out of whack since I'm living in a condo. But I don't feel good when I skip it, so I try to do it without looking like a moron."

They fell silent again.

I'm an idiot for thinking he was hitting on me, Miranda berated herself. *I made a damn fool of myself. What the hell is wrong with me?*

200

"I apologize, Miranda. I did not mean to make you uncomfortable. We can talk about other things. This is not my business," Kareem offered, obviously disappointed.

Miranda took a centering breath.

"No. Please don't apologize. It's my fault. I...thought something else. It was kind of you to want to help me, and I'm sorry you are alone here. I can't invite you to my circle without talking to others first. But if you want, I can ask. We gather on Monday nights." Miranda tried to smile as she fought back her embarrassment and disappointment.

"What did you think?" he asked, eyebrows lifted. "What did you think when I started talking to you yesterday morning?"

She shook her head. "It doesn't matter. Do you—"

"Did you think I was flirting? Because I was. Teasing, too," he clarified, the start of a smile hanging around his mouth.

"Oh."

"I admit I noticed the energy before I noticed you. But I was happy for a reason to talk with you."

"Thank you," she murmured, looking at her plate again. "Do you want me to ask my circle?"

"I would be happy to meet them." Kareem nodded. "I usually end up building my own circles, though I'm interested in seeing the type of circle you stand with that earth energy. But I'm only interested in attending one if you're comfortable with the idea."

Her lips quirked up. "I'm not the one you have to convince."

"No," Micah's voice crackled through the cellphone.

"He's very kind. I don't think he'd ever—" Miranda spoke quickly, unable to finish before he talked over her.

"No, we will not add a random person to the circle at this time, Earth," Micah scolded.

"Would you just come to meet him and tell him that, then? I feel terrible. I completely misread the whole thing and made a fool of myself," Miranda whined.

"No."

"Please?"

"No."

Miranda hesitated. "Okay. Ethan is home anyway. He and I can explain to Kareem together. We'll just—"

"You let him in the apartment?" Micah's voice was quiet and cold, but his outrage was unmistakable.

"Well, no. But I'm sure Kareem would walk me home if I ask. It's only a few blocks…"

The line was silent.

"You're probably right. I can just call Ethan and see if he can join us for dessert." Miranda knew she had Micah's attention.

"This is beneath you," Micah objected.

Miranda grinned, knowing he couldn't see it. "Is it? I don't think it is."

The line was silent again.

"Are you trying not to laugh right now?" she asked.

Micah sighed. "I'll be there shortly. He will not be joining the circle, Miranda. Get the thought out of your head."

Miranda grinned, walking back to the restaurant table to sit across from Kareem.

"After dinner coffee? He'll be here soon."

"I'm enjoying your smile, but it's almost a smirk." Kareem laughed as he nodded in agreement, signaling for the waiter.

Miranda shook her head, grinning. "It's fine. Just a little more manipulative than I'd like, but it confirms things that make me happy. Now, my friend that's going to join us is…well, let's say he's gruff. He says we can't add to our circle, and he might be right. But it's worth a try. Just don't be offended if he's abrupt, okay? He's very protective of things."

"He's worried that *I'm* going to harm *you*? Your energy outclasses mine by several orders of magnitude."

"Yes, well. Things are a little complicated. It'll be fine. If he says no, I'm sure my sister and I can help you form a different circle."

Kareem's brow furrowed in confusion again. "You do not hold the center of your circle? I don't understand."

Miranda shook her head. "I don't hold the center."

"So the one coming to meet us is your center?"

"No." She shook her head again. "He is not technically part of our circle. He stands it but refuses the energy."

"That doesn't make sense."

"I know. He's just diff—"

"We have to go now!" Kareem jumped up. "Please, Miranda. There is trouble here or there is about to be trouble here. We must go—"

"You," Micah groaned, approaching the table from behind Miranda. "I can't believe someone hasn't drained you yet."

"Lord Micah, we'll leave. Whatever trouble comes, we are not part of it. We will leave immediately. We don't mean—"

"Oh, shut up. Are you kidding me with this?" Micah asked, glaring at Miranda.

"Lord Micah?" she asked.

"I have a reputation."

"Coffee?" She smiled.

Micah rolled his eyes, sitting down in the empty chair on her left.

"Sit, fool," he barked at Kareem. "What are you doing here?"

Kareem stood awkwardly beside the table for a moment, apparently undecided if he should run away or sit back down.

"I said sit," Micah growled, voice low as he noticed the waiter approach again.

Miranda grinned at Kareem. "It's fine. I promise. I told you. He's gruff."

"Gruff?" Micah and Kareem asked together.

"You're adorably gruff." Miranda grinned again, patting Micah's arm.

He scowled at her.

"Miranda," Kareem murmured. "This is dangerous. We should leave here."

"Yes," Micah agreed. "You should absolutely leave, fool. Goodbye. Leave the Lady alone."

"Anything else here?" the waiter asked, noticing Kareem's obvious discomfort and unwillingness to sit at the table. He wondered if there was a love triangle unfolding.

"Coffee, Micah?" Miranda asked brightly, smiling to assure the waiter all was well.

"No, I'm not staying."

The waiter nodded then continued on his circuit of tables. Miranda wondered at his disappointed expression.

"Stop it, both of you." Miranda glared between them once the waiter was gone. "Kareem, sit down and relax. He's not going to hurt you."

"Well," Micah qualified her statement. "I would kill you if you hurt her, but you're a pansy."

Miranda snorted, scowling at Micah. "Oh, the irony. That's not nice. Don't use that word like that."

Micah glared furiously at her. "You will stop trying to manipulate me. Right now. You're a better person than that."

She grinned. "I could talk to Ethan for you…"

"What are you doing here, fool?" Micah barked, focused on Kareem again.

"I-I moved here," Kareem muttered. "To be with my girlfriend. But she dumped me."

Micah snorted. "Same girlfriend?"

Kareem gave a small nod.

Micah grinned. "Fool."

Miranda smiled pleasantly. "How do you two know each other?"

Micah's grinned remained fixed. "I saved him from being drained. Several times."

"Three times," Kareem corrected, finally retaking his seat. "And the first time doesn't count."

"How does it not count?" Micah asked, laughing.

"I was eight. I didn't know any better."

"But ten years later—"

"Seven years!" Kareem corrected again.

Micah turned to Miranda. "This makes perfect sense. He should be part of your circle. He's too stupid to be left unattended."

"Can I have a little more detail?" Miranda asked, trying not to laugh. She could see and feel how upset Kareem was with the turn of events.

"Um, Miranda, I'm not sure—" Kareem began.

"You will meet the circle before you decline it, fool."

"My name is Kareem." The words came out more annoyed than Miranda would have expected.

"I don't care." Micah grinned again, happy to annoy someone after being so thoroughly and ham-handedly manipulated. "He has a history of trying to befriend the wrong sort of people, Miranda. He's too stupid to sense danger. If he doesn't find a home in your circle, someone in this city will drain him before long. I'm too busy to keep an eye on him."

Miranda grinned. "You'll let him come to the circle on Monday?"

"I'm fairly certain he belongs to your circle. I'll let Sam know."

Micah stood and left without another word.

"Yay," Miranda cheered. "It's going to be great."

Kareem looked ill.

"You can ride with us," Miranda offered, patting his hand. "Don't worry. Micah's fine. He'll behave around Sam."

"Um. Who is Sam?" Kareem whispered.

16

"You're wrong. Totally wrong," Matthew said while climbing out of Luke's car at their parents' house on Sunday evening. "The Hulk leap is the best."

"The Hulk leap is awesome. Super fun. But I want to work out how to use the energy to Spider-Man crawl up walls. I don't think that's gravity as much as spatial awareness. Maybe something Sam can do…" Luke's words trailed off as he considered the possibilities.

Matthew snorted.

"Come on!" Luke yelled. "It'd be awesome to crawl up the side of a building! There has to be a way to do that!"

"Let me know when—" Matthew started.

"You're fucking it up!" Jake interrupted, charging his younger brothers before they made it to the front door. He smacked Matthew upside the head.

"What's your problem?" Matthew asked, confused. "I didn't do anything."

"I know! That's my problem!" Jake yelled, smacking his brother again. "Hairy chest and nipples on the beach, you fuckup!"

Matthew and Luke shared a look.

"Um, Jake," Luke started. "What are you talking about?"

"Matthew is fucking up his life, and mine, too! I don't want to double date with the hairy chest nipples, Matthew!"

Unable to lock it down, Matthew burst out laughing. "What the ever-living fuck are you talking about?"

"You are such an asshole!" Jake bellowed. "Don't do this. Don't fuck it up!"

"Jake, we have no idea what you're talking about," Luke said calmly. "What's going on?"

Narrowed, irritated eyes turned on Lucas.

"Stop pushing that peace shit at me," Jake growled. "I'm not Noah. You're not going to knock me out. Keep your shit to yourself or I'll push back."

Luke's eyes went wide. "Wow. It didn't affect you at all?"

Jake glared.

"I wasn't trying to knock you out, Jake," Luke said, hands up in defense. "I was just trying to get you to calm down."

"Yeah, well. I just spent an hour in the car listening to Matty and Miranda laugh and joke about the hairy-chested stud that Miranda met while walking on the fucking beach on Friday. She had a date with him last night and everything! You're fucking this up, Matthew!"

"Oh," Luke murmured, turning a glare on his favorite brother. "I agree. You're fucking this up."

"She had a date?" Matthew's eyes lit with excitement.

"Yes, asshole! And it wasn't with you!" Jake yelled, frustrated.

"That's okay," Matthew said. "That's great!"

"Huh?" Jake and Luke said together.

Matthew shrugged. "I thought it'd take her a while to be interested in dating again. It's great that she's interested in someone."

"Matthew." Luke's voice was cold. "It'd be better if she was interested in *you*, don't you think?"

"Oh. No," Matthew replied, shaking his head. "Not at all."

Jake and Luke shared a look.

"Don't do this," Jake pleaded. "Please? We saw it with Adrian. I don't want to watch you go batshit insane, man. You two fit together like puzzle pieces."

"I'm not. I agree. I mean, I fucked it up in college. I don't deny that. But I get it now."

"Then what are you waiting for?" Luke asked, just as confused as Jake.

"Time," Matthew said with a shrug. "It's not quite a full month since she split from the shit-bag. She's not divorced yet. A lot is going on in her life and relationships. I thought I'd give her some time and space to re-center herself. The beach dude is a rebound. I don't want to be the rebound."

"You're risking your window of opportunity, moron," Jake disagreed. "She had a date!"

"I hope she had fun," Matthew said with complete sincerity. "She deserves some fun."

"Matthew," Luke started.

"Luke, it's going to be fine. And if I fuck it up again, that's on me," Matthew said, speeding up to get away from his brothers.

WALKING INTO THE BIG ROOM, Matthew couldn't stop grinning.

I can't believe this. I thought a year. Maybe more. Out-fucking-standing, he mentally cheered. Sure that Miranda would go through a rebound phase, he'd wait for her to be ready before discussing how badly he had screwed up in college. Things were moving along much faster than he thought possible.

Quickly kissing his mom on the head and shaking his dad's hand, Matthew ignored everyone else and made a beeline for Miranda. There was no room on the couch near her, so he plopped down on the floor in front of her.

"You had a date?" he asked, still grinning wide with genuine excitement.

All side conversation in the room stopped as everyone tuned into this tidbit of news. Hank shared a confused glance with Jake and Luke as they made it into the room.

"I did," Miranda replied, searching Matthew's face for some insight into his good mood.

"Tell me! Who is he?"

MIRANDA SHOOK HER HEAD, fighting off a wave of hurt and disappointment so profound she wondered if she was going to be sick.

Eyes traveling the room, they landed on Jake and Luke. Jake's frustration was obvious.

Just friends, Miranda thought. *There's nothing else with Matthew. I told Jake. I know Matthew doesn't want anything else. This is how it is. But, holy cow, my chest hurts.*

Miranda's energy, normally so stable and calm, clawed at the inside of her brain, causing her to wince in pain.

"Miranda? Tell me about the date!" Matthew said again, smiling from ear to ear.

"Oh. Um. His name is Kareem. He moved here recently to be with a girlfriend, but she dumped him right after he got here. I had breakfast with him on Friday morning after I met him and then dinner last night."

"Are you going to see him again?" Matthew asked, no sign of jealousy or malcontent in his expression.

Miranda wasn't sure how to answer. She shot a glance at Micah, who shook his head. Micah had not yet talked to Sam.

Unfamiliar with how new people were introduced to the circle, Miranda didn't want to mention Kareem's addition to the broader group of empowered energy users. That seemed like something Sam or Adaline should approve and then announce.

"Yes, I'll see him again," she said after a pause. "I'll be right back, okay?"

Without waiting for a response, she jumped up and headed toward the door, rushing for the bathroom before she was sick.

"Let's head to the dining room," Darla called, hearing Sam and Adaline in the front foyer. "Everyone's here."

"I WANTED to talk to you earlier," Micah murmured at the dinner table.

Sam and Adaline turned from the conversation at the other end of the table with Matilda, Ethan, Miranda, and Jake.

"What's wrong?" Sam asked, frowning at Micah.

Sitting beside Micah, Matthew tuned in to hear what Micah was up to, hoping for positive signs on the romance front with Ethan.

If Miranda and I figure it out, and Ethan and Micah get a move on, it'll just be Luke left as the lone singleton. What a year. Matthew smiled to himself again, choosing not to think about Luke's dating life. *Maybe Linda? Maybe.*

"I met Miranda's new friend last night. I know him," Micah explained.

Sam's eyebrows shot up. "Oh?"

Oh, man. Please don't let him be a bad guy. I don't want her to get hurt...

"I've helped him in the past. He's easy pickings for drainers, strong in his own right but too sympathetic and understanding to protect himself. I think he may belong to you and the Mistress. I think it would be wise if he stood the circle tomorrow night."

Sam glanced at Adaline before they both nodded in agreement. "I still can't see much, but if you think he should join us, we'll make him welcome."

"I don't want to see him get drained, and he will die without a circle. The goodness radiates from him," Micah replied, a hint of his familiar grin playing on his face. "He is a fool, though."

"He's joining the circle?" Matthew asked, shocked. Joining the circle meant the guy would be around to stay.

Micah shrugged. "I don't know. Attending it tomorrow, at least. He may choose to go back to his old circle. But, if he stays in Chicago, this would be the best place for him."

Oh, shit. Oh, shit. Oh, shit, Matthew repeated in his mind, thinking of the way the circle yanked energy and emotions from him, whether he wanted them shared or not. He thought of what it'd be like to actually *watch* Miranda flirt with someone.

His stomach rolled as his energy awoke, a faint crackle in his ears. *Oh, shit.*

Conversations carried on around him for the next few moments as the family chowed down on beef stew and fresh bread. As the crackling in his ears increased, Matthew tuned out his hearing, aware that the energy was building up to dangerous levels again.

Luke touched his arm, saying something. Matthew stared at him, unable to hear the words or read the question on Luke's lips.

"I'll be right back," he muttered, quietly leaving his seat. Instead of heading for the bathroom, Matthew headed out the back door.

The crackling noise in his ears was drowning out all other sounds, becoming impossible to ignore.

I have to get out of here. I have to get away from here before someone gets hurt, he thought, panting with fear.

Halfway through the vacant land where Jake and Matty's house was being built, he thought he heard William yelling. Afraid to listen, he just kept moving. Sometimes the energy used different voices. He couldn't trust it.

I should have driven myself here. I should drive myself everywhere from now on. I should just drive so I can leave if I have to, he mentally repeated to himself, trying to tune out the noise.

A hand grabbed his shoulder, shocking a wave of energy out of him.

"Jesus!" William yelled as the ground rolled underfoot, knocking them both on their asses. "What happened?"

Oh fuck. Go. Will, just go, Matthew chanted in his head. *He has Emma. He's going to be a dad. Babies are coming. He needs to get away from me!*

"Go, man. Go. Go away. Run," he eventually managed to choke out. "Energy is bad."

"There's enough fear coming off you to drop a crowd of adults, Matthew. What's going on?"

"The energy..." Matthew muttered, trying to hear William without hearing the chaos. Clouds rolled in the sky overhead, blocking the evening lights. The air felt heavy around him.

This can't be good.

"I'll go get Luke?" Will asked.

Matthew didn't respond, didn't seem to hear the words.

WILL PUNCHED Matthew in the face, trying to shake him loose of the mental trap he'd fallen into.

Matthew's eyes remained unfocused.

In his parents' house two hundred yards away, William clearly heard someone yell. At this distance, it was impossible to tell if it was playful yelling or fearful screaming. Will focused on Matthew, wary of the energy lurking in his younger brother.

"Luke? You need Luke, right?" William yelled.

Matthew shook his head, otherwise not responding. He took off at a run, away from William and into the fields beyond where the houses were being built.

"What's going on?" Miranda asked, coming up behind William.

Will shook his head. "I have no idea. Matthew's freaking out. I felt his fear all the way from inside the house and came to help. He just took off into the field. I'm not chasing him out there in the dark. Let's go find Sam and Addy."

"I'll go get him," Miranda said. "I know where he is."

William's eyebrows shot up.

"Can't you feel his energy? I felt it in the house, too. It's every-where," Miranda replied to the unspoken question.

"His energy is difficult to control. He can do a lot of damage if he's lost a grip on it. Let's get Sam and Addy to help. I don't want you to get hurt, Miranda. Come on."

She shook her head, already following in Matthew's wake. "Go get them. I'll go wait with him. It'll be fine."

"MATTHEW," Miranda called. "It's just me."

When she finally saw the outline of him, sitting on the ground in the darkness, she realized she shouldn't have bothered calling to him. Matthew's eyes were wide with panic and glowed with energy. He didn't react to her words at all.

"Matthew, what happened?" she asked.

He didn't look at her.

She crouched down directly in front of him. "Matthew?"

He didn't even blink.

"Matthew?" she repeated, gently touching her cheek.

He groaned at her touch, startling her. She yanked her hand away.

"What happened?" she asked again.

When his eyes met hers, he exhaled in relief before yanking her down into his lap.

"Miranda," he almost sobbed, burying his face in the crease between her neck and shoulder, wrapping her hands with his own to maximize the skin contact. "You're here."

"What happened?" Miranda asked as his energy roughly slammed through her body, easing the splitting headache and sick feeling from earlier in the evening.

"Energy freak-out," he panted.

"Got that part." She laughed. "What happened to cause it? Are you better now?"

"Better. Yes, better," he gasped. "Thank you for helping."

"Matthew, what happened?"

"Can we talk about it later?" he asked.

"Are you sick? You were fine before dinner."

"No, not sick." He shook his head. "Just a little overwhelmed."

"We can talk about you being overwhelmed," she offered.

"I know."

"You can tell me things," Miranda reiterated.

"I know, Randa. I don't want to add to your stress."

"Are you kidding? I'd love to help someone else's stress right now. Mine is so boring." She smiled, snuggling in closer to his chest and enjoying the way it vibrated with suppressed laughter against her cheek.

Matthew didn't respond other than to twirl her long brown hair through his fingers.

"You know, if you keep playing with my hair like that, I'm going to fall asleep," she offered a few moments later.

"Sorry." He stopped.

"I wasn't telling you to stop. I was just warning you."

Matthew sighed. "Thank you for helping me."

"Why'd you head all the way out here if you need help? You could have just stayed by the house. Will is rounding up Sam and Addy to help you level out, but you seem fine now."

"I am," Matthew muttered, itching to run his fingers through her hair again. "I felt it going whacky and didn't want it to hurt anyone, so I left. Everyone's okay in there?"

"Fine," she replied. "You sure you don't want to talk about what happened?"

He nodded as Sam and Adaline appeared next to them in the field.

"What's Will babbling about? You're fine," Sam griped. "I was enjoying chocolate cake, Matthew. Mom made chocolate cake, and I'm not eating it right now. I thought you went to the bathroom."

"Energy went haywire. It's better," Matthew summarized.

"What happened?" Addy asked. Matthew could see her head turning between himself and Miranda, though her expression was hidden by night.

Matthew shook his head with a shrug. "It just went wonky on me. It was an accident."

Adaline's teasing smirk was audible in her voice. "You didn't get upset?"

"Why would I be upset?" Matthew asked, all innocence, eyes narrowed in warning.

Adaline either didn't see the warning glance or didn't care. Her brilliant white grin shone in the dark night, full of mischief. "Because Miranda had a date with a hairy-chested person, and you just realized you're going to end up standing a circle with him."

"What? Matthew!" Miranda gasped.

"I'm not upset!" Matthew yelled immediately. "I swear I'm not, Randa. I'm not upset. I have no right or cause to be upset."

She stared at him for a moment before turning to Sam and Adaline. "Go away."

She could tell Sam's eyebrows shot up, even in the darkness.

"I mean it," Miranda said decisively. "Go away."

"But—"

"Go, Sam!" she yelled.

Sam turned to Adaline. "Why am I getting yelled at? It's not my fault. I could be eating cake right now."

Adaline's grin blazed brightly again before they both disappeared.

ell, fuck, Matthew mentally cursed. *Now what do I do?* Miranda sat stiff and unmoving, still in his lap.

"Spill it."

"I'm not upset. I'm really not, Randa. I would tell you if I was."

"But?" she asked, sensing that Addy was right and there was more to this.

"I don't know how to explain this without sounding like an idiot," he grumped.

"Just tell me, Matthew." The words were a whisper.

How can a whisper sound so hopeful and resigned at the same time? he wondered, pausing to consider his words. *Fuck it.*

"I've loved you from the beginning. You know that, right?" he asked.

Miranda jumped in his lap, exhaling hard. "No," she breathed. "I don't. I didn't."

"I want you to date and have fun and be happy. Honestly, all the happiness you can find. Heal the broken heart from Lawrence, rebound, and re-center. I want nothing but good things for you. But I have no idea how I'm going to stand in a circle with your boyfriend."

She chewed her lip for a minute, considering her words. "Lawrence never had my heart to break. And given a choice between you and anyone else on the planet, I would choose you. But I don't understand what happened, Matthew. Why? Why did things happen like they did in college?"

"Do you want to talk about this right now? We don't have to. You've been through so much, Randa. There's time."

"You have to be kidding me," she said, tone sharp. "I've been hoping and waiting for this conversation for years. We're having this conversation now, Matthew. Start talking."

Matthew tried to swallow, but his mouth was dry.

Where's Luke with like fifteen gallons of water when you need him?

Gathering his thoughts, he started at the very beginning. "I was angry when I walked into that classroom that first day. I wasn't supposed to be leading that section. Another teaching assistant flaked out and withdrew from classes the day after the semester started. I was the only TA that wasn't already booked at that time. The other teaching assistants each got one extra section. I got two because my schedule was more accommodating. I was cursing the fact that I was too nice to tell Dr. Broosh to teach his own damn class. I threw my crap down on the desk, ready to deal with another group of immature high school–minded college freshmen."

"You were very grumpy. I remember that."

"I looked the class over, spotted you by the windows, then had to scold myself about staring at the youngin's."

Miranda snorted. "You're four years older than me. I'm not that much younger than you, Matthew."

He shrugged. "I was the teacher. I wasn't supposed to be scoping out the students. That's just wrong. Nonetheless, I was stuck on you even before you started arguing classic literature with me. You were quoting shit that no one else in the class had even read, let alone memorized. I was crazy about you. I couldn't wait for that semester to end."

"Me too," she admitted. "Over winter break, I plotted and planned how to reconnect with you."

"Did you follow me home that day? When I ran into you by my apartment?" he asked, smiling.

"Yup," she admitted, grinning and unrepentant.

"Miranda, that was downright forward for you. Almost manipulative."

"Still not sorry. You were the best friend I ever had, except for maybe Megan, before Matilda came along."

He squeezed her tighter in a hug.

"I kept waiting for you to make a pass. Trying to encourage you. I was not subtle, Matthew," she prompted.

Matthew sighed. "I ignored it. I was selfish enough to want you in my life. Not selfish enough to have a relationship with you."

"Moron."

He nodded. "I didn't know what the energy was until after Sam found Addy a few months ago. I just knew I caused madness, around me and in others. I can sense it in others, you know? I can feel it when a mind starts to go sideways. Hear it, too.

"I was sure that I had some kind of mental illness when we were in college. I didn't want that for you. But it was so much easier to manage the energy and the sensations when you were around. There was no crackling in my ears. I didn't feel other minds unless I wanted to. It was all easier."

"The energy does seem to feel better when we're together," Miranda agreed. "I didn't notice it then. I used to be good about noticing energy in others. I missed yours. Kareem's, too."

"I tried to keep it back, away from you. It's not the type of energy that slips out unless I've completely lost my grip on it. I have to focus on it, listen to it, for it to affect things around me. So I ignored it around you. It was naturally quieter anyway."

They were both silent for a moment.

"The last night of the semester?" she asked.

Matthew exhaled, laying back in the field. The ground was cold and hard under him.

This is the wrong place to have this conversation. Wrong place, wrong time, he lamented as she laid down next to him, snuggling up to his side.

"I've spent the last four and a half years dreaming of laying with you, having this conversation," she admitted.

Guilt punched Matthew in the gut, making it hard to breathe again.

"I'm so sorry. I made such a mess of things, Miranda. I'm sorry," he whispered, kissing the top of her head.

"Make it up to me," she challenged. "What happened in your mind that last night?"

Matthew smiled, his teeth and eyes visible in the pitch black of the country night. "I got home from proctoring that final exam, expecting you to be in my place with pizza and a movie. I wasn't expecting you to be waiting in your damn underwear."

"It was a negligée."

"It was a heart attack in satin and lace form," he countered. "It was a perfect moment of clarity, when you know you're making a terrible choice that's going to damage you for the rest of your life, and you do it anyway."

"Then why did you do it? Why did you run away?" Her voice broke with the question.

"Miranda, please don't. Don't cry," he whispered, turning on his side to hug her.

"Answer me," she replied, a bite to her words. "I need to know the answer to that."

"I told you. I thought I was going to hurt you. I thought I was bad news, and I wanted better for you.

"That night, my energy was fighting hard against my control. I couldn't get the words out fast enough. I couldn't even hear what you said in response. The energy was raging in my ears so loudly it drowned everything else out. I babbled words, trying to make you understand. I don't even know what I said. I don't know what came out of my mouth. Then I turned around and ran before the building could cave in or the stove could explode or something."

"You literally ran away?" she asked, almost laughing.

"Yes. I ran. Then I got into my car and drove until I was in the middle of nowhere, where I couldn't hurt anyone around me. Then I let it go. It fucking *exploded* out of me. I mean that literally. There was a crater in the middle of that field. The next day, I knocked on the farmer's door and paid him for an entire crop season. I told him I was doing a mad-scientist experiment out there and destroyed his crop on accident."

They were silent for a few minutes again, thinking separate thoughts.

"Where was that field?" Miranda asked suddenly. "What direction did you drive?"

"Huh? I don't know. Why?" Matthew asked, not getting it.

"I'm wondering if we're laying in that field right now."

"Oh! You know," Matthew laughed, "I can't rule it out. We'll have to ask Sam. That's funny."

"Somehow, I wouldn't be surprised."

"I guess I wouldn't, either," Matthew admitted. "I've only been here a handful of times since Sam bought it. It really was nothing but cornfields all around."

"Back to us," Miranda prodded. "What happened after you ran away from me?"

Matthew shrugged. "Eventually, Jake met Matty. Matty led to Lucy in a roundabout way. Adrian fought his energy, trying to spare Lucy. Then William threw down with him. We had a family heart-to-heart and realized a bunch of us were fucked up in some way.

"Once Will started talking about balancing energy and Adrian needing Lucy to feel right, how they'd be sick and miserable apart, I knew exactly how much I messed things up. William sat at my parents' dining room table, eating the mustard out of the fridge, explaining his energy, and all I could think about was you and what I'd done to you and to us."

"Well, more accurately, what you *didn't* do to me," Miranda joked, sensing his remorse. "Will ate mustard? Just mustard?"

Matthew gave a sad little laugh. "Yeah. Will and Adrian 'played superheroes.' On par with Micah gouging out Will's eyes. I still have nightmares about it. I thought they were going to kill each other while we all watched. But, once Adrian balanced his power, they stopped. And then they ate all the food. All of it. One of them even drank the pickle juice."

"That's what Adrian meant when Micah wanted to do training?" Miranda asked. "I didn't entirely follow Adrian's reluctance to train but forgot to ask by the time Ethan and I got home. I was upset for you."

Matthew nodded. They were quiet again for a moment.

"I didn't tell them. Even then, after it was clear that most of us were weird in some way, I didn't fess up to my family. Mine is different than theirs. I didn't come clean until after I met Ava and Jess. They knew what I was immediately."

"You hate it?"

Miranda could hear the sound of his nod against the ground in the darkness and feel it against the earth. "Why? It's energy—not inherently good or bad."

"I've never experienced anything good as a result of it. It doesn't introduce anything positive into the world."

"I fundamentally disagree. Chaos is part of evolution and adaptation. Besides, if you can sense mental illness, you have the opportunity to help someone who's struggling."

Matthew made a sound of agreement. "That's true. I forget about it, but I've done that. I've found children in my class that have mental instability. I helped a mother that was struggling with what I think was postpartum psychosis. She may have hurt herself or her kids otherwise. I forget about that little stuff."

Miranda flinched next to him.

"What's wrong?"

"Holy cow, Matthew. It's not little stuff to the people it affects.

Don't downplay that help. Dealing with mental imbalance can have a serious impact on someone's life."

"Maybe I'm in the wrong profession," he agreed. "Are you really ready to date? I thought you'd need more time after everything with Lawrence. You've made peace with all of that?"

MIRANDA GROANED.

Matthew chuckled into the trailing silence. "What are you thinking?"

"I'm wondering if we can skip this part and get to the making out," Miranda replied archly, grinning in the night.

"I don't make a habit of necking with married women," Matthew replied, laughing.

"The divorce should be final next week," she said, her voice losing some humor. "What a mess I made of things."

"We can argue about who was a bigger contributor later."

She pushed him on his back, curling up under his arm. "It's chilly out here."

The laughter stopped. "We can go back. We'll talk about this later."

"I don't want to go back."

"It is chilly. We can do this another time, Miranda."

"Matthew, don't break the magic of this moment. There's nowhere else I'd rather be than whispering secrets with you in the darkness, even if the topic leaves something to be desired."

He grunted.

The sound took some of the joy out of Miranda. "We can go if you don't want to be here."

"That's not what I was grunting about. I was grunting because there are plenty of other places we could be whispering secrets to each other that are more comfortable than this."

Miranda's cheeks heated and heart leapt at the implication.

"Are you blushing?" Matthew chuckled.

"Say it again?" she breathed, afraid to give too much voice to the words.

Matthew paused, considering. Finally, he turned his head to whisper directly in her ear. "I love you. I have always loved you."

Miranda wiped at the tears dripping down the sides of her face. "I love you, too," she choked out. "I always have, even after you ran away. I was so mad at myself for not being mad at you. But all I could manage was hurt and confused and worried."

Matthew's arms closed around her, nearly pulling her atop himself to be closer. "I'm sorry, Miranda. I thought I was doing the right thing."

As her tears subsided, he smiled. "This isn't getting you out of answering my question."

"Ah, shit." She laughed.

"Do you want more time? Are you ready to start another relationship? Start dating?" he asked again, propping himself up on one arm to see the outline of her in the night.

"Well, I mean, date? Like, date a random person? I don't know. Probably not—"

"Kareem?" Matthew asked.

"I'm ninety-two percent sure we were only ever going to be friends. He's just coming out of a relationship, too."

"You're not ready? We can hit the pause button here," Matthew offered, swallowing his disappointment.

"Being with you is not starting a random relationship, Matthew."

"No," he agreed. "But I don't want to play unless we're playing for keeps. And if you're not there yet, we don't have to cross that line right now."

"I like that you're willing to give me that time. But I don't want it. If Lawrence and I were still together when you and I had this conversation, I'd be filing for a divorce the next day. There was no love between us, Matthew."

Matthew sighed. "I understand that you don't love him. That

doesn't surprise me. But it seems nearly impossible that he doesn't have feelings for you, Randa. I don't know how anyone could know you and spend time with you and not love you on some level."

She gave a huff of laughter. "He was sleeping with other women *before and during* our marriage, Matthew. The man saw me as a career advancement opportunity. He's making out now. He gets to keep the career and not deal with me."

"He may have sucked at showing it and may not have respected you, but he got mad enough to take a swing at you, Miranda. There's some deep emotion there. This thing between us has been brewing for years. It will keep brewing if needed."

"I don't want more time to ponder the inner-workings of not-svelte Larry's mind, Matthew."

"So, what do you want now?" Matthew asked.

"Besides you?" she asked.

Matthew could sense her cheeky grin, even if he couldn't see it. He smiled, tipping his head down to brush his lips against hers.

He missed.

"You just kissed my nose," she said, causing them to crack up in fits of giggles.

"In my defense, it's really dark out here!" Matthew replied, still laughing.

The laughter died when her hand brushed his cheek and her lips touched his. The feather-soft brush of her lips transitioned into a meeting of mouths then quickly escalated as the energy exploded through them, demanding contact and closeness.

He pulled away after a second, touching his forehead to hers. "That freaks the energy out for me. Does it for you, too?"

"Well, that's one way to put it." She grinned.

"Back to my question, miss. What do you want, knowing that you've long since had my love? You spend so much time and energy trying to make everyone else happy. What do you want?"

Miranda pushed against him, rolling him over onto his back again before snuggling back into his chest.

"Did you just mess with gravity?" Matthew asked, eyebrows raised.

"Yes. I did what I want. Be proud of me."

Matthew laughed, pulling his arms tight around her.

"I'm trying to find a way to ask Sam to help me start a business."

There was a moment of silence as they both processed the words she had been avoiding.

"Why do you sound so angry about this if it's what you want?" Matthew asked.

"I wouldn't have to ask for help if Lawrence wasn't such an idiot, but I don't have much choice now. I hate that I have to ask for a handout."

"Sam?" Matthew asked without raising his voice. "Are you done eavesdropping?"

"WHY IS TAKING my help worse than taking Ethan's help?" Sam asked from the darkness about ten feet away. His voice was laced with annoyance. "You called Ethan for help without a problem. I'm a good guy. I'd be happy to help."

"I would rather not have taken anyone's help at all, but I wasn't going to stay with Lawrence after that night," Miranda said defensively. "Ethan and I had just talked about his prior relationship while we were at Matilda and Jake's engagement party. I knew he'd understand and not judge me for needing help."

"Matilda does this, too," Sam grumped. "She hates needing help."

"Where's Addy?" Matthew asked into the awkward silence.

"She went back to the farmhouse to settle bets."

"Bets?" Miranda asked.

"You probably don't want to know," Matthew said, tone laced with amusement. "It's my turn. Sorry in advance."

"Noah and Jake were confident you two were rolling around naked out here. Matty said it was too cold. Hank and Darla were undecided. Everyone else just thinks it's funny."

"Oh my God." Miranda sighed, cheeks heating again.

Matthew laughed. "We heckled Jake for a solid year before he got together with Matty. I thought we might slip by unnoticed since Noah and Talise are still new."

Sam snorted. "Not a chance. They've been betting on you two since the day we met Miranda."

Matthew nodded. "I'm not surprised. Is everyone okay in there?"

"Mhmm," Sam replied.

"Well, I'm not okay. I'm mortified," Miranda complained.

"It'll pass. But right now, nothing is sacred," Matthew replied. "Again, sorry."

"Not true. Lasagna and puppies are sacred," Sam retorted.

"We're adding puppies?" Matthew asked, surprised. "Randa, aren't you allergic to some dogs?"

Sam snorted. "She'd never kick a puppy. We're tolerant of allergies. You know this."

"Fair enough." Matthew nodded, laughing.

The humor left Sam's voice. "What exactly do you need help with, Miranda? What was the goal that you were willing to sacrifice your own happiness to achieve? I'm offended you stayed in that farce of a marriage for money. I told you I'd be happy to help, that you could leave when you were ready. I thought you knew me better than this. I thought you understood that I meant what I said."

Miranda blew out a frustrated sigh, knowing she had wronged Sam in her unwillingness to ask for a handout sooner. "I want to buy some land and start a plant nursery. With the proceeds from that, I intend to start a program to teach kids how to garden for their own healthy, organic food."

Both men went still.

"You want the nursery? That's part of the dream? Or is the dream more to do with teaching kids to garden?" Sam asked.

"I don't know how I'd fund the gardening long-term without the nursery, Sam."

"Miranda," Sam snapped. "We have an entire charitable foundation that does stuff like this. You don't need a handout. You need a *job*. We need to talk to Adrian. He's working with some groups to revive Lucy's old neighborhood. Your idea would fit perfectly in there. Why wouldn't you just ask about it? You have to know we do things like this!"

Miranda blinked in the darkness. "I did ask. Repeatedly. To every social works project I could find or connect with. They weren't interested!"

"Did you ask *me*?" Sam yelled.

"I-I didn't ask, Sam. I'm sorry. You have a protective streak. I figured you would tell me no, that I didn't need to work," she stammered, near tears in the face of his hurt and anger.

"You don't need to work! But what the fuck, Miranda? If you want to work, who am I to tell you no? I don't tell Matilda that she can't work. I would never *dream* of it; she'd gut me!" Sam responded.

"Sam," Matthew breathed in warning. "Calm down. Your voice is going a little bit echo-heavy."

"I hate that we're so fucking lost. I didn't see this!" Sam yelled in frustration. "I should have fucking seen this! I should have seen him taking a swing at you! I should have been able to head this whole thing off at the pass, but I don't know where we are right now!"

"Okay," Matthew breathed into Miranda's ear, rolling her over to put himself between her and Sam. "He's gone full echo. Let's tread carefully."

"A job would be great, Sam. Amazing, actually," Miranda said, injecting cheer into her words. It wasn't false cheer. It was nervous cheer.

The darkness was getting lighter. She couldn't figure out why or where the light was coming from.

"Why is it getting lighter?" she breathed to Matthew.

"Oh. I thought that was just my perception. I don't know."

"Sam!" Miranda barked, interrupting his mental brooding.

His eyes jumped to her.

I can see him clearly now, even ten feet away in what had been pitch-black darkness three minutes ago, she realized.

"What are you doing?" Miranda asked.

"What?" Sam asked, thrown off from his tantrum. "Nothing."

"You are doing something. It's getting lighter," Matthew retorted.

Sam looked around, baffled. "Oh. I don't know. That's not me."

"It's me!" Matilda called, grinning as she approached, holding onto Jake's arm on the uneven ground. "Jake didn't believe you weren't getting it on out here, so we came to check on you. I'm better than a flashlight. She's not even properly mussed, Jake. You lost that bet!"

"He tried to kiss me but missed," Miranda offered, causing Jake and Sam to cackle at their younger brother.

"You're not even glowing. How is the light coming from you?" Matthew asked, trying to move the conversation along.

Matilda scrunched up her face. "I wanted it to be lighter so I could see where we were going. Don't judge my methods. It worked."

"But where is the light coming from?" Miranda asked.

"I don't know. I don't care. I wanted it to be lighter, so it's lighter. Don't bitch," Matilda said with a shrug. "Let's go back. It's cold out here. I suppose I could play with the fire stuff—"

"No!" Sam, Miranda, and Matthew shouted as one as Jake laughed.

18

"*H*i, Kareem, I'm Ethan. Hop in! We have a long ride to the circle and a lot to talk about."

Kareem stood on the sidewalk in front of his apartment building, his stare moving between Ethan and Miranda. "Um. Yeah, okay."

"How are you?" Miranda asked cautiously. She was unsure where things stood with Kareem. But she had no intention of pursuing a relationship outside of being friends.

Kareem opened and closed his mouth a few times before words made their way out. "I'm nervous."

"Don't be nervous," Ethan and Miranda said simultaneously.

"Micah won't bother you," Miranda promised. "You don't need to be afraid of him."

"Lord Micah has never harmed me," Kareem said quietly. "Quite the opposite. I would be dead a few times over. But the man is terrifying. Old, powerful, and terrifying. A sustaining relic of a time long past, when power was distributed differently."

"Well, that's an interesting statement," Ethan said, eyes on the road as he merged on the expressway. "What sort of relic do you think he is?"

"Wait, before we talk about Micah..." Miranda's voice trailed off as she swallowed her nerves.

"What's wrong?" Kareem asked.

"She's super anxious about hurting your feelings because she doesn't want to date you. She's worked out her issues with my younger brother. They're probably going to be a thing."

"Holy crap, Ethan! I didn't mean for *you* to do it!" Miranda yelled.

Ethan shrugged, grinning at the road. "It's done. How're you doing, Kareem? Do I need to take you home so you can pout in private?"

"No," Kareem said slowly. "I'm glad to be friends, Miranda. As I said, I don't know anyone here. I didn't get the feeling you were looking for hot and heavy right now, other than staring at my chest."

"Damn! I forgot." Ethan laughed. "I gotta see the hairy chest at some point."

That caught Kareem off guard. He threw his head back and laughed loudly. "She was all but drooling."

Miranda smiled. "I'm glad you didn't notice the drool. I was overwhelmed."

"This is not what we need to talk about. Or, at least, it's not only what we need to talk about," Ethan said, trying to get back on track.

"Are we going to talk about your energy? Because I've never felt such a pure Joy holder."

"Yes, we can talk about that," Ethan said easily. "But first. What did you mean about Micah being a relic? I think that might play into things."

Miranda was happy to let Ethan lead the conversation, glad that her awkward dumping was done.

"He comes from a time when power was more concentrated in individuals. How old are you, Miranda?"

"Twenty-two."

"Ethan, how old are you?"

"I'll be thirty-two years old in January," Ethan said.

"I didn't know you were that much older than me!" Miranda grinned.

"Clean living and a lack of stress," Ethan joked. "Why do you ask, Kareem?"

"Your energy is different, more like Micah's than mine. I wondered if you were from a similar time."

"No," Miranda said simply. "But we are similarly empowered. Ethan and I are what's known as pillars."

Out of the corner of her eye, Miranda saw Kareem pull a face in the backseat.

"You know what a pillar is?" she asked, smiling.

"I've read the nonsense in the chat groups and message forums," Kareem said, rolling his eyes.

"Oh! That's interesting, too. What chat groups? What do they say?" Ethan asked. "It never occurred to me to ask Jess and Ava how they communicate with other empowered."

"Rumors say that Greggory of Harbor has surrendered his circle to the Walker and Mistress. The man has been obsessed with those legends for most of a century. It's fitting he's fallen prey to such a pair of con artists."

Ethan and Miranda shared a quick grin.

Kareem grew silent and severe. "If I'd not seen you with Lord Micah, Miranda, I'd be wondering if I had again landed myself in a dangerous situation. Where are you taking me?"

"To meet my family," Ethan said. "And the rest of Harbor. There's no con here, Kareem. Sam and Addy are what they are, though they were very reluctant to claim the names. Micah has assigned himself as our guard and trainer, though he still refuses to stand with us. You'll see. But no one means you harm, okay?"

Kareem gave a slow, reluctant nod. "I'm already in the car, Ethan. Lord Micah is right; I trust too easily."

"Well," Miranda gave him a reassuring smile, "it's not misplaced. And if all else fails, you can rip off your shirt to dazzle us with your muscly chest then run away while we're all stunned."

"I'm telling Matthew you said that," Ethan teased.

Miranda grinned. "I dare you to start referring to 'Lord Micah' just so we can watch his reaction."

Ethan's cheeks turned pink. "You really think there's something there?"

"Ethan, he even did the ass synonyms for you. How can you still be unsure about this?"

"I think he just didn't want to make me sad. Like, part of the whole 'Joy' thing, you know?"

"Nope."

"Really?"

"Yep." Miranda laughed, gently touching one of Ethan's grinning dimples. "You're so adorable, even big, bad Micah can't help but love you."

"Eep!" Ethan chirped. "I want to be excited about this, but I don't think I can be yet."

"It's time," Miranda replied, deadpan. "Time for new love, Ethan!"

"I'm not disagreeing. And oh my goodness—Micah. When he grins? Come on! Also, total brooding badass. It's too good to be true, Randa. It's not going to happen."

"Well, not with that attitude." Miranda laughed.

"I'm sorry. Can we back up a minute?" Kareem asked. "Are you suggesting Lord Micah is gay?"

"Got a problem with that?" Miranda asked, losing all traces of humor, her tone abrupt.

"N-no. I mean, not at all. I just didn't consider it before now," Kareem replied, surprised by Miranda's tone.

Ethan's lips twitched up. "I love that you're all timid and unsure when we talk about you, Miranda. But the minute it looks like someone's going to pick on *me*, you get all fierce. You can be fierce for yourself, too, you know?"

"I know," Miranda said quietly. "I guess I struggle with that. I'm working on it."

"We've been in the car for almost an hour." Kareem laughed. "She hasn't apologized once. This is a vast improvement over our first meeting."

"Miranda!" Ethan barked.

"I caught myself," she replied primly. "I was distracted and flustered by the hairy chest."

Kareem shook with laughter, despite his earlier misgivings. "I feel like my muscles are a separate entity in this car."

"Don't take the shirt off while I'm driving. I want to be able to appreciate the view, too." Ethan smiled.

"WHOA!" Kareem yelled, stumbling and falling away from the car in fear as he watched Matthew approach from the farmhouse. "Madness!"

"Meh," Ethan said, smiling as he offered Kareem a hand up. "That's my little brother Matthew and also Miranda's soon-to-be sweetie. Chaos is more accurate. Pandemonium even more so."

Miranda gave a little smile, not turning her head to look at Ethan. She watched Matthew approach, delighted by the fact that he was coming to meet her.

"Hi," Matthew murmured, wrapping her in a hug and kissing the top of her head. "How are you?"

She grinned up at him, secretly wiggling her toes in her shoes in excitement. It was difficult to stand still, but doing a happy dance at that moment would be decidedly out-of-place. "Good. You?"

He smiled then looked around. "Hi, Kareem. Welcome. Thank you."

"H-hello. T-thank you?" Kareem stuttered.

Matthew nodded, offering his hand to shake. "I'm Matthew. It's wonderful to meet you. Miranda says good things about you. And you unknowingly served as a catalyst, giving me an early opportunity to correct a mistake I made years ago. Thank you."

Kareem tentatively shook the offered hand. "Okay? I guess?"

"Fool," Micah called, approaching the car. "That one is scary for his intelligence first and his power second. There are more terrifying ones yet to meet. Get it together. Is everyone well?"

"By everyone, do you mean Ethan?" Miranda asked, grinning.

Micah glared at her.

Her grin remained unapologetic, even after Ethan poked her in the ribs. His cheeks were bright red. "Don't," Ethan muttered.

"We're doing this now?" Matthew whispered to Miranda. "We're pushing?"

She grinned up at him then paused. "I guess I always knew you were tall but never realized you were so tall. You seem...taller. Bigger."

Matthew dragged his feet, not looking at her. "I told you. Micah's been working with me. I'm stronger and my posture's getting better."

"Huh," she muttered, following in Micah's wake as they walked around the back of the house.

"Holy God," Kareem breathed, getting his first glance of the Trellis family.

"I'm sorry! I'm sorry! I'm sorry!" Noah yelled. "I was teasing! Let me up! Please don't break it!"

"What did I tell you?" Beth asked, voice calm. She had Noah pinned on the ground, his right arm contorted behind his body, holding him still.

"We won't joke about it. Fine. Agreed. I promise! I'm sorry!"

Beth climbed off his back after shoving Noah's face in the cold, packed dirt one more time for good measure.

"You are absolutely my scariest sibling!" Noah yelled, climbing to his feet. "I didn't even see her move."

"Are we done?" Ethan asked Beth.

"I'm good for now," Beth said with a straight face. "Unless I get a shot at Micah, I'm calm."

"What did I do? I didn't do anything!" Micah looked appalled.

Beth scowled.

"What did I do?" Micah asked, looking lost.

"Nothing," she said, grinning. "I was just ensuring you still held the proper level of fear. We're good."

Micah winced, swallowing his grin but unable to hide all his laughter.

"She got you pretty good," Ethan acknowledged. "You were scared. I didn't need to be William to know that."

"She's terrifying," Micah muttered, unleashing his grin on Ethan.

Miranda wiggled in place, unable to further contain her excitement as Sam approached from the field.

"Karim," Sam said, head tilted, staring at Kareem. "No. That's not right, is it? That's not your name in this time. I thought you would be Karim, but not in this one. Kareem. You are Kareem now. Oh, shit."

Kareem stood frozen, unable to speak.

"Not con artists," Ethan said quietly. "This is my little brother, Sam, also known as the Walker. I have a lot of brothers but only one sister. Let me know when you're ready for introductions."

Kareem didn't blink as he continued to stare at Sam and Sam continued to stare at him.

After a moment, Sam's eyes went vacant. They glowed faintly in the gathering twilight.

"Sam?" Will called, walking up to join the group from where he'd been standing with Adrian, Lucy, and Beth. "You okay?"

Sam didn't respond.

Ethan scrunched up his face. "I think he's left the building."

"Pure terror is rolling off him," Will said, tone flat. "Are you getting that?"

Before anyone could answer, Adaline's energy radiated from her as she ran from the farmhouse with Luke and Talise.

"*What happened?*" Adaline asked through the mental link she shared with most of the family. Not yet close enough to speak without yelling, she had reverted to mental communication.

Micah started at her unspoken words. "That can't be good. She could have Walked and been here instantly, but she's running. She's that distracted."

Will shook his head. "Nope, probably not good. The last time he was afraid like this, he took the name. New guy, please shut it down. I get that you're new, but we're not going to hurt you unless you mean us harm."

"Fool!" Micah barked. "What did I tell you?"

"I-I-I didn't believe... When I read the chatter about it, I didn't believe it," Kareem stammered, eyes moving between Sam, William, and Adaline as she got closer. "It's real? They're real? I have to go read that message thread about them now! Fuck. I hate gossip!"

"They're literally standing in front of you. You are a fucking idiot," Micah said, shaking his head.

"I don't know what happened, Addy," Will finally answered her unspoken question as she got closer. "He met Miranda's friend then went adrift on us."

Turning to glare at Kareem on her way by, Adaline stepped alongside Sam, touching his face. "Samuel," she murmured, the word imbued with energy. "Come back to us, Sam."

There was no response.

"Can I slap him?" Will asked, a smile lurking around his lips. "He's freaking out."

Adaline glowered at him. "Just wait. He's far afield. He heard me, though."

"What? What's wrong?" Ava yelled, running from the farmhouse with Jess.

"Jess, will you look?" Adaline called. "He's done something to Sam."

"Me?" Kareem almost yelled. "I didn't do anything. I swear to God, I didn't do anything but stand here!"

Adaline sighed. "That's not what I meant."

"Fool," Micah added. "She implied the word 'fool' there."

Jess shook her head. "No influences, no stolen energy. Looks like a lot of kindness, compassion, and generosity."

"And stupidity," Micah added for good measure.

Jess grinned at Micah before turning back to Adaline and Sam. "What happened?"

Sam flinched, blinking his eyes. "Cancel the circle. James and Evelyn are coming. Get everyone out of here. We have less than an hour before they're here."

Adaline's eyebrows shot up.

"I know where we are. Approximately. I know approximately where we are. A third time walker is trying to take shape. Micah is right," Sam continued. "We're in danger. He means to take our circle. He means to take the energy. All of it."

All expression fell from Micah's face. "Who?"

"It's Jared, but not. I don't understand it. We need Evelyn and James. I don't understand."

19

"*S*am, calm down," Adaline shared mentally. "*I am right here. We are all well. Please, you're making me feel sick.*"

"*He means you harm, Addy. You, specifically. He means to trap you. He's going to separate us. He's going to try to take you from me and me from you,*" Sam babbled in her mind, their mental link trembling with his terror. "*We have to stay together. Please. I'm sorry. I have to stay with you. Please. I won't interrupt you and Tali. I won't get in the way when you're doing house stuff with Blake. I promise. Please. We need to—*"

"Sam," she murmured aloud, wrapping him in a hug. "Please. It will be okay."

"No, Addy. No. That's what I'm saying. It's *not* going to be okay," Sam said, louder than he intended. "He's going to hurt you. I couldn't find a future in which he doesn't kill you. It's not going to be okay."

"It's mutable, Sam. Remember? We can change it," she soothed as the rest of the group stared at them in horror.

"I don't know how, Addy. I don't know how to fix it!" Tears dripped down Sam's cheeks. "We should give up the names. Now. Right now."

"No," Addy said. The word was gentle but firm. She brushed her lips against his cheek. Sam's body remained rigid and unresponsive, arms at his sides rather than returning her hug. "We will not give up the names because things get difficult. No. We will work it out. Calm down."

"Adaline, I lose it," Sam said quickly. "I lose control of it. The dreams. The fire dreams and suffocation dreams. I do that. I cause it. When he takes you and then when he kills you. When the accordance snaps and our circle breaks, I take the world apart. I kill everything. It all dies with us. We have to give up the names. Now. We have to give up the names now before it's too late."

"Could you see what happens if you give up the names?"

Sam started at the sound of Micah's voice, reminded at last that others were within earshot. He glanced around, noticing his family and closest friends staring at him in horror.

"No," Sam said after a moment. "I tried. I can't see that."

Micah's expression remained unfixed. "How do you know that giving up the names is correct, then? If you give them up, what if the next pair is less altruistic? What if the third walker can claim the energy you sacrifice?"

"I don't know, but I kill everything, Micah. Everything! We have to stop. We have to give up the names," Sam yelled, words coming so fast they were hard to parse between his gasping breath.

"You're not thinking clearly," Micah said calmly. "Even I know that's not how time works. You don't know for sure. It's not predetermined."

"Micah! There is a significant—" Sam yelled.

"Stop. Sam, stop!" Hank yelled, rushing out of the farmhouse with Darla. Emma trailed behind, having gone into the house to gather the missing members of the family. "They're going. Everyone's leaving. Calm down, okay? Let's wait until things clear out and wait for James and Evelyn."

Sam dug at his hair, yanking hard. "This is it. This is where we are. Oh my God, Adaline. Oh my God. I can't do this. I don't want to do this."

"Sam, shhh," she soothed, trying to hush him. "Sam, look at me."

"Adaline, I don't want to—"

"Samuel," Adaline's voice reverberated through the field. "Sam, come back to me."

"Addy, please. Please don't let this—"

"Samuel," she said again, pulling more power to her voice. "Touch the indifference. You need it right now. *This* is why the indifference exists."

Sam gasped. "Addy—"

"Samuel, please?" she whispered. "Not forever, but for now. We can't walk through the wildflowers like this, Sam. You can't follow the threads in the web like this. There is no danger here. Please."

Between one second and the next, the panic left Sam's eyes, leaving a stranger in its wake.

"MAYBE KAREEM COULD CATCH a ride home with someone else? Or we could order a car?" Ethan suggested as the family filed into the farmhouse living area.

"No," Samuel said, expressionless voice heavy with power. "He is of this circle. He stays."

Noah trailed Samuel into the room with a cautious distance between them. "Why are his footsteps echoing? Sam, why are you doing that?"

"I'm not," Sam said.

"You are. You're doing something. Your footsteps don't usually echo, man," Noah argued, creeped out by the utter lack of expression in his brother's countenance.

"I'm not doing anything, Noah," Sam said again, uninterested.

Adaline sighed. "He usually extends the effort to make it so that doesn't happen, Noah. It's part of how the Space energy works. It's fine. Sit."

"Kareem, speak your name," Sam commanded.

"Kareem?" Kareem said, confused.

"Your other name. Speak it before the Mother and Father are here, else they'll attempt to take you from my circle."

Kareem's eyes shot to Miranda. "I don't understand."

"Speak your name now," Sam said again. "It's almost too late."

"So, it's not complete indifference." Jake laughed. "He's still a bossy prick."

No one responded.

"Yeah, okay. It's fucking creepy," Jake said in the stilted silence. "Addy, tell him to stop."

"He's fine, Jake. Just sit quietly until James and Evelyn are here. He'll need to explain to James," Addy whispered from her spot next to Talise, on the opposite side of the room from Sam.

"Come here," Samuel said to her. "I told you that you were to stay with me."

"No," she said, her smile tense. "You said you were going to stay with me."

"In most futures, you die screaming in a binding circle, drained by your own grandmother, begging for our unborn child's life. Come here. The rest is semantics."

"My mother! Sam, my mother?" Ava demanded, eyes wide. "I can find her. I never severed my binding. We can find her. We can proactively—"

Moving to sit next to Sam, Adaline sighed again, interrupting Ava's panicked planning. "We have time, then. I am not with child."

"See, if you just never have sex again, it'll all be fine." Noah grinned at Sam. The grin was short-lived as Noah backed out of the room, dragging Talise with him. "We'll just wait in the kitchen."

"This is so fucking weird," Jake muttered.

"Shhh," Addy said, sharing peace through the room. "All will be well."

"You know we're incapable of being quiet for more than ten seconds at a time, right?" Luke whispered to her.

"Take your name," Samuel said to Kareem, ignoring everyone else. "They will be here shortly. Within a minute. Take the name."

Kareem shook his head in confusion. "I don't know—"

"Too late," Sam said, eyes turning toward the front door. "They're here. William, open the door."

With a backward glance at his brother, Will moved to open the front door. "When did I become the designated doorman?"

Ethan shrugged. "You seem to do it a lot."

"You know, I was watching *Wheel of*... What's going on? You're all... WOW! LOOK AT YOU!" James cheered at Sam. "All power forward, full of indifference. YES! Evie! Look what we did!"

"Oh, mercy," Evelyn whimpered, backing out of the front door in fear. "Addy, come. Come here, sweet girl."

"I am well, Evelyn," Adaline assured her. "I asked him to use it. He was unwell."

"Addy, please. Please come away," Evelyn asked quietly, just shy of begging. "We shouldn't be here. We should go. You and me. Let's go elsewhere."

"You will not take her from me," Samuel stated.

"LOOK AT YOU! I LOVE THIS! All promises are considered delivered upon. YES! Well worth the wait," James congratulated himself.

"There is a third time walker. Micah was correct that Josiah lives on, though I don't understand how it is so. You will Walk with me to see it," Sam addressed James directly. "Are you ready?"

"Right now? You want to—" James's words cut off as his eyes went vacant in time with Samuel's.

"Samuel was adrift for a few minutes the first time. I don't know how long they'll be. Sit, Evelyn. He will not hurt us," Adaline said.

"Addy, he will kill you if he stays like that for too long," Evelyn said, voice still drenched in anxiety. "We need to draw a trapping circle—"

"No!" Adaline barked, outraged. "He will put the indifference down. If he doesn't do it willingly, I will take it from him. Sit. Now."

With a confused glance around the room, Evelyn sat next to Micah. "This is folly."

"Evelyn, we won't let him hurt you, okay?" Will said, voice soothing. "I can't help with your fear. You're like Sam and Adaline. But I hate seeing someone so terrified, especially of Sam. He won't hurt you."

"William, you are a warm, kind, caring person. You can't understand—" Evelyn started.

James twitched before falling to the floor, convulsing and gagging. "Holy shit! Don't ever do that again!"

"There is a third walker," Sam said again without inflection.

"FUCK! Fuck you, Sam. Don't do that again!" James yelled. "My head is going to explode."

"James?" Evelyn asked, voice small.

"Fine, Evie. Fine," he said, dry heaving where he laid on the floor. "It's fine. Getting better."

"You understand? You saw it?" Samuel asked in the same monotone voice.

"Yeah, Sam. Yeah. I saw."

Taking a long slow breath, Sam blinked, coming back to himself. "It is horrible, and we need to give up the names."

"GAH!" James groaned. "Put the indifference back! You're too fucking dramatic like this. You're badass with it, though—a sight to behold."

"A terrifying sight," Evelyn muttered, only then realizing she was digging her nails into Micah's hand. "Sorry."

"It's fine, Evelyn," Micah murmured back, patting her hand.

Sam sighed. "James, how is that possible? That was Josiah's energy. I went back and looked for him after I saw it the first time. It's him, correct?"

"It's not possible—" Evelyn started.

"Yes, that was his energy," James confirmed, talking over Evelyn. "I don't know how that's possible. His body was destroyed. We did it ourselves."

"Moron," Micah yelled. "I told you this over a month—"

"You can do the I-told-you-so dance later, Micah!" James yelled over him. "Evie, didn't we... What?"

Evelyn started, realizing everyone was staring at her. "Sorry, I just realized there's a new face in the room. Hello, friend." She smiled warmly at Kareem.

James focused on Kareem as well. "You're not bound to them."

Sam sighed, rolling his eyes at Kareem. "I told you to take the damn name before they got here."

"I don't have any idea what's going on," Kareem bitched. "I just got here, and you people started freaking out. Lord Micah, I want to go home!"

With that, Will, Hennessy, and Adrian broke out in simultaneous laughter. Unidentified muffled sounds of suppressed mirth trickled through the room before the family finally broke out combined giggles.

"I agree," Adrian said. "I wanna go home, too!"

"Lord Micah?" Hennessy asked, wiping tears from his eyes.

"Holy shit." Jake laughed. "I'm glad I'm not the only one that caught that. What the fuck, man?"

"Fool." Micah glowered at Kareem, eliciting an actual snort from Beth, which triggered another round of giggles.

"Can we get back on topic?" Sam asked, unamused. "We need to give up the names. I kill everything."

"Oh, yeesh, shut up," James said, rolling his eyes. "There are futures in which I destroy everything. Granted, I don't do it with as much...gusto as you do, but I do it. There's probably a future in which Adaline destroys everything if she has also touched the indifference. Just because it's there doesn't mean it's going to happen. Quit your bitching."

"James," Sam barked, his anger rolling through the room. "You saw the same thing I did. There are a significant number of futures in which I—"

"Yeah, that was really something the way you did that. The way you use it, I see what you mean about losing your place in time," James said, distracted. "That's highly efficient. I don't think I can do that. My brain is not structured to organize like that. But make sure you teach that to your successor. That's next evolutionary step stuff, Sam. Your brain is amazing."

That gave Sam pause. "It's not like that for you? What's it like for you?"

"Me?" James asked, chuckling. "No. Relatively speaking, time is a great big fucking ball of knotted twine for me. I can see the strands and maybe how they relate to each other, but not the beginning or end, not the fine threads. I can't focus on seeing the minor details, and I don't have a quarter of the range. How far out in time do you think we were for the one with William? That had to be a couple hundred years from now."

"But the close ones—" Sam began, confusion written across his face.

"They crop up, Sam. It's hard to see the other Walkers. At least, it is for me. I can't see much of your future, though I can see all of your past. Is it difficult for you to see me as well?"

Sam nodded. "It's difficult to find your past and future, though I haven't tried lately."

"Yeah, I get what you mean about 'finding' now." James nodded. "Time will warn us of our own troubled paths. We can't see each other well, but we can see ourselves. Sometimes it comes through visions, sometimes through dreams or premonitions. It doesn't mean it's going to happen. You've been dreaming of fire since the day you were born. You haven't flamed out yet."

Sam exhaled hard, sagging with relief. He rested his face in his shaking hands, arms propped up on his knees. Adaline pulled him close, weaving her fingers through his hair, resting her forehead against him to murmur soundlessly in his ear.

"I get why you freaked out, but holy shit, don't do that," James said, not unkindly. "You won't always see the stupid things you might do. I didn't see the path in which I tried to take Evie's power. In retrospect, I think that was a 'mistake' that was destined to be made. There was a severe lack of balance between the Walker and Mistress for an extended period. My asinine stunt put an end to that. You and Adaline are now so well balanced, you're almost a single being."

Evelyn rolled her eyes. "I enjoy how you're making getting your ass handed to you out to be some epic, noble gesture."

James grinned at her. "But seriously, I think when the possibility of large-scale destruction is looming in front of us, we get hints and warnings. I consider the fact that it scares you so much to be a *good* thing, a sign that you're still the right person for this gig. When making huge, sweeping changes to civilization stops being a scary thought, we should probably take a breather."

"You know what would have helped in this situation?" Micah asked.

"Oh, shut—"

"If you had taught him *anything* about what he is," Micah roared over James's words, making Kareem flinch badly enough to knock over the lamp on the end table next to him.

Nora glared at Micah. "That was my great-grandmother's lamp, and it's nearly as old as electricity. We will have words."

"It's not broken," Kareem muttered, righting the antique on the table.

James grinned at Kareem. "Oh yeah. Back to that. Hello, new unbound pillar. What's *your* name?"

Kareem's eyes darted around the room, finally landing on Micah. "I'm just going to call a Lyft. You people can do whatever it is that you need to do. I won't get in the way."

Micah sighed. "Such a fool. Will, would you help?"

"I am," Will replied. "He was on his way to a heart attack in the field."

Micah looked at Luke, eyebrows lifted.

Luke's lips twitched. "Naptime or euphoria time?"

"Leave him be," Evelyn cut in. "Let him listen, then he can choose where he wants to stand."

Adrian's face scrunched up. "I thought you couldn't take pillars from other circles."

"We can't." Evelyn gave him a coy, flirty smile. "But he's not yet bound to your circle. He's a free agent, so to speak. You were all bound to Sam and Addy, even before the names. That one is more tied to Micah than anyone else, and even that tie is weak."

"Why not just choose pillars from the other circles over the last three hundred years, then? Why not collect the pillars before each pair declines the names?" Adrian asked, brow furrowed.

"It doesn't work like that," James explained. "The imminent arrival of each pair triggers a new set of pillars. It is excessively rare for a pillar to outlast their pair."

William cleared his throat, looking at Micah with raised eyebrows.

Micah's lips turned up at the corners. "I'll explain another time."

"You haven't...?" Evelyn asked, shocked.

"Obviously not," Micah murmured.

James grinned smugly. "Sure, talk to me about training and then leave out your own history lesson."

An awkward silence persisted as everyone stared at Micah. Micah looked back with a politely closed expression on his face.

"Anyway," James continued. "The new guy exists because of Sam and Addy, but he's not bound to them yet. He can come to hang out with us if he wants. In the unlikely event we outlast Sam and Addy, he might have trouble."

"I would advise against it, fool," Micah offered, looking at Kareem.

Evelyn made a ticking sound. "Don't be like that, Micah. It's hard to do this without pillars. And Sam and Addy have already collected way more pillars than they need."

"How many pillars are there?" Matthew asked.

James smiled. "How many distinct emotions and factors that affect life are there? How many elemental forces? If you can think of a word for it, there's probably a pillar for it. Not all of them surface or survive. The traditional circle of the Mistress and Walker includes twenty pillars. It took Evie and me almost fifty years to gather eighteen. There are already sixteen in this circle, not counting the unclaimed one."

"Don't count me," Micah said. "I don't stand with them."

James rolled his eyes. "You're as tightly bound to the Mistress as the rest of them, and Sam only slightly less so. Let go of the polite fiction, Micah."

"I don't have a name," Micah argued, eyes flashing.

Sam sighed in time with James.

"Even if we don't count Micah," James said, "you're still at fifteen in a matter of months. This will be a giant circle."

"Adaline said thirty-two," Greggory offered quietly. "I asked them right after they took the names."

Evelyn shook her head. "That's terrifying. That many empowered pillars standing a single circle—I can't fathom that level of energy."

James nodded in agreement. "There will be enough new energy to balance things and promote growth, even with the current deficits and hotspots. Especially because they push it all out into the world. You people have yet to close a circle and keep your energy."

"Why keep it? What would we do with it?" Luke asked, confused.

"I love that you don't even know why you'd keep it." Evelyn smiled. "Micah, you're doing a good job of teaching them without corrupting them."

Micah grinned at her, acknowledging the compliment. "It's a fine line. They haven't even been curious before now. I'm guessing that's about to change."

Hank snorted in disgust from where he sat with Darla, Ava, and Jess.

"Or not." Micah nodded.

"Regardless," James sighed, "we'll be joining the training. They need to learn how to pull the circle from the center. The Walker over there outclasses me by several orders of magnitude. I can't take him down if he goes batshit insane."

Micah's eyebrows shot up. "You're going to let them practice draining you?"

"Well, you don't have to sound so gleeful about it." James glowered. "Can you think of another way?"

After a pause, Micah shook his head. "No, but I'm really looking forward to training now!"

"What about my mother? And the extra Walker?" Ava asked, sounding sick.

"I don't know," James admitted. "We need more information."

"He's not a walker in truth, yet. However Josiah came to be part of him, Jared cannot walk through time. He seems to be able to move through space, though," Sam said. "Ava, you think you can find him?"

"I can find my mother," Ava replied. "If she's with Jared now, I guess so."

"I can probably find Jared," Ben offered. "I can still find his mind when I look for it, though it's closed to me."

"We don't know enough to pick that fight yet," James said. "We need more information. And you need more preparation. There is time. Several things from that branch in time have yet to surface."

"Yeah," Noah said, grinning at Sam from the doorway. "Like I said. No more sex for you!"

20

"$\mathcal{I}$ cannot believe you came home with me last night," Ethan said the following morning. "Why didn't you get in the car with Luke and Matthew?"

Miranda grinned. "Mostly because I felt bad for Kareem. But, also, I'm getting divorced today. Might as well make it official!"

"Hurrah! So long not-svelte shit-bag Larry!" They shared a high-five.

"Poor Kareem, though." Ethan laughed. "He seems like such a nice guy. Matthew nailed it, calling him a catalyst."

"That was scary last night. I'm not sure I'll ever look at Sam the same way," Miranda admitted, more subdued.

Ethan nodded. "Before he took the name, we referred to the part of the energy that would peek out at us occasionally as 'Spooky Samuel.' It's an apt name. Still Sam, though."

"You weren't afraid of him?"

"No," Ethan said, shaking his head. "I've seen that lack of emotion twice before last night. Jake has, too. It was much worse after I was attacked. Still Sam, though. If it scared you, remind yourself that he willingly set the otherness aside as soon as he could. He hates and fears it more than you do."

"True," Miranda admitted. "Poor Sam. So many blessings but also so much hardship."

Ethan nodded in agreement. "What do you think Kareem is going to do?"

"I think he's going to try to convince himself it was a bad dream." Miranda grinned, only partly kidding.

Ethan sighed. "Are you ready for today?"

"As ready as I'll ever be," Miranda said, her good mood deflating.

"I'll go with you," Ethan offered again. "I wish you'd let Matty and me be there with you."

Miranda shook her head. "I want to do this on my own. I'm done with emotional dependence for a while."

"Being independent doesn't mean you have to be without friends, Randa."

"I know," she said, tearing up a bit. "Thank you, Ethan. For everything."

Nodding in acceptance, Ethan scrunched up his face. "You're not coming home tonight, right? Please say no."

"No." She laughed. "Not if I can help it."

"Does Matthew know this?" Ethan grinned. "Should I warn him?"

Miranda's grin returned. "Please don't. If he runs away again, I'm going to be crushed. I think my odds are better if I surprise him."

"I think your odds are good no matter what," Ethan said, kissing her cheek before heading out for the office.

THE MALICE and hatred rolling off Lawrence toward Miranda were strong enough to make everyone uncomfortable.

"Mr. Suffolk," the judge said to Lawrence's attorney. "Before I declare these proceedings concluded, I'd like to remind you and your client of a few things. First, you laid out the terms for this divorce. These terms are fair and, I would even say, favorable to your client.

Second, no current criminal charges are pending. Finally, there are repercussions to our actions. Please consider how you move forward. If necessary, I will grant a restraining order as part of this settlement."

Lawrence's lawyer shifted uncomfortably, unsure how to respond to the judge's unusual admonishment. "There is no cause for a restraining order, your honor."

"Please don't create a reason for one," the judge said directly to Lawrence. "As both parties have agreed, I hereby grant the permanent legal separation of..."

Miranda sat stiff and unmoving in her chair, unwilling to make eye contact with anyone, even her own attorney.

How can he hate me this much? How is this my fault? she wondered before reminding herself that she knew better than to marry him in the first place. *Short-term convenience rarely turns into long-term gain. Lesson learned.*

Before she knew it, the proceedings were done. Her lawyer was shaking hands with Lawrence's lawyer.

Miranda stood to gather her coat and bag.

"You goddamn whore," Lawrence muttered from behind her. "I told you that fag was after your ass and now you live with him. Directly from my bed to his, you're completely useless on your own. I hope you know that."

The absurdity of the words caught Miranda by surprise. Unable to stop it, she burst out laughing.

The rage displayed on Lawrence's face doubled, drawing alarmed attention from both lawyers.

"Have a good life, Larry," she said quietly, still laughing, before preceding her lawyer out of the room.

MATTHEW SMILED TO HIMSELF, watching Miranda hesitate on his doorstep through the security camera.

Unwilling to push for things to move along, he didn't question why she went home with Ethan on Sunday night. He didn't wonder at Miranda leaving the farmhouse with Ethan again after Monday's failed circle.

Today was a big day—her final day tied to Lawrence. Today she was free.

"Are you sure? I can be an adult. I'll be there..." Matthew had texted earlier that morning.

"Absolutely not!" she had replied back immediately.

While he wasn't sure when she'd surface, Matthew was confident she would show up at some point, aiming to surprise him.

There would be no surprises this time. He was waiting for her.

She lifted her hand to ring the doorbell, hesitated again, and put the arm back at her side.

"Are you ready to ring that bell or not? That was your third failed attempt. Maybe I shouldn't open the door if you're this unsure," he yelled.

She paused, looking around. Spotting the tiny camera, she pulled a face. "How come I'm the one making a move on you? Again."

Matthew threw the door open, smiling at her. "You're not. You just think you are."

"That's crap! I'm the one..." Miranda's words trailed off as he presented her with a single long-stemmed red rose.

He grinned at her expression before stepping back, out of the doorway. "I promise I won't run away this time. Are you ready for this or not?"

"What? What did you do?" she whispered. "I can feel...but what did you do?"

He lifted an eyebrow in challenge.

"Fine." She grinned, stepping into Matthew's little A-frame house. Her mouth dropped open in surprise.

"I've managed not to kill them over the last two days."

She didn't respond, looking around her in wonder.

"The struggle has been real, though."

No response.

"Miranda? Do you like it?" The uncertainty in his voice must have pulled her back to reality.

"Your version of wooing me is to buy twenty-three living plants for me to take care of?" she asked, scowling.

Matthew's mouth dropped open. "I thought— I don't know. I thought you'd like it. I-I was going to do traditional flowers. But flowers are already dying when they're cut, and I didn't think you'd like that. Um, I thought. I don't know. I can..."

His panicked babbling trailed off at the sight of her grin.

"I don't like it. I love it," she admitted, smiling as she fidgeted with her hands.

"That was slightly evil, Miranda," Matthew muttered, exhaling in relief.

"I know. But it lasted like thirty seconds. I could have run away for four years," she teased.

"Did I say I was sorry for running away? I think I said that at some point. I did, right?" Matthew asked, suddenly nervous.

"You did," she confirmed, nodding as her heart raced in her chest.

They stared at each other in awkward silence for a moment.

"I love you," he said.

"Good," she replied, still nodding.

"Fuck it," he said, seizing her mouth and sweeping her off her feet up into his arms.

"Matthew?" she muttered against his lips, voice quaking a bit.

"You're going to make a joke about me missing your mouth on Sunday, aren't you?"

"Did you water the plants this morning?"

Matthew raised his eyebrows. "You're worried about this right now?"

She squirmed in his arms. "Some of the soil is dry."

"You're nervous." It wasn't a question.

"Fuck, yes," she squeaked. "Aren't you?"

He set her down.

"No!" she gasped, jumping to wrap her arms and legs around him. "I'm not that nervous."

"Randa—"

She slammed her lips against his, trying to show the longing and excitement she felt. Matthew's arms tightened around her, holding her legs in place around his waist.

"No rush," he gasped, pulling away from the kiss.

"Rush," she encouraged, kissing him again.

"Randa—" he tried again.

"You win all the nice-guy understanding points on the planet," she cut him off. "That's not what I want right now, though. Nervous doesn't mean undecided."

He groaned as she nibbled at his ear. "Sure?"

"Very," she breathed, brushing his earlobe with her tongue.

"Holy fuck. Energy," he gasped. "Too much."

"So good." Miranda panted. "Feels so good."

Kissing her, Matthew's hand slid up the back of her blouse to caress her smooth, soft skin.

Her legs dropped from around his waist. Standing on her own two feet, she kicked off her heels and ran her hands under the front edge of his t-shirt.

"Huh?" she breathed, pushing his shirt up. "Muscles!"

Matthew laughed, kissing her again. "Happens."

She broke the kiss off, offended. "Chest muscles! Sexy chest hair and muscles!"

"I told you. Micah and I have been beating the crap out of each other daily for a solid month now." He grinned. "Don't look so upset."

"We could have been naked together days ago!"

Matthew threw his head back, laughing as he pulled off his t-shirt. "We'll make up for the lost time."

Sweeping her feet from under her again, he turned out of the entryway. "House tour later."

"I love you," she whispered as he set her down on his bed.

Touching his forehead to hers again, he smiled. "I love you, too."

Words slipped away as he unbuttoned her blouse and she undid his jeans. Slowly, they each let go of their nerves, exploring with gentle kisses and bold touches.

Finally, Matthew gasped, rolling away from her. "Stop. Too much. Energy. Too much energy. Dangerous for—"

"Foreplay over," Miranda murmured, rolling to straddle him.

"Wait. Too much energy. Wait, Miranda—"

She didn't wait.

She didn't even pause.

They exhaled slowly together as their bodies joined.

Matthew grabbed her hips, holding her still. "Wait. Please. Wait."

Miranda counted to thirty in her mind, watching him struggle to breathe as he fought with the energy.

"It's energy, Matthew," she murmured, bending to kiss him.

He gasped with the increased contact. "Hurt you. It'll hurt you. No control. Chaos."

"You don't know that it'll hurt me," she whispered, shifting.

"Might," he panted.

"Might not," she sighed, moving slowly. "No more waiting. Enough waiting."

Matthew's eyes closed as he shifted with her.

Miranda kissed him again, eliciting a gasp of surprise and a spike of energy that nearly sent her speeding over the edge to oblivion. He paused, looking up at her with raised eyebrows.

"Definitely didn't hurt," she panted, fighting back laughter as she leaned over to nibble his ear again.

"Holy hell," Matthew breathed, shifting to gain leverage and speed as he tried to control the energy.

"Let go," Miranda whispered. "Just let it go."

When he didn't respond, Miranda pulled her own energy forward, pushing it into him.

Matthew's eyes flew wide open in surprise. He groaned in pleasure as the energy cycled through them, making everything tingle. He flipped them in one smooth motion.

"I wasn't prepared for that." Miranda smiled.

"Too late." The words came out deeper than Matthew's normal voice, slightly echoing in the room, laced with power. He was glowing faintly in the dim bedroom light.

"Let go," she said again. "Matthew, let go."

She touched his cheek, drawing his attention to her. Without warning, the energy exploded from him, cycling freely between them, cavorting with her own power as the ground shook.

While he was distracted, she flipped them quickly, slowing the pace again.

Matthew grunted in frustration before flipping her again.

"Hey, gravity. You shouldn't have been able to do that," she gasped, digging her fingers into his back as he moved quickly, driving them both closer to the finish.

"Chaos." His lips twitched into a teasing smirk as he slowed things down again. "No accounting for it."

She shifted under him, searching for leverage. He moved with her.

"More like 'no fun,'" she murmured, poking him in the side.

Matthew gave a gasp of quiet laughter, flicking gentle fingers in sensitive places to send her over the edge. "I object to that assessment."

Still working on catching her post-orgasm breath, Miranda gave a huff of surprised laughter, running her hands up his chest. With a wicked little grin, she twisted her body so she could scrape her teeth across his nipple while forcing the rampant energy back into him.

"Fuck," he gasped, moving with more speed and focus.

Miranda's lips slammed into Matthew's.

Raw energy poured through them, into the room, then out into the world on its own accord.

Shifted into a headspace beyond thoughts and words, their bodies took over. Twisting and sighing together, they slid over the edge into oblivion as one.

TWENTY MINUTES LATER, Matthew and Miranda were tangled in bed together, adrift in sleepy musings.

"What are you thinking?" Matthew murmured, playing with her hair.

"Mmm, nothing," she muttered, turning slightly pink.

"That was not convincing."

She turned her head away, fighting back laughter.

Matthew's eyes narrowed. "Were you thinking about grilled cheese?"

"Gah! How'd you know? Why would you assume that? I could have been thinking sexy thoughts. Don't assume that!"

"Because I was thinking about it, too. I'm starving. Are you hungry?"

"Yes." She laughed. "I have that gross belly burn feeling that comes with being too hungry!"

"Food!" Matthew yelled, grinning as he kissed her. "All the food. Someone order the lady a pizza."

Miranda laughed, grinning back.

"Sandwiches? Pizza? Asian? Fried Chicken?" Matthew asked.

"Fried Chicken?" Miranda's mouth dropped open.

"Spicy fried chicken with the mashed potatoes and spicy gravy… you love that."

Miranda grinned. "I forgot all about that. I haven't had that since we were both in school."

"Miranda!" Matthew gasped, only slightly exaggerating his indignation. "It was your *favorite!*"

"I know, but it's terrible for me."

"We're getting fried—"

Matthew's words were cut off by a frantic pounding on the front door.

"What the hell?" he muttered as he slid out of bed and pulled on clothes.

Just as he buttoned his jeans, the front door slammed open fast enough to bang the wall.

"Hello!" Luke yelled. "Matthew, are you—?"

"Oh, shit! Don't come in here, you nosey prick!" Matthew yelled back, tossing Miranda a shirt.

Miranda burst out laughing. "Nothing is sacred."

"Oh, fuck!" Luke called from the living room. "You're fine. Hi, Randa. Um. I'm going."

"Why are you here?" Matthew said, stumbling over Miranda's discarded bra as he walked into the hallway.

"Your energy was going batshit. Sorry. I thought there was trouble," Luke replied, voice muffled with embarrassment. "I didn't consider... Anyway. I should have."

"Huh. That's interesting," Matthew said. "We should ask Micah about why you would feel that. But you could have fucking called, Luke."

"Didn't think about that," Luke replied, sheepish.

"Idiot." Matthew laughed.

"Hey, Miranda," Luke called down the hall to her in the bedroom. "He really loves being called by lovey-dovey nicknames. Snookums, honey pie, sweetheart, sugar plum...like that. He'll never admit it, but it's his most favorite thing ever."

"'Sugar plum' it is," Miranda replied, not missing a beat. "But only when he's mean to you."

"I really do love you," Luke called back.

"Hey," Matthew said, struck with an idea. "Since you're here, go get us fried chicken."

"And strawberry soda!" Miranda yelled. "Love you, too!"

21

*M*atthew and Miranda picked up Luke for the car ride out Nora's farmhouse on Wednesday evening.

"We could have picked up Noah and Tali, too. We'd fit fine," Miranda observed.

"Yes, but then we'd have to sit in the car with Noah heckling me for ninety minutes. No, thank you," Matthew replied, his lips twitching in a small smile. "I think he's trying to win over her dad, anyway. He went over to their house early to rake leaves and do fall yard cleanup."

Miranda grinned. "That is so freaking sweet. You love him. Admit it."

"I do. I love all of my family. They're amazing. But he's not my favorite brother." Matthew grinned back.

"That's me. I'm the favorite!" Luke raised his hand in the back seat. "Likewise, bro."

"Why pick a favorite?"

"Why not?" Luke asked, laughing. "We joke about it, but we're a little bit clique-ish when you get down to it. Matthew and me. Will, Hennessy, and Adrian. Sam, Jake, and Ethan. Though Ethan hangs out with everyone. Noah floats back and forth between groups. We take turns spending time with him to avoid getting snappish over his baiting. He understands. We need breaks."

"What about Beth?" Miranda asked.

Matthew grinned, eyes still on the road. "Beth does as she pleases, though she spends more time with Will, Adrian, and Hennessy now."

"Meh," Luke said. "I would argue she's more like Ethan. Welcome everywhere, but also happy to be on her own. I have lunch with her at least once a week. You should get in on that now that you're not teaching."

Matthew's lips pressed together.

"You heard Sam on Monday night," Luke continued. "There is trouble coming, and some number of sinister people mean us harm. Are you still serious about going back to class? You're going to paint a target on your back and surround yourself with helpless kids?"

"It doesn't need to be decided right now," Matthew muttered, frustration written on his face. "I wasn't supposed to go back until January anyway."

Miranda touched his arm in sympathy. She hadn't considered what Monday's events meant for their daily lives. "We don't know anything yet."

Matthew sighed. "I won't risk the kids, but I'm still hoping we have a better grasp on things before the holidays. Halloween is next week; we have two months before I need to decide anything."

They fell silent as Matthew turned into a parking space at the farmhouse.

"In a couple more weeks, we can do this in Sam's backyard. It's kind of Nora to let us use her property like this," Matthew noted.

Luke snorted. "We're unleashing incredible amounts of energy into the world, with her farm as the epicenter. She's doing it to be helpful and supportive. That's just who she is. But this farm is going to have amazingly bountiful crops for the next thousand years. The whole community is benefiting from this."

"You think?" Miranda asked, surprised.

"Yes, Lady Earth." Luke laughed. "I think your energy, in particular, is driving a legendarily profitable harvest. Livestock is healthier and more fertile. In general, people are happier here, too. I'm glad we're doing this in an area that is primarily owned by small farmers."

No one moved to get out of the car, though it was parked and turned off.

"It's hilarious that Noah's doing yard work to woo Mike. It's good for him to have to work at building a relationship with someone else. He gets along so easily with everyone," Luke admitted, sounding like he'd been considering it the entire car ride. "I still hate that they're together, though."

"You need to let that go," Matthew said, tone firm and unmoving. "They're happy."

"I know," Luke muttered. "I just didn't see it coming. You know?"

"Don't be that guy," Miranda chided.

"What guy?" Luke asked.

"The guy that doesn't want her but also doesn't want to see her with someone else," Miranda explained.

Luke's brow furrowed in confusion. "I'm not upset that she's with someone. I'm struggling with the fact that she's with *Noah*. She's smart, sharp-witted, and relatively innocent. He is none of those things. I'm assuming he's going to fuck it up and hurt her. I don't want to watch that happen."

"Lucas," Miranda scolded. "He did yard work to help her dad. It's time to consider that he's playing for keeps."

"Yeah," Luke muttered, finally opening his car door. "Let's go. We can continue this conversation on the way home—after he's spent two hours making fun of you and Matthew for finally hooking up."

"I win!" Noah yelled at the sight of Miranda's fingers woven with Matthew's as they walked back to the field together.

SATURDAY MORNING STARTED LAZILY. Miranda sat at the breakfast bar in Matthew's kitchen, wearing nothing but his oversized t-shirt. Matthew shuffled around in pajama pants, hair properly mussed, putting together something that might be pancake batter.

"You're not wrong." She smiled.

"Of course, I'm not!" he agreed immediately. "What am I not wrong about?"

"Ethan is much better at this."

Matthew quirked an eyebrow. "Do you want to do this?"

Miranda grinned. "If you leave it to me, we're having black coffee and dry toast."

"That hurts my heart." Matthew sighed dramatically, leaning over to kiss her cheek. "I'm shirtless. Admire the view. I'll be done making a mess in a few minutes."

She laughed, focusing her phone to take a picture of shirtless Matthew. "Now I also have this shirtless morning memory properly captured to savor later. Oh."

"Oh?"

"I'm okay. My mom texted last night. I missed it."

MEGAN: Sweetheart, your daddy and I miss you. How are you now that everything is done?

After pondering for a moment, Miranda sent her mother the picture of shirtless Matthew. The response was instantaneous.

MEGAN: RANDA! I'm so happy! I'm actually crying. Sweetheart. I'm so happy for you. Are you happy? Please tell me you're happy!
MIRANDA: I'm ridiculously happy, Mom. How are you?
MEGAN: Sobbing. I'm sobbing at the breakfast table.
MIRANDA: Don't cry. I'm doing well. I promise everything is good.
MEGAN: I don't doubt it, Randa. Please give Matthew a hug from me and tell him how happy I am.
MIRANDA: Will do. Maybe lunch next week?

MEGAN: I just told your father. He's over the moon excited for you, sweetheart. We've been so worried. We understood about Lawrence. Once the work stuff calmed down and he had time to think about it, your father was devastated over the way things went at brunch a few weeks ago. Come to brunch tomorrow, sweetheart! You and Matthew. Please come to brunch!

"What do you think?" Miranda asked Matthew.

"Sure." Matthew shrugged. "I've never met your brother. But, Randa, I'm not going to take shit from them. They're your family. I'll be respectful, but they're not going to give us a hard time."

"We'll leave immediately if things go sideways." She nodded, typing a reply to her mom.

MIRANDA: We'll see you tomorrow. Love you and Dad.

22

$\mathcal{M}$iranda's father, Charles, was hopping down the Gold Coast mansion's front steps while Matthew was still helping Miranda out of the car.

"Baby girl!" he crowed, swinging her around in a hug almost before she had her feet under her. "We missed you so much."

"Hi, Daddy," Miranda muttered, trying to catch her breath in Charles's crushing hug.

"I'm so sorry, sweetheart. I'm sorry for the way things went a few weeks ago. That's not what I wanted. No one wants you to be miserable."

Once again standing on her own, Miranda shot her father and sardonic look of disbelief.

"Your grandfather doesn't want you to be miserable," Charles admonished. "He just doesn't care if you're happy."

Miranda grinned at that. "I missed you, too, Dad. Say hello to Matthew and be nice."

"Do I have to? Being nice takes most of the fun out of him being here." With a genuine smile, he extended a hand to Matthew. As

Matthew took the offered hand, Charles pulled him into a hug. "Thank you for coming to brunch and for giving us another chance."

Miranda smiled, knowing Matthew could have refused the handshake and the hug without effort.

"No second chance needed, Charles. I never harbored ill will against you. I thought you hated me," Matthew replied, working to not smirk.

Charles scrunched up his face. "Hate? No."

Matthew raised his eyebrows, throwing his own sardonic look at Charles.

Miranda's dad shifted uncomfortably. "I have never wanted anything but for Miranda to be cared for and happy. I didn't believe you were capable of providing for her in life."

"Did it ever occur to you that she might want to provide for herself?" Matthew asked, honestly curious.

Charles nodded, turning so he was looking at both Matthew and Miranda. "Your mother and I had a long talk after the last time you were here for that horrible brunch. We want you to be happy. If that means working, fine. You're capable. I know you're not a little girl anymore. I know you were unhappy with Lawrence. Thinking back on it, I'm not sure either of you were ever happy together.

"Regardless, whatever happiness looks like for you, we support it no matter what your grandfather says, okay?"

Miranda's lips quirked. "You and Mom had a nasty fight, huh?"

"One for the record books." Charles nodded, sighing. "She wouldn't speak to me for almost a week. I've had a lot of time to think about the last few months. I'm not proud of my actions in retrospect."

"Thank you for saying that," Miranda murmured, dabbing at her eyes.

"Baby girl," Charles murmured, hugging her again. "I'm sorry."

"Are you officially out of the doghouse now?" Miranda chuckled.

"I think so." Charles grinned. "She seemed to know when I realized the error of my ways. She laughed at me, watching at the window for you both. I wanted to talk before going into the house."

"Good plan." Miranda nodded. "No telling how Grandfather is going to react to this."

"Am I 'this?'" Matthew asked, eyebrows raised.

She grinned at him. "Oh, yes. Ready to step into the Twilight Zone? Just remember: Sunday brunch is the polar opposite of Sunday dinner."

"RANDA!" Megan exclaimed, yanking her younger daughter into a hug immediately. "You're okay? Of course, you're okay. Look at you—positively glowing with happiness!"

"Hi, Mom." Miranda laughed. "I'm good. Are you okay?"

"Better now," Megan murmured, wiping at tears as she turned toward Matthew.

Without a word, Matthew lifted Megan into a foot-swinging hug, surprising a giggle from her.

"Hi, Matthew," Megan said, grinning as she kissed his cheek. "I'm so happy. Also, have you been working out?"

Miranda burst out laughing.

"I mean, the picture. Muscles!" Megan teased. "I had no idea."

Matthew sighed, turning red. "I'm sorry," he said to Charles.

"Me, too." Charles laughed. "Come on. Max and Shelly are in the sitting room with your grandfather."

Entering the sitting room, Matthew's gaze traveled between Max and Miranda. Some of the facial features were similar, but Max was even more smarmy than Lawrence, and that was saying something.

"Hey, there he is!" Max called, voice loaded with false cheer. "Good to finally meet you, Matthew!"

Matthew hesitated. "Likewise, Max. I'm sorry we didn't see you at your sister's engagement party."

"Yeah, I couldn't make it. Decidedly under the weather. Didn't want to spread my germs, you know?" Max replied, not even hesitating in the lie. Matthew knew Max and his wife had outright declined the invitation to Jake and Matilda's party.

Letting it go, Matthew turned to the old man sitting in the straight back chair, openly scowling at everyone in the room. "Hello, sir," Matthew said, extending his hand to shake with the crotchety geezer.

Miranda's grandfather didn't move to accept the handshake or return the greeting.

Matthew sighed, putting his arm down. "This is going to be great," he whispered to Miranda.

"Let's sit down to the table," Megan said, subdued by her father's rudeness.

BRUNCH WAS AN UNCOMFORTABLE, silent affair for the first twenty minutes.

"What is it you do again?" Benjamin demanded of Matthew. "Some sort of child care?"

Maybe I should tell him I'm a nanny, just to see what he says, Matthew thought, chuckling to himself.

"I teach second grade, sir."

The old man snorted. "If that brother of yours didn't make an ungodly sum of money in the last decade, you'd be a pauper, begging for scraps at this table."

Matthew smiled. "Well, Sam is Sam, but I don't think I'd be begging for anything. We weren't wealthy growing up. I can live within my means and still be happy. Money only buys so much."

"Maybe you can't buy happiness," Benjamin disagreed. "But it's hard to be happy without it."

"Peace and security without basic necessities are challenging. Happiness is a choice."

Benjamin snorted again, turning his sneer on Miranda. "Now that you've ditched your husband and shacked up with someone new, I'll ask again. What do you intend to do now?"

Come on, Randa. You can do this, Matthew mentally cheered for her.

Miranda coolly met her grandfather's eyes without flinching or cowering.

Matthew smiled to himself again. *It didn't take long for her to find her footing,* he realized, noticing the strength of spirit he so admired when they were in school.

"I'm going to start a non-profit to help children learn how to grow their own food. It's knowledge that is lost in urban—"

Benjamin cackled. "You and your grandmother spent all that time screwing around in the yard. No one wants to know how to do that, you moron. We've evolved beyond that."

Matthew's temper flared for a moment.

Miranda actually smiled at the old man. "We've not grown beyond needing food, Grandfather, unless you've learned how to sustain yourself on malice?"

Megan actually gasped, choking on a surprised laugh. She grinned at Matthew.

"You ungrateful little—"

"Don't," Miranda spoke over him. Matthew started, realizing her word crackled with something other than earth energy.

Oh, shit. Was that mine? My energy? Did that slip out? I'm not that mad. Matthew took several calming breaths.

"I'm done with being a doormat, Grandfather. You're not going to call me names or bully me. No more. I'll give just as well as I receive. Understand?"

"No wonder you couldn't keep your husband in your bed, you stupid girl. All you're good for is living off other people. You're a parasite..." The old man's words trailed off as he noticed a shift in the air.

Oh, fuck, Matthew thought, desperately trying to pull back his energy. It took him a moment to realize his energy was well under control.

Miranda is doing this. Holy hell, she's pulling my energy. Does she know she's doing this? Matthew stared at her, eyes wide in panic.

Miranda met his stare with a quirked smile.

I don't know what that means! Matthew thought. *We have to get out of here.*

Then family brunch went from hostile to weird.

CHARLES LAUGHED A MOCKING CHUCKLE. "Parasite? Miranda? You're calling her a parasite when all she ever tries to do is make us happy? No, you're the one that sucks the life out of us, Benjamin."

Matthew's eyes shot to Charles.

"I mean, really, Daddy, could you be any more miserable? You're why I ran away from home when I was a teenager. You blame Mom for that, but you're absurd. I never would have come back if Matilda didn't need me to leave."

Miranda started at that, staring at her mother. "What?"

Max's wife, Shelly, sighed. "I hate all of you. I'm pregnant with another man's baby, but Max would never divorce me over it because of the gossip that would follow."

Max nodded. "It's true. I know it's another man's baby, too. We haven't had sex in almost a year."

Miranda's mouth dropped open in shock before she turned to stare at Matthew.

He gave his head a small shake, making a subdued gesture to Miranda.

She burst out laughing.

"Well, I wouldn't be so miserable if you people weren't such a bunch of screw-ups. I built this empire from the ground up—"

Charles choked on his laughter. "You married a woman with money and then tried to invest it. We'd be wealthier now if you had saved the money and invested it with standard market returns."

Megan burst out laughing. "Really?"

"I did the math several years ago." Charles nodded. "Also, I secretly call you Benji in my head."

"I knew you had an affair last year," Megan said to Charles. "Even after we agreed you would never do that again. I was just too much of a coward to call you on it."

"I think I might be gay," Max mused. "I'm not sure. I've never tried it. But I think I should."

"Bisexual is a thing," Matthew added, biting his lip to hide his grin. This was, by far, the best manifestation that had ever come from his energy.

"Your grandmother had a girlfriend for almost thirty years," Benjamin said. "I blame her. But it was fun to watch."

"Oh my God!" Miranda exclaimed, bursting out into giggles.

"There's nothing wrong with that," Megan chided, looking at her daughter. "Don't judge."

"I'm not. Just surprised. I wish Gram had told me. I wish I knew her girlfriend." Miranda laughed.

"She was ashamed. It was a different time. But you met Aunt Gert."

"Aunt Gert! Seriously?" Miranda cackled. After a moment, she grinned. "I could see that!"

"We kept all kinds of things from you. It was for the best." Megan sighed.

That gave Miranda pause. Her laughter stopped. "What else did you keep from me?" Her tone was curious instead of accusatory.

"Oh. It doesn't matter now. You figured out where you're supposed to be. It's good." Megan waved a hand in dismissal.

"No, really. What other deep dark secrets are you hiding?"

"I can start a fire with my mind." Megan grinned.

Max went still. "I can make the wind blow."

"Freak. I thought you were too ashamed to admit that." Shelly laughed.

"Umm," Matthew said, unsure what to do with the knowledge.

"You could have told me that," Miranda scolded her mother. "You know about my earth stuff."

Megan shook her head. "I couldn't tell you that. Nope. There are repercussions to our actions, and I knew that I couldn't tell you that."

"Why didn't you tell me about Matilda?" Miranda asked. If the social filters were gone, she might as well ask.

Megan froze, her face suddenly guarded. "She had to stay safe. Hidden. Until she found her way, she had to be safe. I can't talk about that."

"Doh! Vague hinting sucks," Matthew exclaimed. "Just tell us. She found her way."

"No, Matthew. I won't risk it. I won't risk her. Ask Sam."

"Oh, that's even worse." Miranda groaned.

"I have no idea what you people are talking about," Charles said, the euphoric look on his face fading a bit.

"My head is killing me," Shelly said, resting her forehead on her hand. "I don't think the baby likes Eggs Benedict."

"I like Lawrence more than this one." Benjamin pouted, waving a hand at Matthew. "At least he kisses my ass. This one isn't even a little bit intimidated by me."

"Nope," Matthew confirmed. "I don't give a flying fuck."

Miranda grinned at him. "Potty mouth."

"I'm channeling my inner Jake right now." He grinned back.

"I'm telling Lawrence about this," Benjamin whined.

Miranda snorted. "We're divorced. He's living with his girlfriend. He didn't care about me when we were married. Why would he start now?"

"He won't care about you," Benjamin confirmed. "But you're all being mean to me. He cares about me."

Charles rolled his eyes. "He cares about your money. There's a difference."

"Not really," Benjamin retorted. "Works out the same for me."

23

$\mathcal{M}$atthew and Miranda were sprawled together, breathing steadily in a deep sleep several hours later when Matthew sat bolt upright in bed.

"What the fuck?" he yelled, pulling himself out of bed as he looked for his pants. "Stay here. Stay right here!"

"Matthew?" Miranda asked, groggy and confused as she also tried to get out of bed.

"Miranda, stay here!"

Then he was gone.

Miranda waited, paying attention to all her senses. She could feel Matthew and his agitation, but she couldn't tell what was happening.

After about two minutes, she caught a whiff of something. She sniffed again.

Is that...gasoline? Miranda wondered, climbing out of bed and pulling her own clothes on as she made her way to the living room.

"...do this, Lawrence. It's going to be fine. Relax, okay? It's over with now, and you're done with it," Matthew's voice came to her. "I understand, I do. I would be devastated, too. But help is coming."

Lawrence?!?

There was a bellow of rage and pain. Miranda couldn't make out the words.

"No," Matthew scolded in his teacher's voice. "You're not going to reach for that. Just leave it there. Stop this. Help will be here soon."

"What is happen—?" Miranda asked, walking up behind Matthew at the front door.

"SHIT!" Matthew roared, diving off the front porch to tackle someone in the front yard.

The last thing Miranda recalled was fire exploding around her.

IN THE HALF-SECOND it took Matthew to launch himself from his porch to Lawrence, he realized he was too late. The radiant heat of fire washed against his face as he tackled Lawrence, throwing him to the ground.

Miranda! Miranda's still in the house!

Moving before the thought registered, Matthew was back on his feet, running towards the wall of flames engulfing his unassuming, quiet little house.

"MIRANDA!" he bellowed.

She's still in there! The thought sucked the breath from his lungs.

Charging through the flames, back up the porch steps and into the house, he scooped Miranda out of the entryway without conscious thought.

She didn't react. She was dead weight in his arms.

FUCKING LARRY! FUCKING BURNING HOUSE!

The house exploded into a fireball as he jumped off the porch and ran away from it again.

"MATTHEW!" Adaline's voice bellowed in his head.

"Addy?"

"What has happened? Jake is screaming for you. What happened?"

"My house. Lawrence blew up my house. Randa is unconscious. Hurt. Oh, fuck, Addy!"

"Are you safe?" Addy asked. *"I called to you several times before you responded. Are you hurt?"*

"I'm in my neighbor's yard, waiting for help. How do I do this? How do I help her?" Matthew demanded, ignoring Adaline's other question while trying to quell his panic.

THERE WAS energy pulsing into her. Miranda could feel it.

"Hold still," Adaline said without her voice.

Miranda tried to speak.

"Be still. Don't move. He's pushing energy into you before the paramedics get there. It'll be over in a moment."

"Miranda, can you hear me?" Matthew whispered.

"Okay, Adaline says you can hear me. Okay. Okay. Holy shit. Holy fuck," Matthew breathed. "Okay."

"Little ears," Miranda mumbled. But laughing at her own joke was painful. "Ow."

"Holy shit," Matthew exhaled, collapsing next to her.

"Snuggle?"

Matthew shook with laughter. "What do you remember? Do you remember anything? The sirens are getting closer. Help will be here soon."

"What happened?" she asked, forcing her eyes open. "I feel weird."

"Everything is okay," Matthew mumbled. "Everything's fine, okay? I'm just going to rest for a minute."

"YOU'RE all moving to the cornfield houses now. No more of this!"

"Sam, we don't know what happened yet," Adrian said, voice calm.

Matthew tried to pull his eyes open. It didn't work the first time. Or the second time. But the third time did the trick.

"Matthew!" Darla yelled, her panicked pale face appearing in the edge of his vision.

"Hi, Mom."

"DON'T YOU 'HI, MOM' ME! YOU'RE GROUNDED!" she yelled.

Wait. I'm grown up, right? I think I'm grown up. Is this a dream? he wondered.

Hank appeared alongside Darla in Matthew's vision. "You can't ground him. He's an adult."

"You fucking asshole!" Luke bellowed. There was a sharp jab in Matthew's side.

"Ow," Matthew muttered.

"I'm going to fucking call you 'sugar plum' for the next decade!" Luke swore.

"Oh man," Adrian breathed. "We gotta make that stick."

"Randa?" Matthew asked.

"They'll move her up here as soon as they can," Hank said. "She'll be fine. Do you remember what happened?"

"Fucking shit-bag," Matthew slurred.

"Yeah, Lawrence. What happened?" William asked.

Holy shit. Is my entire family here? Where am I?

"Hospital?" he asked.

"Absolutely," Adrian snorted. "Anyone else would be dead. What happened?"

"Randa's okay?"

"She'll be fine," Hank assured him. "Little bit of smoke inhalation and some burns. Addy, Emma, and Ethan are sitting with her in the emergency triage area. They moved you to a room immediately."

"I don't deserve that glare, Dad," Sam complained. "We can't speak freely in an emergency room triage bay."

"What happened?" Adrian asked again.

"Fire," Matthew mumbled, finally starting to process normal thoughts.

"No shit, Sugar Plum," Will said, laughing. "How did it happen?"

The sound of Adrian's laughter was clearly audible.

Hank shifted out of Matthew's field of vision.

Fuck my life. They're going to call me Sugar Plum now. Even Dad's laughing about it.

Matthew tried to move his head.

"What are you doing? Stop moving!" Darla scolded.

"Who's here?" Matthew asked, realizing he couldn't move. There was a brace around his neck, and he was strapped to a board.

Hank nodded, coming back into view. "Just us right now. The doctor will be back shortly, I imagine."

Matthew tried to nod and failed because of the neck brace. Restrained as he was, he couldn't even open his mouth to speak normally.

It's fine, he thought. *Gives me an excuse if my words are still slurred.*

"We were sleeping. Felt shit-bag's mind crumbling. Told her to stay. Went to help him. He poured gasoline everywhere. Over himself, too. Tried talking him down while we waited on help. He saw Randa. Snapped. Boom. Dead?"

"Nope," William replied. "Barely singed, actually. You knocked him more than ten feet away from the fire. Then he rolled around in the neighbors' yard until the fire was out."

Matthew grunted, trying to free himself from some of the medical restraints.

"Just leave it for now," Adrian said. "The doctor's waiting on scan results to make sure your spine didn't get damaged from the explosion. Just chill for a bit."

Matthew grunted again, making his displeasure known.

"Do you remember running back into the house?" Hank asked.

"Randa."

"I'll take that as a 'yes,'" Hank muttered.

"Cornfield houses," Sam said again. "We're bunking up until the houses are all done."

NOVEMBER

24

"I'm not living with you. No," Ethan said. "It was fine when we were both single, but you're not single anymore. I don't want to see your bare ass wandering around at night. No."

"Don't worry, Ethan. He can't have sex. No sex for Sam!" Noah taunted. "There's no risk of seeing the all-powerful Walker's bare bum in the moonlight. His shorts are staying on."

Ethan fought back the laughter that he knew would just make Sam more irrational.

Sam turned narrowed eyes on Noah. "I'm telling Talise's dad there are rubbers stashed in your car."

Noah looked horrified. "Why would you even know that?"

Adaline cackled.

"Nothing is sacred!" Talise yelled, pointing at Adaline.

Addy shrugged, grinning.

"What the fuck?" Luke demanded, giving Noah a horrified expression. "You literally have unlimited money—all the money you could ever want to spend. Why would you get it on in the damn car?"

"Because it's fun," Talise said, grinning at Luke's bright red cheeks, much to Adaline's enjoyment.

"Oh my God," Luke groaned, trying not to laugh. "Get a hotel! Buy a condo!"

"I keep telling her we should move in together!" Noah bitched.

"Too soon," Luke and Talise said together, before sharing a smile.

"It's not safe!" Sam complained at Ethan, getting back on topic. "Live with Mom and Dad, then."

"Nope, not doing that, either," Ethan said, shaking his head. "Matthew and Miranda are already staying there. I'm not moving until my house is done. It's like two weeks. Get over it."

Sam groaned in frustration.

Early November was cold behind Nora's farmhouse where the circles were held. The family was bundled up, awaiting training on Wednesday evening.

A little over a week since the fire, Miranda and Matthew were both healed, each sporting a new, shorter haircut. It would be a while before Matthew's eyebrows fully grew in again.

"It's not safe to stay so far from everyone else," Micah argued.

"My apartment is literally an armed fortress, Micah. I don't even have neighbors."

Micah blinked. "I thought you lived in a condo?"

"I do," Ethan said, irrationally pleased that Micah would know such a detail. "But Sam's nuts."

"I am not!" Sam yelled.

"He is not," Matthew agreed immediately.

"Listen here, Sugar Plum." Ethan grinned. "You stay out of this. You're the reason I'm getting yelled at in the first place."

"I am not," Matthew said, decidedly not rolling his eyes over being called "Sugar Plum." He was relatively certain his family would forget about it in time if he didn't react.

"What? You're full of crap!" Ethan yelled.

"It is not my fault. It's Miranda's fault. She's too adorable to resist." Matthew grinned.

Miranda sighed. "I'm so—"

"Don't say it!" Matthew and Ethan yelled together.

"I was teasing," Matthew clarified, kissing the top of her head. "Well, I was teasing about it being your fault. You're absolutely, addictively adorable."

"It is my fault," she mumbled.

"Booo!" the Trellis family bellowed as one.

Micah shook with laughter. "It's like you people plan that shit. What's worse is that I knew it was coming."

"You didn't tell the shit-bag to impersonate a human torch," Will said to Miranda. "He did that all on his own. And now he'll be enjoying some much-needed inpatient care. No one was irreparably hurt. It's done."

Ethan shook his head. "I think getting involved with our energy roasts normal brains."

Miranda nodded in agreement. "He wasn't always like that."

"I'm going to fucking roast his brain for real if I get the chance," Matilda murmured, hugging Miranda again, just because she could.

"They're coming," Sam said. "We'll continue this later."

"No, we won't," Ethan muttered as James and Evelyn appeared in the field.

"Oh, Sugar Plum. I'm glad you're okay," James cooed at Matthew with a straight face.

"I would have gone with 'Hewy' for a nickname," Evelyn chimed in.

"WHAT ARE YOU THINKING?" Matthew asked later that night.

"Hmm?" Miranda asked, tuning back into reality.

"What are you thinking?"

"Mmm," she said, yanking off her shoes and putting them in the closet. "I think that I somehow managed to make an even bigger mess of things."

"Miranda, I was teasing," Matthew said, guilt making his chest tight. "I had no idea you were blaming yourself. I'm sorry."

She shook her head. "Don't be. I know I didn't start the fire and it's not my fault. But I think I probably should have asked you to go with me to court. He was unbalanced there. The judge told him off. If you were there with me, maybe he would have been triggered before any real damage could be done. Or maybe you would have sensed it sooner. I don't know."

"Pretty sure I would have sensed it." Matthew nodded. "You're right—my fault. I should have gone with you. I wanted to. It was hard to stay home and wait. I should have gone, and then it wouldn't have happened."

"You're doing that thing again."

Matthew frowned. "I'm not trying to distract you."

"No, you're trying to take the blame for things that can't reasonably be your fault."

He pulled a face. "You started it."

"Mmm," she replied before ducking into the attached bathroom. "If Ethan's right, it is my fault. Literally. If he's right, I affected Lawrence's thought process."

"Eh, I don't know that Ethan is right on that, Randa. Jake and Noah have had lots and lots of girlfriends throughout the years. None of them tried to light anyone on fire."

"Matty told me about Jake's old girlfriend—"

"Bella started out that way." Matthew shook his head, ending that conversation before it began.

"And Noah never really had a lasting relationship, right?"

"Ask Micah if it's really bothering you. He probably knows."

They were quiet while Miranda pulled on pajamas.

"He wouldn't have blown things up if I had done what you told me to do and stayed in bed," she eventually said, voice shaking with emotion.

Matthew sighed, pulling her down onto the bed then wrapping himself around her. "I've had nightmares about that."

"About me causing fires?" Miranda asked, confused.

Matthew kissed her gently, swallowing his grief. "If you had done what I told you to do, I might not have gotten to you in time."

The truth of his words silenced their conversation for a moment.

"He was losing it before you came into view. I was yelling at him about the lighter before you called out to me."

"Thank you for saving him," Miranda murmured, kissing Matthew. "And me."

"I felt his mind snapping. I thought I could get to him before he managed to light up. I was wrong." Matthew swallowed hard again.

"What?" Miranda asked, knowing he wasn't saying something.

"The energy exploded the house. As I was pulling you through the front door, it made the house explode."

"Matthew, the house was already on fire. You didn't cause that."

"I know," he replied. "That's not what I'm saying."

"Then, what?"

"When I realized that the shit-bag was safe, but you were still in the burning house, I was pissed. Pissed at him. Pissed at myself. And super pissed off at the actual house. I was pissed off at the physical structure. I remember that clearly."

Miranda's brow furrowed.

"I think I know how to direct the energy now. I've always known how to affect someone's thought process with it. But thinking back, I directed it at Noah right after Matty and Jake's party. He was nagging me about you. I was mad. One of the ceiling tiles fell right where he was standing. I can direct it more than I imagined."

"I WAS SLEEPING," Ethan yelled, walking out of his bedroom to answer the knock at the front door.

I just know this is Sam. If it's not Sam, this is Sam's doing. Like middle of the night, "surprise" movers or some strange shit. I know it, he cursed. *Security didn't call up here. Sam gave the garage code to movers, and I'm going to be fucking swept away out to the cornfield houses in the middle of the night. I just fucking know it. We need an intervention. Again.*

"I'm not moving in the middle of the fucking night!" Ethan snapped, throwing open the door without checking the security camera.

"Fine," Micah replied. "But you shouldn't be alone here, either."

THANK YOU FOR READING!

The final installment in the *Building the Circle* series, The Close, will be available on November 19, 2020, and is available now for pre-order.

For alerts on new releases and other book news, join my email list at https://maggielilybooks.com/sign-up.

Finally, your Amazon review of this novel would be much appreciated. Reviews are critical to the success of brand-new authors (like me!)

GLOSSARY & CHARACTER REFERENCE

GLOSSARY

THE CIRCLE - Based on the premise that all energy, including the power of time, is recycled in some form, the Circle is a conduit for gathering energy and dispersing it through the world.

THE WALKER - A man of immense power, including walking through time and space without limits. The Walker is historically known to be a force of destruction and indifference. He can also access the power of elements: fire, wind, water, and earth.

THE MISTRESS - Caretaker of all Life energy, the Mistress stands with the Walker at the Center of their power circle. She is his counterpoint and can control the forces that drive life, including emotions.

FATHER TIME - When a new Walker takes the name, the former Walker is promoted to the role of Father Time. This being can walk through time and space.

MOTHER LIFE - When a new Mistress takes the name, the former Mistress is promoted to the role of Mother Life. This being can control the energy of life.

CENTER - Gatekeepers of a circle's energy, the people standing at the center control the type of energy produced in the circle and how it is distributed.

CORNERS - The foundational cornerstones of the circle, the corners are pillars that dictate the flow of energy throughout the Circle.

PILLARS - The support beams of the circle, the pillars produce and cycle the specific type of energy they control. Any pillar can stand as a corner. When used as a title, Pillar refers to a person with absolute control over a specific power element.

CHARACTER REFERENCE

THE TRELLIS FAMILY

HANK - Hank is the Trellis family's patriarch, known for integrity and doing what's right.

DARLA - Darla is the Trellis family's matriarch, known for her strong commitment to her family and their happiness.

WILLIAM - Oldest Trellis sibling and former military man, William is married to Emma. He's referred to as William, Will, or Reap (as in Grim Reaper). He stands the circle as the Pillar of Terror.

ADRIAN - Doctor and philanthropist, Adrian is involved with Lucy. He stands the circle as the Pillar of Rage.

JACOB - Foul-mouth with a short fuse, Jake is engaged to Matilda and serves as the anchor of the family's natural circle.

ETHAN - Unattached, Ethan is Sam's favorite brother and stands as the Pillar of Joy.

SAMUEL - Sam is the Walker. He's only referred to as Samuel when he's scary.

NOAH - Noah is the Pillar of Lust and involved with Talise.

MATTHEW - Matthew is the Pillar of Chaos.

LUCAS - Lucas is the Pillar of Peace and usually goes by Luke.

BETHANY - Beth is the youngest Trellis sibling and only girl. She stands as the Pillar of Hope with her fiancé, Hennessy.

SIGNIFICANT OTHERS

EMMA GRACEN - Former movie star, Emma Gracen married William Trellis and is expecting the first Trellis grandchildren—twins. While most people call her Emma, William has a habit of calling her Pip. She is also the Pillar of Love.

LUCY - Lucinda is Ree's primary caregiver and is cohabitating with Adrian. She is the Pillar of Wind in the circle.

MATILDA - Matty is engaged to Jake Trellis and stands as Lady Light. She's also Miranda's older sister.

ADALINE - Mistress Life is Samuel Trellis's life partner and better half. She goes by Addy or Adaline when she's not infused with the energy of all living things.

TALISE - Pillar of Water, Tali also controls life energy, giving her the ability to sense emotions around her. She's involved with Noah.

MIRANDA - Randa stands as the Pillar of Earth. She is Matilda's younger sister and Matthew Trellis's long-time crush.

HENNESSY - Jessup Garland is William Trellis's best friend and Bethany Trellis's fiancé. A former military man, he works as a private investigator and stands the circle as Loyalty. He's known by his favorite after-dinner drink, Hennessy cognac, unless he's in trouble.

SUNDAY DINNER ATTENDEES

MICAH - Former Pillar of Hate, Micah broke with his circle more than two thousand years ago. He has a reputation for hunting down and ending people that steal energy from others.

REE - Adopted son of Lucy and biological son of Linda, Ree is five years old.

LINDA - Lucy's foster sister, Linda is also Ree's mom. She stands the circle as the Pillar of Perseverance.

AVA - Adaline's mother and a strong life energy holder.

CLYDE - Ava's husband, father to Jess and Adaline.

JESS - Adaline's older sister, empowered with all-sight, the ability to see energy, ties, bindings, and influences between living beings.

BLAKE - Jess's husband, father to Mia and Meg.

MIA - Daughter of Jess and Blake, Adaline's niece.

MEG - Daughter of Jess and Blake, Adaline's niece.

GREGGORY - A powerful life energy holder, Greggory is the former leader of the Harbor circle. He gave up his position to Sam and Adaline but remains part of the leadership as a guide and scribe.

BEN - Former corner of the Harbor circle, Ben has the rare ability to interpret and affect thoughts.

NORA - A strong elemental fire holder, Nora is a former corner of Harbor and long time, secret significant other of Greggory.

OTHER PRIMARY CHARACTERS

JAMES - Father Time has a fondness for cable TV.

EVELYN - Mother Life.

JARED - Former corner of the Harbor circle, Jared has abilities the family was unaware of until the end of The Corners.

SECONDARY CHARACTERS (OR CHARACTERS THAT ARE NOT YET PRIMARY)

LAWRENCE - Miranda's husband.

MIKE - Talise's father, who is very fond of Lucas and not fond of Noah.

MONICA - Talise's mother.

CHARLES - Miranda's father.

MEGAN - Matilda and Miranda's mother.

BENJAMIN - Megan's father, Matilda and Miranda's grandfather.

MAX - Matilda and Miranda's brother.

SHELLY - Max's wife.

ELEANOR - Matilda's best friend, married to Charlie.

CHARLIE - Eleanor's husband and Matilda's dear friend.

ERIC - Matilda's other best friend. Attempts to form a love match between Eric and Ethan Trellis have fallen short.

KAREEM - A skeptic and catalyst.

ALSO BY MAGGIE M LILY

BUILDING THE CIRCLE SERIES

Building the Circle - Volume 1

The Call

The Power

The Center

Building the Circle - Volume 2

The Corners

The Pillars

The Close

Becoming Hank - A Trellis Family Novella

PEACEKEEPER'S HARMONY SERIES

Ransom

Reaping

Rise